D1094122

BOYS DON'T CRY

Praise for Malorie Blackman:

Noughts & Crosses
'A book which will linger in the mind long after it has been read and which will challenge children to think again and again about the clichés and stereotypes with which they are presented' *Observer*

Knife Edge
'A powerful story of race and prejudice' *Sunday Times*

Checkmate
'Another emotional hard-hitter . . . bluntly told and ingeniously constructed' *Sunday Times*

Double Cross
'Blackman "gets" people . . . she "gets" humanity as a whole, too. Most of all, she writes a stonking good story' *Guardian*

Pig-Heart Boy
'A powerful story about friendship, loyalty and family' *Guardian*

Hacker
'Refreshingly new . . . Malorie Blackman writes with such winsome vitality' *Telegraph*

A.N.T.I.D.O.T.E.
'Strong characterisation and pacy dialogue make this a real winner' *Independent*

Thief!
'. . . impossible to put down' *Sunday Telegraph*

Dangerous Reality
'A whodunnit, a cyber-thriller and a family drama: readers of nine or over won't be able to resist the suspense' *Sunday Times*

Unheard Voices
'This excellent collection of stories, poems and first-hand accounts is published to commemorate the 200th anniversary of the abolition of the Slave Trade Act' *Carousel*

BOYS DON'T CRY

MALORIE BLACKMAN

DOUBLEDAY

BOYS DON'T CRY
A DOUBLEDAY BOOK 978 0 385 60479 6
TRADE PAPERBACK 978 0 385 61930 1

Published in Great Britain by Doubleday,
an imprint of Random House Children's Books
A Random House Group Company

This edition published 2010

1 3 5 7 9 10 8 6 4 2

The Random House Group Limited supports the Forest Stewardship
Council (FSC), the leading international forest certification organization.
All our titles that are printed on Greenpeace-approved FSC-certified paper
carry the FSC logo. Our paper procurement policy can be found at
www.rbooks.co.uk/environment.

Mixed Sources
Product group from well-managed
forests and other controlled sources
www.fsc.org Cert no. TT-COC-2139
FSC © 1996 Forest Stewardship Council

Set in 12.5/15 pt Bembo by Falcon Oast Graphic Art Ltd.

RANDOM HOUSE CHILDREN'S BOOKS
61-63 Uxbridge Road, London W5 5SA

www.kidsatrandomhouse.co.uk
www.rbooks.co.uk

Addresses for companies within The Random House Group Limited
can be found at: www.randomhouse.co.uk/offices.htm

THE RANDOM HOUSE GROUP
Limited Reg. No. 954009

A CIP catalogue record for this book is available from the British Library.

Printed and bound in the UK by Clays Ltd, St Ives plc

For Neil and Lizzy,
with love – as always

Dante

Good luck today. Hope you get what you want and need. ☺

Phone in hand, I smiled at the text my girl Collette had sent me. My smile didn't last long though. I was too wound up. Thursday. A level results day! I must admit, I didn't expect to be quite so nervous. I knew for certain I'd done well. What I mean is, I *almost* knew for certain. But it was the *almost* that was the killer. Between having my exam papers collected and having them marked, there was a world of possibilities. The person doing the marking might've pranged their car or had a fight with their partner – anything might've happened to put the test marker in a really bad mood which they would then take out on my exam papers. Hell! A cosmic ray could've hit my exam papers and changed all the answers – and not for the better – for all I knew.

'Don't be a plank – you've passed,' I told myself.

It was simple. I had to pass. There was no other choice.

Four good A level grades, that was what I needed. Then it was off to university. Up, up and out of here. And a year earlier than all my friends.

You've passed . . .

Positive thinking. I tried to dredge up confidence from somewhere deep inside. Then I felt like even more of a plank and stopped trying. But it was like Dad constantly said: '*Temptation leans on the doorbell, but opportunity knocks only once.*' And I knew only too well that my A levels were my best opportunity to not just hit the ground running but to take off and *fly*. Dad was full of fortune cookie quotes like that. His 'life lessons' as he called them were all tedious homilies that my brother Adam and I had heard at least a thousand times before. But every time we tried to tell that to Dad, he replied, 'I wasted all the chances that life threw my way. I'm damned if I'm going to let my sons do the same.' In other words, *Tough!*

Dante, stop worrying. You've passed . . .

University was just a means to an end. I mean, yes, I was looking forward to college; meeting new people, learning new things, being somewhere different and being totally independent. But I was looking way beyond that. Once I had a decent job, things would be different – or at least they would when I'd paid off my student loan. But the point was, my family wouldn't have to scratch for every penny. I couldn't even remember the last time we'd had a holiday abroad.

Three impatient strides took me to the sitting-room window. Pushing aside the grimy-grey doily-effect net curtains, I stared up and down the road. The August morning was already bright and sunny. Maybe that was a good omen – if anyone believed in such things. Out loud, I didn't.

Where the hell was the postman?

Didn't he know he held my whole future in his satchel? Funny how one sheet of paper was going to change the rest of my life.

I need to pass my exams . . . I really need to pass . . .

The words played through my mind like a recurring phrase from a really irritating song. I'd never, ever wanted anything so badly in my life. Maybe because my A level exam results *were* my life. My whole future rested on a slip of paper and a few letters at the beginning of the alphabet – the closer to the top of the alphabet the better.

I let the net curtain fall back into place, wiping my dusty hands on my jeans. What was it about the dust on grubby net curtains that made them seem almost sticky? I eyed the curtains critically. When was the last time they'd seen detergent and water? When was the first time, come to that? They'd been hanging there since I'd helped Mum put them up. When was that? About nine years ago, or thereabouts? Whenever it was my turn to vacuum, I'd suck the curtains down the vacuum cleaner hose, hoping to get rid of some of the dust that way. But the nets had become too fragile to withstand that sort of treatment any more. Dad kept promising to take them down and wash them or to buy some new ones, but somehow he never got round to either. Looking around the room, I wondered what I could do to pass the time? Something to occupy my mind . . . something to take my thoughts off—

The doorbell rang – as if on cue. I was at the door in a heartbeat, throwing it open with eager trepidation.

It wasn't the postman.

It was Melanie.

I stared at her. It took a couple of seconds to register the fact that she wasn't alone. I stared down at the contents of the buggy beside her.

'Hello, Dante.'

I didn't say a word. The baby in the buggy had all of my attention.

'C-can I come in?'

'Er . . . yeah. Of course.' I stepped to one side. Melanie wheeled the buggy past me. I closed the door behind her, frowning. She stood in the hallway, biting the corner of her bottom lip. She watched me expectantly, like an actress waiting for her cue. But she knew where the sitting room was, she'd been here before.

'Go through.' I indicated the open door.

Following her, my thoughts flitted like dancing bees. What was she doing here? I hadn't seen her in . . . it had to be well over a year and a half. What did she want?

'Are you babysitting?' I pointed to the bundle in the buggy.

'Yeah, you could say that,' Melanie said, looking at the many family photos Dad had placed on the windowsill, on either side of Mum's favourite lead-crystal vase, and around the room. Some were of me; more were of Adam; most were of my mum. But there were none of her during that last year before she died. I remember that Dad had wanted to take some – he was always taking photos – but Mum wouldn't let him. And after she died, Dad hadn't picked up the camera again. Mel flitted from photo to

4

photo, studying each intently before moving on. To be honest, I didn't see what was so fascinating.

Whilst Melanie was looking at the photos, I used the opportunity to eye her. She looked the same as ever, maybe a little slimmer but that was all. She was dressed in black jeans and a dark blue jacket over a light blue T-shirt. Her dark brown hair was shorter than the last time I'd seen her, shorter and spikier. But she was still stunning, with the biggest brown eyes I'd ever seen framed by the longest, darkest lashes. I glanced down at the bundle in the buggy which was staring up in fascination at the light-fitting in the middle of the ceiling.

'What's its name?'

'*Her* name is Emma.' Pause. 'D'you want to hold her?'

'*No*. I mean, er . . . no, thank you.' The words came out in a panicked rush. Was Melanie barking mad or what? No way did I want to hold a baby. And she still hadn't said what she was doing here. Not that I wasn't pleased to see her. It'd just been a long time, that was all. Melanie had dropped out of school over a year and a half ago and I hadn't seen or heard from her since. As far as I knew, no one had.

And now she was in my house.

As if reading my mind, Melanie said, 'I went away to live with my aunt. I'm back for the day visiting a friend and, as I was just passing by, I thought I'd pop in and say hi. I hope you don't mind.'

I shook my head and dredged up a smile, feeling unexpectedly awkward.

'I'm going away today actually,' Melanie continued.

'Back to your aunt's,' I assumed.

'No. Up north. I'll be staying with friends for a while.'

'That's nice.'

Silence.

'Can I get you something? A drink?' I said at last.

'Er . . . some water? Some water would be good.'

I headed for the kitchen and filled a tumbler from the tap. 'There you are.' I handed it to her once I got back to the sitting room.

The glass shook slightly on its way to her lips. Melanie took two or three sips then put it down on the windowsill. She retrieved a box from her jacket pocket and took out a cigarette, pushing it between her lips. 'D'you mind if I smoke?' she asked, the flame from her lighter already approaching the cigarette end.

'Er . . . I don't, but my dad and Adam will. Especially Adam. He's an anti-cigarette fascist and they'll both be back soon.'

'How soon?' Melanie asked sharply.

I shrugged. 'Thirty minutes or so.'

Why the urgent tone to her voice? For a second there she'd looked almost . . . panicky.

'Oh, OK. Well, the smell will be gone by then,' said Mel, lighting up anyway.

Damn it. To tell the truth, I wasn't keen on cigarettes either. Melanie drew on the cigarette like she was trying to suck all the tobacco in it down her throat. She closed her eyes for a few seconds, then a rush of swirling grey vapour shot out of her nostrils. Minging. And the smell was already filling the room. I sighed inwardly. Adam was

6

going to do his nut. Melanie opened her eyes to look at me, but she didn't say a word. She inhaled from her cigarette again like it was an oxygen tube and her only source of air.

'I didn't know you smoked,' I said.

'I started almost a year ago. It's one of the few pleasures I have left,' said Melanie.

We regarded each other. The silence stretched between us like taut elastic. Oh God. What was I supposed to say now?

'So . . . how are you? What've you been up to?' It wasn't much but it was all I could find to ask.

'I've been looking after Emma,' Melanie replied.

'I mean, apart from that?' I persisted a little desperately.

A slight smile curved one corner of Melanie's mouth. She shrugged but didn't reply. She turned her head to carry on looking around the room.

Silence.

The baby started gurgling.

Some noise to break the scratchy quiet. Thank goodness for that.

'What about you?' Melanie asked, removing the baby from the buggy and holding it on the left side of her body as she moved the cigarette to the right side of her lips. 'What've you been up to?' Her eyes weren't on me though. She was looking into the face of the thing in her arms. The thing gurgled louder, trying to wriggle closer into her. 'What are your plans now you've done your A levels, Dante?'

For the first time since she'd arrived, she looked directly at me and didn't immediately turn her gaze away. And the

7

look in her eyes was startling. Her face hadn't changed that much since the last time I'd seen her, but her eyes had. They seemed . . . older somehow. And sadder. I shook my head. There went my imagination, running off in all directions again. Melanie had aged by exactly the same amount of time that I had.

'I'm waiting for my exam results,' I said. 'They're supposed to arrive today.'

'How do you think you've done?'

Crossing my fingers, I held them up. 'I worked my butt off, but if you tell anyone, I'll hunt you down!'

'God forbid that anyone should find out you actually . . . revised. Don't worry, your secret is safe with me,' smiled Melanie.

'If I've passed, I'm off to university to do history.'

'And after that?'

'Journalism. I want to be a reporter. I want to write stuff that everyone wants to read.'

'You want to work for one of those gossip magazines?' queried Melanie.

'Hell, no! Not a celebrity reporter. How boring would that be, interviewing talentless airheads who are famous for absolutely nothing except being famous? No, thank you,' I said, warming to my theme. 'I want to cover proper news. Wars and politics and stuff like that.'

'Ah, that sounds more like the Dante I know,' said Melanie. 'Why?'

The question took me by surprise. 'Pardon?'

'Why does reporting on that kind of stuff appeal to you so much?'

I shrugged. 'I like the truth, I guess. Someone needs to make sure that the truth gets told.'

'And that someone is you?'

How pompous must I have sounded? Embarrassed, I smiled. 'Didn't you know? Dante Leon Bridgeman is only my Earth name. On my home planet I'm known as Dantel-Eon, fighting for truth, justice and free computer games for all.'

Melanie shook her head, her lips twitching. 'I'm beginning to remember why I used to like you so much.'

Used to? 'Past tense?'

She glanced down at the baby in her arms. 'I've had other things on my mind since we split up, Dante.'

'Like.'

'Like Emma for one.'

'Whose baby is she? Is she a relative?'

Just at that moment, the baby started to grizzle. Hell! It sounded like the thing was winding up for a long, loud bawl.

'Her nappy needs changing,' said Melanie. 'Hold her for a second. I need to get rid of my cigarette.'

Melanie thrust the baby at me and was already turning so I had no choice but to take it. She headed out of the room and made her way to the kitchen. Getting rid of her cigarette was now academic. The whole room stank. I held the baby at arm's length, pulling back my head like a turtle to put maximum distance between myself and the thing. There was the sound of running water from the tap, then the bang of the bin lid snapping shut. My hearing was switched up to maximum as I waited for the second I could pass back this thing in my hands.

Mel re-entered the room. With a practised hand, she opened the outsized navy-blue bag hanging on the back of the buggy and removed a pale yellow plastic baby mat decorated with multicoloured flowers. She lay it down on the ground, smoothing it out. Next came a disposable nappy, a small orange plastic bag and some baby skin wipes. With a rueful smile, Melanie took the baby from my unresisting hands. My sigh of relief was unintentionally audible. But damn! I didn't want to do that again in a hurry. I watched as Melanie knelt down on the carpet to lay the baby on the plastic mat. Whilst I opened the windows, Mel started talking a whole heap of rubbish.

Words like: 'Am I going to change your nappy now? Yes, I am. Oh yes, I am!'

And it was getting worse. Stricken, I watched as Melanie undid the yellow, all-in-one baby-gro, gently extracting the baby's legs from the outfit. She wasn't seriously going to change the baby's nappy on our carpet, was she? It looked like she was. Gross! I wanted to stop her but what could I say? I watched in horror as Melanie unfastened the disposable nappy.

Urgh!

It was filled to overflowing with poo. Sticky, nasty, ultra-smelly baby poo. I was amazed I managed to hold down my breakfast. But I backed up and backed off double fast. I couldn't have moved faster if the nappy had suddenly sprouted legs and started chasing me round the room.

'You should watch this,' Melanie said. 'You might learn something.'

Yeah, right!

'It's quite straightforward,' Melanie continued. 'You lift up her legs slightly by the ankles till her bum is off the nappy, then wipe her off till she's nice and clean.' Melanie dropped the wipes on the soiled nappy. 'Then you whip out the old nappy and place a clean one under her. After that you just fasten it like this, making sure it's not too tight and not too loose. See. It's so simple even you could do it.'

'Yes, but why would I want to?' I asked.

I mean, duh!

After placing the soiled nappy in the orange bag and tying a knot at the top of it, Melanie refastened the baby-gro before holding Emma to her, rocking it gently. The baby's impossibly long eyelashes fluttered against its cheeks as its eyes closed. Melanie handed me the soiled nappy bag. I recoiled in horror.

'Could you put that in your bin, please?' she smiled.

'Er . . . the kitchen is in the same place. Help yourself.'

'Would you mind holding Emma then?'

Oh God. Poo or a baby? A baby or poo?

I took the nappy bag out of Mel's hand, holding it at arm's length between my thumb and index fingertip. I started off carrying it gingerly but decided that speed would be better. Much better. So I sprinted to the kitchen, dropped it in the pedal bin, then washed my hands in the kitchen sink like I was scrubbing up to perform surgery. I headed back to the sitting room, Mel's laughter ringing in my ears. Melanie looked at me and smiled, her eyes crinkling with amusement. I didn't quite see what was so funny, but Mel's toothy smile brought back a rush of unbidden memories. Memories of things that I hadn't exactly forgotten, but memories I'd buried somewhere where they weren't easily accessible. I sat down, more puzzled than ever. What was Melanie doing here? Just passing by didn't quite ring true somehow.

'Mel, why . . . ?'

'Shush. She's fallen asleep,' Melanie whispered. She placed the baby back in its buggy and she was so gentle, the baby didn't stir once. Melanie straightened up, biting repeatedly on one side of her bottom lip. I remained seated. Abruptly, as if deciding something on the spur of the moment, Melanie dug into her oversized baby bag and withdrew a folded sheet of beige-pink paper.

'Read this,' she said, thrusting the paper at me.

I hesitated. 'What is it?'

'Read it.'

Frowning, I took it from her unresisting hand and unfolded it.

CERTIFIED COPY Pursuant to the Births and		OF AN ENTRY Deaths Registration Act 1953

CHILD		
Name and surname Emma Cassandra Angelina Dyson		Sex Female
FATHER		
Name and surname		
Place of birth		
Occupation		
MOTHER		
Name and surname Melanie Marie Dyson		
Place of birth London England		
Occupation Student		

I stared at her. 'You . . . you're the baby's mother?'

Melanie nodded slowly. 'Dante, I . . . I don't know how to say this without . . . well, without just saying it.'

She didn't have to say anything. The birth certificate explained so much and said so little. Melanie had had a baby. She was a mum. I had trouble taking it in. Melanie was my age. And she had a kid?

'Dante, I need to tell you something . . .'

Mel wasn't even nineteen yet. How could she have been stupid enough to have a kid at our age? Hadn't she ever heard of the pill? Kids were for people in their late thirties who had mortgages and steady jobs and serious savings in the bank. Kids were for those sad people who didn't have anything else to do with their lives.

'Dante, are you listening?'

'Huh?' I was still trying to wrap my head around the fact that Melanie was a mum.

Melanie took a deep breath, closely followed by another. 'Dante, you're the dad. Emma is our daughter.'

2

Adam

How much did this suck? I'd woken up with a splitting headache and my morning was rapidly going downhill from there. I made the mistake of not hiding how much my head was hurting when I came down for breakfast.

'Adam, another headache?' Dad frowned at me as I sat at the kitchen table.

I nodded. Thousands of wildebeest were stampeding through my head. Again.

'Is it a bad one?' asked Dad.

'It's not good.' I rubbed my fingers back and forth across my temple. For the last couple of weeks, I'd been getting irregular but really bad headaches.

'Why don't you get over yourself and take some painkillers?' my brother Dante grumbled.

'Because my body is a temple,' I informed him. 'You know I don't believe in popping pills.'

'It's hardly popping pills to take a couple of paracetamol when your head is hurting,' Dante argued.

'I'm not taking any tablets. OK?' I snapped.

'Suffer then,' said Dante evenly.

'Enough is enough, Adam,' said Dad. 'It's time for you to go to the doctor.'

No way. I mean, *no way*. 'It's not that bad, Dad,' I denied quickly.

'Adam, you've been having far too many headaches recently.'

'It's the heat,' I said, pushing away my bowl of corn-flakes. Just the sight of them made me want to upchuck. 'I just need to lie down for a while. It feels like the beginnings of a migraine.'

'You've been having headaches since the match against Colliers Green School,' said Dante thoughtfully. 'Are you sure you're . . . ?'

'Don't you start nagging too,' I said.

Dante gave me a frosty look. 'Well, excuse me for giving a damn.'

'I don't need you clucking round me like a mother hen,' I told my brother. It was a bit unfair, I know. But the only word worse than 'doctor' in my vocabulary was 'hospital'. Beads of sweat were already breaking out all over my body – and I hate sweating.

'What match?' asked Dad.

'It was no big deal,' I said. I really didn't want to get into this now.

'Apparently the ball hit Adam on the head,' said Dante. 'Luckily his head is totally empty, so no harm was done.'

'Adam, you never told me that,' frowned Dad.

'There was nothing to tell,' I replied. 'I just headed the ball when I should've ducked.'

'I'm surprised they picked you for the match,' said

Dante. 'Scraping the underside of the barrel there.'

'Listen, Dante, why don't you—?' I was winding up for a full and frank.

'Dante, that really isn't helping,' Dad interrupted.

'I'll shut up then,' said Dante, focusing once again on his bowl of wheat flakes.

'Dad, I don't need to go to the doctor. It's just a headache.' Which both Dad and Dante were making worse. I just needed somewhere dark and quiet.

Dad shook his head. 'Adam, what is it with you and anything medicinal?'

'Not all things medicinal. I'm more than happy to wear medicated plasters.'

Dad stood up. 'Nope. Not this time, Adam. Get your shoes on. I'm taking you to the doctor.'

No. *No.* NO.

'But you have to go to work. If we go to the doctor's now, we'll have to wait at least an hour before we get seen,' I said, desperation creeping into my voice.

'Can't be helped,' said Dad stonily. 'As you can't be trusted to go on your own, I'll just have to take you.' He stood up. 'I'll phone work and tell them I'll be late. Adam, go and get yourself ready.'

As Dad left the room, Dante raised his head and grinned at me.

'Dante, you've got to get me out of this,' I pleaded.

'No can do, mate. Not this time. Sorry,' grinned Dante, not sorry at all. 'Look at it this way, at least you're only going to the doctor's, not the dreaded "H" word.'

'Thanks a bunch,' I scowled.

'Any time, scab-face,' said my brother. 'Any time.'

So here I was sitting in our car on my way to the doctor's, and for the life of me I couldn't think of a single thing I could do to get out of it.

3

Dante

Melanie's words hit me like a bullet between the eyes. I stared, searching her expression for a sign, some sign, any sign that this was some kind of joke. But Melanie's expression didn't change. I leaped out of the armchair ready to fling her words back at her, only my legs started to dissolve so I collapsed back down. My gaze never left Melanie's face. I didn't speak. Couldn't speak. Couldn't think, certainly not over the sound of my heart pounding like a heavyweight boxer's blows.

I sat waiting, willing, wishing for Melanie to take back her words.

Ha! Not really.

Just kidding.

April fool.

Had you going though.

But she didn't say any of those things.

It wasn't true.

How could it be true?

My stomach was heaving. Dry heaving. My body started to shake, starting deep inside and working outwards like ripples on the surface of a pond. My heart wasn't the only thing that was pounding. My head was beginning to hurt.

I started to remember things I didn't want to.

The night of my friend Rick's party. The day after Boxing Day, almost two years ago now. Nineteen, no, twenty months ago to be exact. Rick's parents were away on holiday, leaving Rick and his older sister home alone. Except Rick's sister had decided to spend a few days with her boyfriend. Leaving Rick all alone, to party. I'd drunk far too much that night. But then so had Melanie. So had everyone.

I remember that night like viewing a series of snapshots. And as the night got later, the snapshots get blurrier. Melanie and I had only been going out a couple of months. And I'd had a great Christmas. I'd got the electric guitar I'd been pestering Dad for, even though I knew he couldn't really afford it. Melanie bought me a watch. I bought her a necklace. On the way to the party, I warned her that the necklace would probably turn her neck green.

'That's OK,' she smiled. 'You'll need a tetanus shot before you wear the watch. Just thought I'd warn you.'

We both laughed and started exchanging kisses, which by the time we got to Rick's house had grown into one long, long kiss, before Rick flung open his front door and dragged us both inside.

We danced.

And drank.

And snogged.

We danced some more.

We drank some more.

We snogged some more.

Someone called out that we should get a room. So a few minutes later, for a laugh, we snuck off and did just that. I remember Melanie giggling as we went up the stairs. We were holding hands, I think, but I'm not really sure. And I had a bottle in my other hand. Something alcoholic but I can't remember what. We went into the first room we came to and shut the door. And I took another swig of my drink. And Melanie giggled. And we started kissing.

More snapshots.

It'd been the first time – for both of us.

The one and only time.

And the whole thing . . . well, it was over before it'd barely begun. It had been a blink-and-you'd-miss-it sprint, not a practised and polished marathon. To tell the truth, it'd kind of put me off. I remember thinking, *Is that it then? All there is to it?* So how could *one* encounter that lasted . . . No, that was the wrong word. It hadn't *lasted*. It wasn't meant to last. And certainly not in the shape of a . . . of a . . .

'Oh my God . . .'

My gaze fell away from Melanie to the still-sleeping contents of the buggy.

A baby.

A child.

My child?

'I don't believe you.' I was on my feet again. 'My name's not even on the birth certificate. How can you be sure it's mine?'

4

Adam

'Dad, I really don't need to be here.' The desperation in my voice was very evident but I couldn't help it.

'Adam, you really need to get over this phobia you have of doctors.' Dad frowned. 'We'll see Doctor Planter and then leave. OK?'

No, it wasn't OK.

If I jumped up and ran, how long before Dad would catch up with me?

I gave the answer some serious thought, but finally decided against it. I had speed but Dad had endurance. He'd just wait me out and then he'd drag me back here. And on top of that, he'd be pissed at me.

Hang in there, Adam. In less than ten minutes, it'll all be over. The doctor will tell me to take some painkillers and throw us out and that'll be that. And then at least Dad will be off my back.

I looked around the doctor's waiting room, which contained six rows of five chairs, and health posters covering up as much of the disastrous lime-green painted walls as possible. The waiting room was half-full, mostly with mums and their kids or old gimmers of forty plus. And half the people in the room were coughing. I mean, what's up with that? It's August, for God's sake. Who gets a cold in August? God only knew what germs I was breathing in.

What were we even doing here? I had a headache, plain and simple. Since when did anyone need to see a doctor about a headache? I'd tried to tell Dad that throughout the ten-minute car journey to get here, but he wouldn't listen. Once he gets a bee in his boxers about anything, that's it. Case closed. End of story. Dante is just the same.

'Adam Bridgeman to room five, please. Adam Bridgeman to room five, please.'

The announcement came over the PA system and the scrolling electronic messaging system on the wall at the front of the waiting room said the same thing. Dad was already on his feet.

'You can wait here if you like, Dad. I'll go in by myself.'

Dad raised an eyebrow. 'That's OK, son. I'll go in with you.'

I sighed and got to my feet. That was exactly what I was afraid of. This was turning out to be a really crappy day – and it wasn't even noon yet.

5

Dante

Melanie's lips tightened; her brown eyes turned obsidian dark. Her expression hardened like she'd been turned to stone.

'I don't sleep around, Dante. Plus I've never been with anyone but you,' she stated icily. 'And if you say that again, I'll slap your face. For your information, I couldn't put your name down on the birth certificate because you weren't there with me when I went to register Emma's birth. I was told I could only put your name down as the dad if we were married or if you were present.'

She glared at me. I stared at her, finding it harder and harder to breathe. Then Melanie sighed. 'Look, I . . . I didn't come here to argue with you. That wasn't my intention.'

'Then why did you come?'

Melanie fished in her pocket for her cigarettes. She took one out and it was almost at her lips when she unexpectedly snapped it in two. Tobacco drizzled onto the carpet. Mel dropped the two ends into her pocket before running a shaky hand through her hair.

'Dante, I need to talk to you but I'm running out of time.'

'I don't understand.'

I didn't understand a lot of things. Melanie had turned up at my house and thrown a bomb into my whole life. A bomb that was still sleeping peacefully in its buggy.

'How . . . how come you didn't have an abortion?'

Melanie regarded me, then shrugged. A shrug which was meant to mean very little but, combined with her sombre expression, showed just the opposite. 'Dante, I did think about it. I thought of nothing else for days and weeks. I even went to my doctor so he could send me to my local hospital to have it done. But in the end I didn't.'

'Why not?'

'Because from the time I found out I was pregnant, Emma never felt anything less than real to me. So how could I go through with it? I just couldn't do it.'

'Did you . . . did you think about giving her up for adoption when she was born?'

Melanie studied me, her face a mask. 'You blame me,' she said quietly.

'No. No, I don't. I just . . . I'm trying to wrap my head around all this.' Trying. And failing.

'I took one look at Emma and I couldn't do that either. My aunt did her best to persuade me to give her up but I just couldn't. My mum had already chucked me out for getting pregnant and my aunt only agreed to let me stay because I said I'd have the baby adopted once it was born.' Melanie's eyes shimmered with unshed tears. 'But the first time I looked at Emma, she felt like the only thing I had left in the whole world. If I lost her, I'd have nothing . . .'

'Your mum kicked you out?' I didn't know what to say,

how to react to that. How could ten forgettable minutes of not much turn both our lives inside out and upside down like this? 'Why didn't you let me know?'

The faintest of smiles. 'What would you have done, Dante?'

'I . . . I . . . I have no idea. But to go through all that alone . . .'

'Dante, you had trouble holding a bag containing a pooey nappy. You held Emma like she was a ticking bomb. So what is it that you think you could've done?'

My blank look was answer enough, I guess.

'Exactly,' said Melanie. 'That's why I didn't even give your name to the child support people when they asked about the father.'

'But your aunt let you stay after the baby was born?'

'Yeah. Only temporarily though,' said Mel. 'But I've found somewhere else to live now.'

'Is that why you and the baby are heading north? Because of your aunt?' I asked.

Melanie nodded. She glanced down at her watch. 'Dante, could you do me a favour?'

'What?'

'Could you look after Emma for a while? I need to pop to the shops and buy more nappies and some other stuff.'

Hell, no! 'Why can't you take it with you?'

'Stop calling her "it". And Emma doesn't like to be moved so soon after falling asleep. She'll wake up and cry and get really miserable.'

How exactly was that my problem?

Except that the baby was supposed to be . . . my . . .

my . . . mine. I started to turn to look at it, but I couldn't. If I didn't look, didn't . . . acknowledge it, then it wouldn't be real. None of this would be real. How I wished there was someone standing in front of me to tell me what to think and how to feel. Because I didn't have a clue. All I felt was . . . scared. Scratch that – terrified. Heart-thumping, cold-sweating, sick-to-my-stomach, mind-numbingly terrified. What did Melanie want from me?

I started to shake my head.

'Please, Dante,' Melanie wheedled. 'I'll be back long before Emma wakes up, I promise. She'll sleep for a good couple of hours now.'

'Melanie, if she wakes up, I wouldn't have a clue what to do.' And God knows, that was the truth.

'You won't have to do anything. I'll be back in fifteen minutes or less. OK?' Melanie was already heading out of the sitting room and towards the front door.

'You can't just dump her on me,' I protested.

'At least you're calling Emma "her" now rather than "it".'

'Melanie, I'm serious,' I said. 'No way are you leaving a baby here.'

'Oh, get over yourself, Dante. I'm coming back, aren't I?'

'You can't leave your baby here,' I insisted, my tone broken-glass sharp with panic. 'I was going out.'

'Yeah, but not immediately. You said you were waiting for your exam results. I'll be back soon.' Melanie was at the now-open front door. 'And she's not just "my" baby. She's yours too. Remember that.'

'Melanie, hang on. This isn't right. You can't just—'

But she was already heading along the pavement. 'See you in a minute.'

'Why don't I shop for the things you need and you can look after your baby?' I called after her.

Melanie turned round but didn't come any closer. Her gaze kept skidding away from mine. If I didn't know better, I would've thought she was only a breath away from tears. 'Dante, what brand of nappies do I buy? What kind of food does Emma like? What do I put on her skin each night after her bath? What cream do I use when she has nappy rash? What book do I read to her every evening before she goes to sleep?'

'Well, you're not going to get all that now, are you?' I pointed out. 'So just tell me what to buy and I'll get it.'

'Dante, what's wrong with you? Are you worried she's going to jump up and bite your ankles or something? I'll be back soon. OK? And then we can have a proper talk.'

No, it wasn't OK. And I didn't want to talk or anything else with Melanie. I wanted, *needed* her to go away with her baby and never come back. If only I could just go back to bed and erase my morning, wake up and start all over again. With increasing frustration, I watched as Melanie carried on walking. With each step she took away from me, the knot inside my stomach grew tighter. I went back indoors. I wanted to slam the front door and keep on slamming it until the thing fell off its hinges, but I couldn't handle the baby waking up before Melanie returned.

I had a kid. Called Emma. My daughter . . .

Oh God . . .

What was I going to do?

Dad . . .

What was Dad going to say?

And my brother?

And my friends?

Oh God . . .

The doorbell rang.

Melanie. She'd come back. Thank goodness. But that was quick . . . Oh . . . I got it now. She was going to tell me it was all a joke. Probably set up by my mate, Joshua. This was just the kind of stunt he would pull. Josh by name and josh by nature. If this was his idea of a wind-up, then when I got hold of him, it'd be on! I wrenched open the door.

'Hiya. Package for your dad that needs signing for and some letters,' said the postman cheerily.

In a daze, I scribbled across the electronic signature box with the inkless pen the postman held out. He handed me an A4-sized padded envelope and an assortment of letters. The top letter was addressed to me. I raised my head to thank the postman but he was already on his way to the next house.

Shutting the front door, I half fell, half leaned against it. I didn't want to move from the spot. And I certainly didn't want to go into the sitting room. To tell the truth, I was petrified to go back in there. And if I stayed still, closed my eyes and waited, then maybe, just maybe, none of this would be real.

I placed Dad's padded envelope and what looked like two utility bills on the telephone table in the hall. On autopilot, I tore open the envelope addressed to me. It was my exam results. Feeling icy-cold and very alone, I looked down at the sheet of paper in my hand.

Four A-stars.

In the sitting room, the baby started to cry.

6

Dante

I sat in the armchair opposite the buggy and watched the baby's scrunched-up face, tears flowing like rivulets from its eyes and down its cheeks. It watched me just as I watched it. It struck me that at that moment, the baby and I were feeling exactly the same. And I mean *exactly* the same. The baby cried and cried and then cried some more. It was lucky. God knows I wanted to join in. But I couldn't. Boys don't cry – that's what Dad had always told me and my brother. And besides, what good would it have done?

Two minutes turned into five turned into ten, and if anything it was getting louder. My head was about to explode. I couldn't stay in the same room any longer, I just couldn't. Jumping to my feet, I left the room, closing the door firmly behind me. Heading for the kitchen, I poured myself a glass of apple juice and downed it in one, counting the moments till the doorbell rang. Where the hell was Melanie? Fifteen minutes had come and gone and practically doubled in size. The noise in the sitting room was still going on, but the strident wail had been replaced by something more tired and resentful. I paced the hallway, still trying to wrap my head around how my life was threatening to dissolve about me.

Keep it together, Dante. Panicking won't help anything.

Melanie would be back soon. She'd take the baby and head north and no one would ever know either of them had been here. No one would be any the wiser. I could get on with my life and she could get on with hers.

Somewhere around my fiftieth circuit of the hall my mobile buzzed in my pocket. The caller was unknown.

'Hello?'

'Dante, it's me. Melanie.'

'Where the hell are you? You said you'd be fifteen minutes. That was over an hour ago.'

Silence.

Calm down, Dante. I forced myself to take a deep breath. 'Mel, where are you?'

'I'm really sorry.' And Melanie really did sound genuinely upset.

'Well, as long as you're on your way back now.'

'I'm not.'

What the . . . ? 'Pardon?'

'I'm not on my way back.'

'Well, how much longer are you going to be then?'

'Dante, I'm not coming back.'

'Huh?'

'I can't cope, Dante. I've tried and I've tried but I can't. I need some time to get my head together. So I reckon Emma will be better off with you, as you're her dad.'

Falling from a plane without a parachute. Tumbling over and over, the ground rushing upwards to meet me. I can't think of any other way to describe that moment. Falling hard and fast and knowing there was no escape . . .

'Melanie, you can't do this. You can't just dump it on me because you're having a bad day.'

'A bad day? You think that's all this is?'

'Look, just come back and we can talk about it,' I said, still trying desperately to keep calm.

'Do you think I want to do this?' The constant sound of sniffing over Mel's words told me that if she wasn't already crying, she was very close to it. 'I hate leaving Emma, but I don't have a choice.'

'What're you talking about? You do have a choice. It's your daughter.'

'She's your daughter too.'

'But you're its mum.'

'And you're her dad,' Melanie shot back. 'What do I know about bringing up a kid? It's not like my dad cared enough about me or my sister to stick around and my mum had to work at two jobs just to put food on the table. I brought myself up, Dante. I don't know how to bring up anyone else and I . . . I love Emma too much to ruin her life.'

'Melanie, you can't leave it here.'

'Dante, I have to. If she stays with me, I'm afraid . . .'

'Afraid of what?'

Melanie didn't reply.

'Answer me. Afraid of what?' I shouted.

'Of what might happen . . . of what I might do . . .' Melanie's voice was barely above a whisper now.

'I don't understand . . .'

'Dante, I love our daughter. I do. I'd die for her. But I have no life. Emma and I live in one bedroom in my aunt's cupboard-under-the-stairs-sized flat with no chance of getting anything better. I gave up my life, my friends, my dreams for Emma, and sometimes when it's just me and her and she won't stop crying . . . Sometimes the thoughts in my head scare me. The things I do . . . the things I want to do scare me. Emma deserves to be with someone who can look after her properly.'

Oh my God . . . 'That's not me,' I protested, barely taking in what Mel was saying. 'I don't know the first thing about babies.'

'Maybe not, but you'll learn. You always had more patience than me. And you've got your dad and your brother and a big house and your friends.'

She had to be joking. 'Mel, don't do this . . .'

'I'm sorry, Dante. I'm going away now, up north for a while.'

I shook my head frantically. 'Melanie, please. You can't. You can't just leave . . .'

'I'm so sorry, Dante. Tell Emma . . . tell her I love her.'

'Melanie . . .'

But she hung up. I immediately tried to recall her but her number was blocked. I stared down at my phone, unable and unwilling to believe what had just happened. It took a few moments to realize that I was shaking, actually shaking.

Was this some kind of sick joke?

The painful, constant twisting of my stomach told me otherwise.

Dumped. Melanie had dumped her baby on me and was now God only knew where. She was free and clear. And me? I'd been lumbered with a kid that was supposedly mine. Well, hell no. I was off to university in less than a month and there was no way I was going to let Melanie and some baby ruin my plans, not to mention my life. No way.

The baby was getting louder and louder. My world was spiralling round and out of control like water down a plughole. I had to do something about that damned noise. Going over to the buggy, I looked down at the thing which was supposed to be my child . . . my daughter. The word set off an earthquake inside me with a magnitude of ten on the Richter scale. How could I have a kid? Ten minutes of not much with Melanie and now I had this thing screaming up at me? And it was so loud I couldn't hear myself think.

'Could you please stop crying – just for five minutes?' The words were out of my mouth before I realized how ridiculous they were. Like the thing in the buggy could be reasoned with.

Oh God, the noise.

Do something – fast.

I pushed the buggy so it was in front of the window. Maybe if the thing looked outside, it would find something to distract it and would stop crying. I broke out my phone and headed for the kitchen where the baby's wailing couldn't be overheard.

'Collette, d'you remember Melanie? Melanie Dyson,' I launched in before she'd barely said hello.

'The girl who disappeared after Christmas a while ago?'

'Yeah, that's her.'

''Course I remember her. What about her?'

'You two were friends, weren't you?'

'Well, we weren't enemies but we didn't swap diaries either if that's what you mean.'

'I . . . don't suppose you've got her current mobile number or her aunt's phone number or address, do you?'

'No. And why on earth would I have Mel's aunt's contact details?' I could imagine Collette's frown.

'Well, Mel went to live with her aunt so I thought you might . . .'

'How d'you know that?'

'Mel told me.'

'When did she tell you that?'

Dammit. 'Er . . . a while ago.'

'Hang on, she was your girlfriend back in the day, wasn't she? Why're you suddenly so keen to get in touch with her?'

'No particular reason,' I replied feebly. 'I was just wondering about her, that's all.'

'Funny time to wonder about her,' Collette commented.

'So would you know how I can get in touch with her?' I asked again, trying to rein in my impatience.

'Nope. Sorry, Dante. Haven't a clue.'

'Oh, OK. D'you know anyone who might know then?'

'No. As far as I know, Melanie didn't keep in touch with anyone.'

Damn it. What was I going to do now?

'Got your exam results?' asked Collette.

'Yeah. Four A-stars,' I dismissed.

'That's fantastic. 'Grats. I knew you would walk the exams though, Mr Boffin of Egghead Lane!'

'Thanks – I think.'

What was I going to do?

'Well?' Collette prompted.

'What?'

'Aren't you going to ask me about my exam results then?' she asked, sounding a little peeved.

'Yeah, of course. I was just about to. Did you get the grades you wanted?'

'Yep. Three A-stars and an A.' The warmth in Collette's voice left me cold. 'So we'll be going to the same university. Different faculties but the same uni. I can't wait.'

'Neither can I,' I replied faintly.

Collette and I had applied to the same university more by luck than design. She wanted to study Computer Science with a view to becoming a games designer. Collette was determined to have a career that would make her name and her fortune. Her older sister Veronica was a social worker who, according to Collette, got paid a whole heap of nothing for doing a totally thankless job. It sounded really unappealing.

'I'm going to learn from my sister's career mistakes,' Collette had told me, more than once.

Me? I'd wanted to be a journalist ever since Mum died. Our first choice of university was over two hundred and forty kilometres away, which suited me fine. I longed to leave home and be independent. And more than that, if I'm honest, I longed to only have to worry about Adam long-distance. He was my brother and I cared about him – but God knows he was hard work.

'It's going to be so great,' Collette enthused. 'You still ready to celebrate tomorrow night? It'll be fun to see everyone again before we all scatter to the four corners of the earth. I never understood that phrase. The earth is a sphere. So how can it have four corners?'

'Doorbell,' I lied. 'Got to go. Talk later.' I hung up before Collette could get out another word.

What was I going to do?

I had to do something . . . I glanced down at my watch. Dad and Adam would be back soon. I had an hour or less to try and sort out this mess. Maybe . . . maybe I could hide it until I managed to track down Melanie?

What a stupid idea. How on earth was I going to hide a baby? But I couldn't arrange my thoughts in any sort of sensible order. I never realized it before but panic was a living, breathing thing and it had taken root inside me and was ruthlessly and relentlessly eating away at my entire body. I opened the kitchen door.

At least the baby had stopped crying now.

Dammit. My mistake. It was obviously just taking a breather to get back its energy and to refill its lungs, because it was now bawling even louder than before. I shut the kitchen door again.

I spent the next ten minutes phoning around friends and friends of friends, trying to find someone, anyone who could give me more information about where Melanie might be. I was out of luck. When she'd left school, she'd cut contact with not just me, but with everyone we both knew. After twenty minutes, I had to admit defeat. Those who did remember her didn't have a clue as to her current whereabouts. Then I had another idea. I used my phone to check out Facebook. If Mel was on Facebook, maybe I could send her a message or find out if we had any mutual friends who might know her location. But she wasn't on Facebook either. I tried every variation of her name I could think of – Mel, Melanie, Lanie, Lani, her first name, her middle name and her surname and everything in-between – but still no luck.

I was well and truly stuffed.

I had to get away.

I headed for the front door, the sound of the crying baby wrapping itself all around me. Gripping me. Smothering me. I opened the door, every instinct telling me to *run*.

Get out of there.

Escape.

But the baby was still sobbing in the sitting room . . .

Slamming the front door, I turned and took the stairs two or three at a time until I reached my bedroom. I flung myself down on my bed, staring up at the Beyoncé poster on my ceiling.

What was I going to do?

I couldn't just lie there, doing nothing.

I needed to get Melanie to come back and take her child away. But how, when I didn't have her current mobile number or the address where she was going? I didn't even have her aunt's name, never mind any other contact details. The walls were closing in on me and there was nothing I could do about it.

I stared past the ceiling into nothing – and waited.

For an idea.

For inspiration.

For Mel's return.

For this nightmare to end.

For my alarm to ring and wake me up.

For a way out . . .

And I waited.

After about ten minutes, the noise downstairs finally faded away before ceasing altogether. I didn't move. I counted every fraction of a second after that, waiting for the clink of metal against metal, for the sound of a key turning in the front door.

7

Adam

'I'm not going to go, Dad.'

'Oh, for heaven's sake.' Dad's grip on the steering wheel tightened noticeably. 'Adam, you're just going to have a blood test and a scan. That's it. Why are you making such a drama out of it?'

'I'm not going.'

Dad's sigh was long and heartfelt, but if he thought I was joking, he had another thought coming. Wild horses couldn't drag me into a hospital again. Did Dad really think I was too young to remember what had happened to Mum in one of those places? If so, then he was wrong. I'd watched my mum waste away in front of my eyes whilst the doctors and the hospital had sucked the life out of her. Dad didn't understand. Neither did Dante. They had thought I was too young to know what was going on at the time so they'd never answered my questions properly or they'd just fobbed me off whenever I'd wanted to know about Mum and her illness. I'm not stupid. I know Mum died of cervical cancer. I know that. But she'd wanted to come home. She hated it in hospital, she'd told me so. And they hadn't let her leave.

'Doctor Planter said she was only sending you for some tests as a precaution,' said Dad.

'She also said it was probably nothing, just a combination of the weather, fatigue and the extra stress I felt about my exams,' I reminded Dad.

'Yeah, but having the tests won't hurt,' Dad argued.

I turned to look out of the window. It was pointless arguing. And anyway, my headaches would probably have stopped by the time we got the scan appointment.

Dad remembered to switch on the radio just as we turned into our road. Why bother when we'd be indoors in under a minute? It wasn't as if we'd hear more than a verse at most. Dad burst into song the moment he recognized the tune. And it sounded bloody awful. He couldn't carry a tune in a bucket.

'Dad, your singing sucks,' I told him.

We pulled up outside the house and Dad switched off the engine. 'You kids just don't appreciate my unique musical stylings,' he informed me loftily.

'Keep telling yourself that.' I opened the door and hopped out of the car, unable to take that unbearable racket any more. I looked at our semi-detached house with its dark blue front door, painted-white bay-window frames and its tall wooden gate at the side. Like a well-worn but comfortable coat, our house was special in a way that wasn't immediately obvious. It was something that couldn't be seen, only felt. And wasn't luxurious by any means but I was glad to see it. Even though Mum wasn't around any more, sometimes when I was at home alone or in a room just by myself, I'd swear I could almost hear her, almost smell the perfume she used to wear, almost hear her laughter like she was only a room away.

Almost.

That's why I loved our home. That's why as far as I was concerned, I never wanted to live anywhere else. I headed up the garden path and turned my key in the front door, with Dad following behind, still subjecting me to his musical stylings. I swear he was making my head hurt worse.

8

Dante

I sat up slowly, my toes curling into the blue carpet.

'Dante, we're back.' Adam's voice rang out from the hallway. 'Did your exam results arrive? How did you do? I bet you passed the lot.'

'Did you pass?' Dad's voice followed Adam's upstairs.

I headed for the top of the stairs, where I sat down. My heart was punching against my ribs. Dad and Adam looked up at me expectantly.

'So how did you do?' Adam asked with impatience.

'Four A-stars.'

'I knew it!' said Adam, a huge grin on his face.

'So you managed to pass, did you?' said Dad.

I swallowed down the disappointment flaring up inside me. But what did I expect? Praise for getting my A levels at seventeen instead of eighteen? Praise for working my butt off? Some hope.

'Yes. I managed to pass.'

'Good for you.'

Don't strain yourself, Dad, I thought sourly.

We regarded each other. Adam looked from Dad to me and back again, puzzled – the way my brother was always puzzled whenever Dad and I had a 'conversation'.

'You'll be going to university then?' said Dad.

I forced myself not to look in the direction of the sitting room. 'That's the plan.'

Dad gave a snort before heading for the kitchen. 'If I had your chances, I'd be a millionaire by now.'

And if I had one pound for every time I'd heard that, I'd be a billionaire by now.

Dad turned back to face my younger brother. 'Adam, I'm making myself a coffee before I head off to work. D'you want one? You can use it to wash down a couple of painkillers.'

'No, thanks,' my brother replied.

'D'you want a drink, Dante?'

I was an afterthought. 'No thanks, Dad.'

My fists were clenched, and for the life of me I couldn't get my hands to relax. Would it have killed Dad to show just a little more enthusiasm?

'So that means you're out of here and I get to move into your bedroom. Yes!' Adam punched the air. Then his hand flew to his temple and he let out a groan. Serve him right!

I frowned. 'Try not to miss me too much.'

'Are you kidding? I won't miss you at all,' Adam scoffed, still rubbing his temple. 'Dad, can I repaint Dante's room when he leaves?' he called towards the kitchen, before he turned back to me. 'All those pathetic posters of yours can come down for a start.'

'To be replaced by what? Posters of butterflies?'

'Butterflies and hurricanes,' said Adam, making a reference to a song by his favourite band.

44

'Butterflies and kittens with big eyes, you mean.'

Adam had a quick look around to make sure Dad wasn't looking, before waving two fingers in my direction. If only Dad could see what Adam, his little angel, got up to behind his back.

And all the time, in the sitting room . . .

This was unbearable – like waiting for the other shoe to drop. A concrete shoe, dropped from a great height and plummeting straight for the top of my head. I glanced towards the slightly ajar sitting-room door. Adam started up the stairs, grinning away at the prospect of getting my bedroom.

'So what did the doctor say, scab-face?' I asked.

My brother's smile vanished. 'She wants to send me to the local hospital for a blood test.'

'What's wrong with you?'

'Nothing – apart from the fact that you're my brother,' Adam replied.

I was about to give Adam the reply he deserved when an unmistakable sound came from the sitting room. Nothing as robust as before, but still just as audible and unwelcome. Adam's head whipped round towards the direction of the noise. And the fact that the noise had just abruptly started meant it couldn't be the TV or the stereo. There was no bluffing my way out of this one.

'What on earth . . . ?' Dad emerged from the kitchen.

I stood up slowly, my heart leaping and my stomach flipping. Dad headed into the sitting room, closely followed by Adam. I headed downstairs, each step leaden.

'Dante, what's going on? Why is there a baby in here?'

45

I stood in the sitting-room doorway as Dad frowned down at the baby. He turned to me when I didn't answer.

'Dante?'

'It's . . . Melanie brought it round. Earlier this morning. D'you remember her? Melanie Dyson. Its name . . . the baby's name is Emma. Emma Dyson.'

'Melanie's here?' Dad looked up at the ceiling with a frown. 'Is she upstairs?'

'Ooh! Dante's upstairs with a girlfriend.' Adam grinned.

At that moment I really, *really* wanted to pummel him.

'She's not my girlfriend. And she's not upstairs. She's gone . . .'

'Gone where?' asked Dad.

'She said she was going for some nappies and other stuff for the baby,' I replied. 'But she . . . she . . .'

'What?' Dad's frown deepened.

I swallowed hard. 'She's not coming back.'

'What the hell—?' Dad looked from me to the baby and back again. 'Why would she leave her little sister here? Has there been an accident?'

'It's not her sister.' I took a deep breath. 'It's her daughter.'

'Her daughter? Why on earth would she . . . ?' Dad studied me, his eyes narrowing. 'Adam, go upstairs to your room and do something.'

'Like what?'

'I don't know. Find something,' Dad snapped. 'And shut the door behind you.'

Dad's glare swept over me like a searchlight, leaving me with nowhere to hide.

9

Adam

Dad didn't often snap at me so I knew it was serious. I looked from Dad to Dante and back again. They were watching each other. Me and my headache were forgotten. But at least my headache was beginning to fade away, thank goodness. And from now on, any more headaches and I'd keep that information strictly to myself.

What was going on?

I headed out of the room, closing but not shutting the door. I stomped up and down on the first two stairs, making my steps quieter and quieter to simulate going all the way up the stairs. Then I tiptoed back to the slightly ajar sitting-room door. No way was I going to miss this. I had any number of questions tumbling in my head and I didn't believe in wallowing happily in ignorance. I didn't have a clue what was going on, but I was going to make sure I found out.

10

Dante

Reluctantly, I moved to sit down in the armchair. Dad moved back to the buggy, staring down at its contents as the seconds ticked past. How I wished I could tell what he was thinking. The baby looked up at him just as intently, its arms outstretched. Dad took the now-sniffling baby out of its buggy and held it close against his chest. The crying stopped almost at once. It laid its head on Dad's shoulder. Dad looked out of the window, his back towards me. Time passed in hollow heartbeats. He finally turned round.

'Dante, what's going on?' Dad asked softly.

'Melanie came round this morning—' I began.

'You've already said that,' Dad interrupted. 'Why did she leave her baby here? And what d'you mean, she's not coming back?'

'Mel left it here 'cause she said . . . she can't cope.' I didn't look at Dad any more. I couldn't. I was leaning forward, talking to the carpet, almost bent double by the weight on my shoulders.

'Why would she leave her daughter here, Dante?'

Silence.

'Dante, I asked you a question.'

'She said . . . Melanie said . . . she said it's my daughter too. She said I'm the dad.'

The prolonged, profound silence that followed forced my head up, albeit reluctantly. I sat up slowly. I needed to know what Dad was thinking and feeling at that moment, no matter how painful it might be. Dad stared at me, his eyes wide, his mouth hanging open in shocked surprise. With some effort he got it together.

'This is your daughter?' he asked, his eyes locked on my face.

'I don't know.'

'But she could be?'

'. . . Yes,' I mumbled.

'You stupid bloody idiot,' Dad said with intensity. 'You stupid, stupid . . .'

His voice was too soft. Too quiet. More. He should shout more.

Dad's eyes closed and he turned his face away from me. He opened his eyes but he still couldn't look at me. And damn but it hurt to breathe as I watched him. When he finally looked at me again, his laser gaze pinned me to the armchair. He shook his head slowly.

Come on, Dad. Rant at me, call me all the names under the sun. Moronic . . . careless . . . irresponsible . . . foolish . . . reckless – those were just a few of the words already rattling around in my head.

'How could you be so damned stupid?'

Ah, here it came. The temperature in his voice was rising.

49

'I never worried about you the way I worry about Adam because I thought you had common sense. Your mum always said you were the sensible one. She said Adam was the idealist, the dreamer, and that you were the one with your head screwed on straight.' Dad's contemptuous glare had me bleeding internally. 'D'you want to know something? For the first time ever, I'm glad your mum isn't around to see this.'

The last barb found its target more than any of Dad's other criticisms. That one cut deep.

Dad's voice was unnaturally quiet again. 'Dante, I don't know what to say to you. I am so disappointed in you. You've let me down, but far worse, you've let yourself down.'

Like I didn't already know that.

Dad shook his head. 'You just don't get it, do you? I wanted you to aspire to something higher than having a kid at seventeen, for God's sake. I thought I'd brought you up to be more than just a cliché.'

Is this really what Dad thought I wanted for myself? I wanted to do something with my life, be someone. I didn't want any of this. Didn't he understand that?

Dad looked down at the squirming bundle in his arms. 'So her mother has run off and left you holding the baby?'

I nodded.

Dad smiled grimly. 'How ironic.'

'What d'you mean?'

'Doing a runner is usually the man's province, not the woman's,' said Dad. He walked over to me. 'Go on. Take her.'

'What?'

'Have you held your daughter yet?'

I shook my head. Only at arm's length, when Mel had gone into the kitchen. 'Not really,' I said. Nor did I want to. Couldn't he see that?

'Take her from me, Dante.'

'Suppose I drop her?'

'You won't,' said Dad. 'Just hold her like you mean it.'

I didn't move. I didn't want to hold that thing. But one of us had to budge and I knew it wasn't going to be Dad. I took the thing, holding it awkwardly. It wriggled in my hands, on the verge of crying again.

'Hold her properly,' said Dad.

How the hell did that work? Terrified I was going to drop it, I brought it closer to my chest and readjusted my grip until its cheek was against my shoulder. Luckily it settled and was still. It brought up one tiny hand clenched in a fist to rest against my T-shirt. It was giving off a baby smell, like baby lotion and milk. Its body was warm against mine. Its hair was soft and silky under my chin.

And I hated it.

Dad sat down on the sofa. 'Tell me everything that happened this morning,' he said, his voice steely.

So I told him – the edited lowlights, but even those sounded damning.

When I finished, he shook his head again, his eyes narrowing as he contemplated me. He was beyond angry, but unlike most normal human beings, the more angry he became, the quieter he got.

'You and Melanie were regularly sleeping together?'

My face began to burn. This was not the sort of thing I wanted to be discussing with my father.

'It was once, Dad. Just once. At Rick's party. And we'd both been drinking.'

'Not too drunk to have sex but too drunk to use a condom?' said Dad scathingly.

'It was just once . . .' I muttered.

'Once is enough, Dante. You're holding the proof of that in your arms,' said Dad. 'Or is Collette or some other girl going to turn up on my doorstep holding another kid of yours in their arms?'

'No, Dad. I've only . . . done it with Melanie, and it was only the once.' My voice was somewhere below a whisper. Dad only just managed to hear me. But damn it, my face was so hot I could've provided central heating for the whole city. Dad scrutinized me. He obviously decided that I was telling the truth – which I was – because his expression relaxed, but only slightly. 'I can't believe you and Melanie had a child and I'm only hearing about it now.'

'I only heard about it for the first time today too.' I tried to defend myself.

'You didn't know Mel was pregnant?' Dad asked, his voice sharp.

I shook my head.

'Did you ever take the trouble to find out?'

My face burned even more at that. My silence was answer enough for both of us.

'Dante, I thought I'd brought you up, not dragged you up. We had the talk about taking precautions and being

52

responsible when you're in a relationship. Why the hell didn't you listen?' To be honest, the disillusionment in his voice cut far deeper than any loud, angry words could've done. I'd have to climb to the top of Mount Everest to reach the status of lowlife.

'It never occurred to me that she might be pregnant,' I protested.

'Don't you know how babies are made then?' asked Dad. 'You kept insisting that *we* didn't need to talk about the birds and the bees because it was being covered at school. Did you lie?'

My whole body was so burning hot now, at any moment I might spontaneously combust.

'It was covered at school,' I replied.

'Did you skip those lessons?'

'No, Dad.'

'Then why didn't it occur to you?'

'I thought . . . I thought Mel must be on the pill or something.' Which sounded totally pathetic, even to my ears. 'She never told me she was pregnant. She never even mentioned the possibility. And then she left school and that was that.'

'It takes two to make a baby, Dante. It doesn't matter what you thought or assumed, you should've damn well made sure she couldn't get pregnant by using a condom.'

The baby in my arms was stirring. I pulled my face away from its head, wanting to make as little contact as possible.

'Dante, hold your daughter properly. She's not a smelly bag of rubbish.'

I took a deep breath and stopped pulling away. The

room was quiet as Dad and I both tried to grasp what was happening.

'Dad, what am I going to do?' The words wobbled as they left my mouth. But I was stuck and struck and stuffed and couldn't for the life of me think of a way out. Inside, I was trembling and I couldn't figure out how to make it stop. 'I'm off to uni in a few weeks. How can I look after a baby if I'm off to uni?'

He stared straight through me.

'Dad?' I whispered after a long pause.

I had his attention once more.

He shook his head. 'Dante, you have a child now, a daughter. Take a good look at her. Her name is Emma.'

I glanced at it, then looked away. I could hardly breathe. My throat was hurting so badly, like I'd been punched in it. And my head was pounding. I was holding a *baby*. A real, live, living, breathing person. That realization terrified me more than anything before.

'I can't look after it, Dad.'

'You've got no choice, son.'

'Maybe I could put it up for adoption or to be fostered?'

The words had barely left my mouth before I realized I'd made a mistake – by saying them out loud.

'You'd give up your own flesh and blood because she's . . . inconvenient?' asked Dad. 'And adoption means giving up your own daughter for good. Is that what you really want?'

Yes. I'm seventeen, for God's sake.

Of course I didn't want to be saddled with a kid at seventeen. An acid wave of guilt swept through me, but I couldn't help it. I didn't want or need Dad's opinion of me to sink any lower. Though God knows, my opinion of myself was somewhere at the bottom of the Mariana Trench. But the kid in my arms was like a brick wall between me and the rest of my life. I wanted it removed. I wasn't going to let this thing in my arms ruin all my plans, ruin my whole future, ruin my entire *life*.

'Besides, there's no way you can put your daughter up for adoption without her mother's consent. And you said you don't know where Melanie is.' Dad scowled. 'And as for fostering, I doubt if you can even do that without Melanie's say-so. So what's your plan? To leave your own daughter on some doorstep somewhere?'

'Of course not,' I denied, shocked.

Did Dad really think me capable of such a thing? Just when I thought his opinion of me couldn't sink any lower.

'Dante, if your daughter wasn't in this room right here, right now . . .' Dad's lips compressed into a bloodless line. 'I don't know what I would do. I still can't believe you could be so stupid. You think this only affects you? It doesn't. We're all going to have to live with the consequences of your actions.'

'I'm not sitting here congratulating myself, Dad,' I told him.

Silence.

'I really don't see that you have many choices here, Dante,' said Dad slowly.

I instantly knew what he was driving at. 'Dad, I have no money, no job, no way of looking after it. I've only just got my A level results, for God's sake.'

55

'Dante, stop and take a deep breath and listen very carefully. You have a child. Whether you give her up or keep her, your world has now changed and it's going to stay that way. Nothing you do or say is going to alter the fact that you have a daughter. You need to wrap your mind around that fact and accept it, just like I'm having to.'

'What on earth can I give a baby?'

'The same thing I gave you – and your brother. A roof over your head, food on the table and . . . and being there. That counts for one hell of a lot.'

But I hardly heard him. Why wasn't he listening to me? I had to sort out my own life first. Until I'd done that, how could I be responsible for anyone else's?

'So will you look after the baby whilst I go to uni then?' I asked.

Dad started to laugh, a harsh parody of the real thing. 'I have a full-time job, Dante. How exactly am I supposed to work and look after *your* daughter at the same time?'

'How am I supposed to go to uni and look after a baby at the same time?' I protested, throwing his words back at him.

'You can't . . .' said Dad. His brown eyes darkened as they regarded me.

'I . . . I . . .' I looked at the child in my arms, now sleeping peacefully. The words Dad had left unsaid clanged in my head like a giant bell. 'If someone can't cope, I'm sure it's OK for the kid to be taken away and placed with foster parents – just for a little while.' I still wasn't ready to give up on that option.

Dad regarded me. 'So you want to do the same as Mel and dump your daughter? On strangers?'

'I'm a stranger to her,' I pointed out.

'But you don't have to be, Dante. You've got a decision to make – probably the most important decision of your life.'

'But what about uni?'

'What about Emma?' Dad replied.

'But I don't have a clue how to look after it.' Dad still wasn't listening.

'You'll just have to learn,' said Dad. 'You want to play grown-up games? Well, this right here is what comes along with it.'

Oh God . . .

Dad contemplated me and the baby in my arms. 'Dan, d'you remember when you were eight and kept asking me and your mum for a dog?'

Here it came. The life lesson. The analogy. The 'this case is the same as that one' – when it so obviously wasn't.

'Yes, Dad. I remember,' I sighed.

And I did remember – unfortunately. I'd begged and begged Mum and Dad for a dog. Any kind of dog, I wasn't fussed.

Yes, I would look after it.

Yes, I would walk it every day.

Yes, I would feed it and brush it and take care of it.

No, I wouldn't ever neglect it. Never ever.

So Dad made a decision. He didn't ask for my opinion. He didn't talk to me about it first. He came home with a goldfish. A goldfish! How was a goldfish even close to being anything like a dog? How was I supposed to bond with a fish?

'You kept on and on at us till our heads were ringing,' Dad continued. 'And what deal did we finally reach?'

'*We* didn't reach a deal,' I muttered.

'Yes, we did,' Dad argued. 'I told you that if you could look after the goldfish for three months, just three months, then we'd get you a dog for your next birthday.'

'How has that got anything to do with this?' I asked. The petulance in my voice made me sound like Adam, but I couldn't help it.

'How long did the goldfish live, Dante?'

'I don't see—'

'How long?' Dad interrupted.

'Two weeks,' I replied reluctantly.

'Eight days,' Dad corrected.

Getting a dog was never mentioned again.

'Dan, you have a daughter now. Her name is Emma. And you need to get to grips with that fact – fast. She's not a goldfish that you can neglect and then flush down the loo when it doesn't work out. She's not a dog you can take back to a pet shop or to a dog shelter when you've had enough. She's a human being that you made. You don't get to walk away, not this time, not without even trying to make it work first. Life doesn't work that way – not even at seventeen.'

'Plenty of other guys walk away in similar circumstances,' I pointed out.

'You're not "other guys",' said Dad. 'You're my son and I know I've brought you up better than that. You don't run away like some kind of coward when you're faced with a problem, especially one of your own making.'

'So what am I supposed to do?'

'You take a deep breath, you grow up and you man up. You have a daughter now . . .'

Dad and I regarded each other. Not a word was spoken. But I knew what he was saying. In a contest between going to university and looking after some baby that was supposed to be mine, as far as Dad was concerned, there was no contest. I closed my eyes. It didn't help.

'Dante?'

'Dad, I know what you want me to do,' I snapped. 'But then what? Serve burgers or sweep the streets for the rest of my life?' Or sit behind a desk all day juggling insurance claims and bored out of my skull like my dad?

'If that's what it takes, yes,' Dad replied. 'You do whatever is legal and necessary to make money. Even if Melanie came back right this minute and took Emma away, you'd still be financially responsible for your daughter for the next eighteen years. You think about that. And there's no shame in taking any job you can get to support your family.'

Family? Dad and Adam were my family. I didn't want or need anyone else. This baby would never belong, would never be wanted by me.

If Dad wasn't here I would've put the thing in my arms down on the ground and punched the walls until my hands bled.

'Dante, look at your daughter,' said Dad.

'What?'

59

Dad stood up and walked over to me. He adjusted my hold of the baby until it was lying in the crook of my arm, its eyes closed, its face turned up towards mine. It was the first time I'd had to look at it, properly look at it. Its face was round, with plump cheeks and a tiny pink mouth. Such a lot of noise could come from that mouth. Its black hair framed its head like a swimming hat. And it had the longest eyelashes that swept down its cheeks as it slept. It was warm and still in my arms, as exhausted from all that crying as I was. I don't know what Dad was expecting. Did he think I'd look down at it and decide that flipping burgers for the rest of my life was a small price to pay for having this thing in my life? Did he think I'd hold it in my arms and suddenly realize just how much I loved it? Well, I didn't. I felt nothing.

And that, more than anything else, scared the hell out of me the most.

Adam

Oh. My. God! Was I hearing this right?
   Dante has a kid?
   Uh-oh. Someone's heading my way.
   Time to make myself scarce. Temporarily, of course.

12

Dante

Dad ran a weary hand over his head. 'God, what a mess,' he said more to himself than to me. 'And I'm already late for work. I told them I'd be in by noon at the latest.' He headed for the door.

'Dad . . .' I struggled to speak but couldn't say another word. I wanted to shout out to him to stay, to help me, to fix this. I didn't want him to leave. At that moment, I might have been the sole living creature on planet Jupiter. I'd felt that way ever since Emma had come into my life.

Emma . . .

And now Dad had abandoned me to my stupidity. And God knows I didn't deserve any better, but I needed someone, somewhere, to help me.

'Hi, Ian, it's me – Tyler. I'm sorry, but something has come up. I won't be able to make it back to work this afternoon after all . . . No, no, Adam is fine. Well, he's been sent to hospital for further tests but he's no worse. No . . . I mean, yes, but I'll explain when I see you, OK? No, nothing like that . . . Yeah, see you tomorrow.' The phone in the hall beeped as it was put back on its stand on the table only seconds before Dad re-entered the room.

'Thanks.' The word was little more than a whisper, but it was heartfelt.

'Oh, Dante,' Dad sighed. 'You're supposed to be smarter than . . .'

Pause. I frowned, not following him. 'Than . . . ?'

'Smarter than . . . that, Dante. You're supposed to know that actions have consequences. You're supposed to be smarter than to end up with a kid at your age.'

But I wasn't smarter, so what was the point of going on about it?

Dad headed over to the buggy and pulled the oversized bag off the buggy handles. Sitting on the sofa, he opened the bag and started taking out the contents. Formula milk, a baby bottle, a few disposable nappies, a book with chewed corners, an A5 envelope bulging with papers, an all-in-one baby-gro thing with poppers down the front, a couple of baby wipes in a plastic bag loosely knotted at the top, a feeding cup, a couple of jars of baby food. Dad pulled out a wodge of papers from the envelope, glowering as he sifted through them.

'What are they?' I asked.

'Medical records, from the look of it.' He pushed the papers back where he'd found them. 'They can wait. I need to think.'

What did he need to think about? I was the one neck deep in crap.

Dad must've read my expression because he answered my unspoken question. 'Priorities, Dante. We both need to concentrate on the priorities now.' He gave a sigh. 'I wish your mum was here. She was always much better than me at being practical.'

'What kind of priorities d'you mean?' I asked.

'Well, for a start, Emma needs food and somewhere to sleep.'

I hadn't even got that far in my thinking. 'You mean, like a cot?'

'Of course.'

I looked around the sitting room doubtfully. 'A cot is going to look a bit out of place in here.'

Dad nodded. 'That's why it will be at the foot of your bed.'

Was he kidding? 'What? No . . .'

'Where else is it going to go, Dante?' Dad glanced down at his watch. 'I'd better head for the shopping centre now, otherwise I won't find anywhere to park.'

'It's sleeping in my room?' I asked, aghast.

'Of course. That way, if Emma cries in the night you can get up and change her or feed her and rock her till she goes back to sleep.'

Oh, hell. 'I'm a guy who needs his eight hours a night – uninterrupted.'

'Welcome to the world of parenting,' said Dad, a knowing smile on his face. He strode towards the door, turning back to face me as he reached it. 'Oh, and Dante?'

'Yes, Dad?'

'You can call Emma "it" instead of "she" until she's collecting her pension, but that's not going to change a damned thing. Now, are you going to be OK for an hour or so?'

No.

'Dante?' Dad came back into the room. 'I know this is a bit of a shock, son. Hell, it's a shock for all of us, including Emma. But you can and will get through this — if you don't do anything stupid.'

'Like what?' What did he mean?

'Just . . . hang in there. OK? I'll be back soon.' And with that, he left the room. Then . . . 'Adam, what the hell? When I'm having a private conversation, don't listen at the bloody door. D'you hear?'

'Yes, Dad,' came the contrite reply, as fake as silicon boobs.

My brother was the nosiest. Adam loved to know everyone else's business. But there was no way to hide what was going on.

'I'll be back as soon as I can. Dante, take care of your brother and Emma till I return.'

'Yes, Dad.' I stood up to put the baby back in its buggy, but it immediately started to stir and to grizzle plaintively, even though it was still half-asleep. I gave in and sat back down again. The baby quietened down at once.

The moment the front door closed, the sitting-room door opened.

'Did I hear right?' Adam asked, his eyes round and bright as a full moon.

'What did you hear?'

'You've got a daughter?'

I've got a daughter . . .

I shrugged. I still wasn't ready to admit to that, not without a bit more than just Melanie's word for it. 'This is Emma.'

'Whoa . . .' Adam stared at me, eyes still wide, eyebrows raised, mouth open in the shape of a capital O. His expression was a confused cocktail of disbelief, astonishment and awe. 'Can I hold her?' He tiptoed over to me as if his footfall would wake up the baby.

I stood up again, already stretching out my arms to hand it over. But then I hesitated.

'Er . . . you'd better sit down first,' I advised.

Adam sat down immediately, no argument. He stretched out his arms, impatient to hold it. And yet I hesitated.

'I won't drop her,' Adam promised. 'Please, can I hold her?'

I placed the baby in his arms. It shuffled and stirred, kicking out one leg, but it didn't wake up. Adam carefully readjusted his grip so the baby lay securely in his arms. He rocked it slowly before kissing its forehead.

'She's lovely,' said Adam. 'Hello, Emma. Aren't you beautiful? That must be from your mum 'cause you sure didn't get your good looks from your dad.'

'You're my brother, Adam, so what does that say about you?' I pointed out.

'Good looks bypassed you and waited for me to be born,' Adam informed me. 'She's gorgeous. She smells all fresh.' My brother raised his head to grin at me, but only for a second. He couldn't bear to tear his gaze away from the baby. He carried on speaking, his voice only just above a whisper. 'Hello, Emma. I'm Adam. I'm your dad's brother. Hang on . . . Wow! I'm an uncle. Emma, I'm your uncle Adam.'

That made me start. My brother was an uncle. At

sixteen years old. Damn. And Adam was so happy – not just his face but his whole body seemed to fizz with joy. The baby opened its eyes. Oh no! I held my breath, waiting for the cacophony to kick off. The baby looked straight at my brother – and smiled. Then it closed its eyes and went straight back to sleep.

'I'm your uncle Adam and I love you.' Adam kissed Emma once again on the forehead before holding the baby closer.

Emma had smiled at him. And I'd never heard Adam say he loved anyone. But just like that, he loved the baby. How did that work? And why did it make me feel so . . . so empty?

13

Dante

Adam didn't want to give Emma back which, to be honest, was fine with me. I had things to do – like desperately trying to find a way out of my predicament.

I went on the Internet and looked up adoption, fostering, Melanie Dyson and paternity tests. It seemed that Dad was right about adoption – it would be bloody difficult, if not impossible, without Melanie's agreement. Finding information about fostering was even harder. From the info I did manage to find, fostering seemed more likely than adoption, but even that was involved and convoluted. There was website after website about becoming a foster carer, but precious little about putting a child into foster care. All sorts of health workers and social workers had to get involved apparently. More people to witness the mess I'd made. And it seemed that the vast majority of kids were taken into foster care *because* of their parents, not put into foster care *by* their parents.

Every page I scanned about fostering made me feel more and more sub-human. This was supposed to be my child, my daughter, and here I was searching for ways to get rid of it. But I wasn't just thinking of myself, I swear I

68

wasn't. I mean, what did I have to offer a baby? In spite of what Dad said, it'd be far better off without me.

But first things first. I wouldn't have a legal leg to stand on until I established once and for all whether or not the baby was really mine. That meant a DNA test. But how did I get one of those done without going on one of those shows where people told the whole nation their private business only to be lectured and harangued by the host before the DNA results were produced. Didn't fancy that – at all. I Googled DNA tests, not expecting much. To my surprise there were loads of online organizations who carried out DNA tests to establish paternity. I scrutinized the details. It looked straightforward enough. If I coughed up most of my hard-earned money, they'd send me a DNA paternity kit. I had to swab the inside of my mouth for cheek cells – what they called a buccal swab – with what looked like a cotton bud. And I had to do the same with the baby, then send off the swabs. Five days after that, they'd send me the results and I'd know once and for all whether or not I was the baby's dad. It's not that I didn't believe Melanie exactly, but she might've made a mistake. She must've made a mistake, in spite of what she said. It was possible. I had to know for sure. Nothing else could happen until I knew one way or another. I phoned the number provided by one site which seemed more slick and professional than all the others. Lowering my voice so I'd sound more . . . mature, I gave the woman at the other end of the line my details and the number of my one and only debit card. The fee was more than half of all the money I had in the world but I figured that if the outcome was the one I wanted, it would be a small price to pay.

When I'd finished on my computer, I headed back downstairs. Adam was exactly where I'd left him. As I entered the room, he grinned at me, whispering, 'She's still asleep.'

Dad already had an action plan which he was following up and Adam was so accepting. They were both swimming. I was the only one drowning. I flopped down in the chair opposite Adam and watched how he held the baby so naturally, like it was no big deal, like he'd been doing it for years. Like it was the easiest thing in the world.

'She's lovely,' Adam said softly. 'You're so lucky.'

'Lucky?' Was he kidding?

'Yeah. You get to be loved unconditionally – at least until Emma realizes what a crap-head you are, which will probably happen when she's a teenager. That's when most kids realize their parents are crap-heads.'

'Oh yeah?' I said dryly. 'You know a lot about it for a half-pint sixteen-year-old.'

'I may be shorter, thinner and younger than you, but in everything else I am greater.'

I laughed, and it felt and sounded strange – and good. This day had already lasted for ever and I hadn't even been on the same planet as a smile since I woke up.

'Modest as ever, Adam,' I said.

But the thing was, he was right. Adam was one of those gits who breezed through exams with the minimum of effort. Actually, it wasn't just exams but life in general. I, on the other hand, had to slog my guts out. Funny, smart and good-looking, everything came so easily to him.

'One day I'm going to be a famous actor.' Adam had regaled Dad and me with his plans for his acting career from the time he was twelve. 'I want to be an actor more than anything else in the world. I live, eat, breathe and dream of being an actor.'

I mean, please! 'Is that like the way I dream of being a pop star?' I'd scoffed.

'No, 'cause yours is just a dream. You sing like a creaking door. Dad's gene! But my dream will become reality one day,' Adam replied. 'Look at me. I'm gorgeous and can act the spots off anyone else at school. In fact, it's only my modesty that stops me from being perfect!'

I mean, pleeease! 'Ladies and gentlemen, the ego has landed.'

'Adam, don't set your heart on being an actor. It's very unlikely,' Dad told him.

Adam had drawn himself up to face Dad directly. 'So was going to the moon, or inventing penicillin, but it was still done. Unlikely things happen every day. And if I want it enough, I'll get it – in spite of what you think.'

'You should have a backup plan, in case it doesn't happen,' Dad warned when it became apparent that Adam was actually serious.

Adam just shook his head. 'A backup plan means somewhere in my head, I think I might fail and that word is not in my vocabulary. Plus I'm too talented to fail.'

Dad and I had exchanged a look at that one.

And as for using the bathroom each morning, forget it! If Dad or I wanted to stand any chance of using it before midday, we had to put on jet packs to get in there before my brother. Once Adam hit the bathroom, that was it. As my brother explained it, he had to cleanse, tone and moisturize to stop his skin looking like a gravel path – his words – only it usually took a good thirty to forty minutes minimum. I mean, no one has that much skin, for God's sake!

My brother, Adam.

He grinned at me now, turning back to Emma. 'D'you want to hold her for a while?'

'Nah, it's OK. You're doing fine,' I replied.

Adam sighed, looking almost . . . sad.

'What's the matter?' I asked.

'I'd love to be a dad some day,' said Adam. 'It's not going to happen though.'

'There's nothing to stop you meeting the right girl some day, settling down and having a whole football team of kids if you want.'

Adam regarded me. 'Do I look like the kind of guy who's going to settle down with a good woman?'

'Stranger things have happened.' I shrugged.

'If I settle down, it won't be with a good woman and what's more—'

'Fine,' I interrupted. 'Go for a bad woman then. They're supposed to be more fun anyway.'

'It wouldn't be with a woman at all . . .' Adam began.

'Adam, I don't want to talk about this.' I turned away.

'No,' said Adam thoughtfully. 'You never do.'

That wasn't fair. 'You're too young to know who or what you really are,' I told him.

'How old were you when you figured out who and what you really are?' asked Adam.

'Damn it, Adam,' I snapped.

'Ah! D'you know you always bite my head off when I ask you something you can't answer?'

'I do not,' I protested. 'And all I'm saying is, this is a phase you're going through and you'll grow out of it.'

'Did you go through this phase?'

'Well, no, but I read somewhere or other that a lot of boys do.'

'Hmmm . . . a phase? So when d'you plan to grow out of yours?'

'Huh?'

'This heterosexual phase you're currently going through?'

'Damn it, Adam.'

'I'm only asking,' said Adam. 'Tell you what – when you grow out of yours, I'll grow out of mine.'

I glared at him. 'My situation is entirely different – and you know it.'

'Why? Because there are more of you? There are more brunettes than people with red hair. Does that make red-heads abnormal just because they're not in the majority?'

'You're deliberately misunderstanding what I'm trying to say.'

'No, I understand you perfectly,' said Adam. 'I'm just curious about this age of enlightenment you keep going on about. This mysterious age when I turn into you.'

'I just don't want to see you get hurt.'

My brother regarded me, a faint smile on his face.

'I know, Dante. But this is my life, not yours. What're you so scared of? What I am isn't contagious.'

'Don't be stupid. I just . . .' I began, then shook my head. 'Never mind.'

'Go on. Say it.'

'I'm concerned about you – OK?' I admitted. 'You need to be more . . .'

'In the closet?'

'No. Of course not. Well, not exactly. You just need to pick your moments.'

Adam frowned. 'The moments to talk about stuff that's important to me? Or the moments when you'd rather I didn't?'

He was deliberately twisting my words. 'I'm not the bad guy here, Adam.'

'Neither am I,' my brother informed me.

Silence.

'I know that,' I said at last.

'I'm glad to hear it.'

'Damn, but you're hard work,' I sighed.

'No swearing in front of your daughter, please. Sewer-mouth!'

I laughed, then stopped abruptly. Hang on a sec . . . Since when was 'damn' swearing? But then, I didn't want Emma to turn into the kind of toddler who went round effing and jeffing.

A toddler . . . Damn it, what was I thinking? This baby would be long gone out of my life before it had the chance to toddle anywhere.

'Did you love Melanie?' asked Adam unexpectedly.

74

There was no pause before I shook my head.

'That's a shame,' said Adam.

'Why?'

'Well, someone as special as your daughter should've been . . . made with love.'

'She shouldn't have been made at all.'

'Coulda, woulda, shoulda,' Adam pointed out. 'She's here now and she's not going anywhere.'

'The jury is still out on that one,' I said.

'D'you think that Melanie will come back for her then?'

'If there's a God,' I replied.

My brother opened his mouth to speak, only to close it again without saying a word. We both sat in silence for a while. I don't know what was on Adam's mind but his words kept buzzing in my head. I regarded the baby as it lay asleep in his arms – so small, so helpless.

My daughter, Emma . . .

Should've been made with love . . .

Yeah, it . . . *she* should've been.

There it was again – that pain like I'd been punched in the throat. I closed my eyes, waiting impatiently until I could open them again without embarrassing myself. And what was the first thing I saw? Adam kissing Emma on the forehead. Again. How I envied my brother. His default state of mind was to trust everyone and accept everything until he had a reason to do otherwise. That's what made me so anxious about him. He was so naive. Next to him, I felt like the most cynical bastard in the universe.

14

Adam

Poor Dante. I can't help feeling sorry for him. I know it must be one hell of a shock to suddenly find out you're a dad and a single parent all on the same day, but he looks like he's teetering on the edge of a cliff and believes that no matter what he does, he's going to fall. He can't see how beautiful his daughter is – which is really surprising considering who her father is.

And his face when I said I was unlikely ever to be a dad! I don't hide what I am, but my family don't exactly encourage me to be open about it either. Dad just ignores the fact that I'm gay, like it's some strange beast in the room and if he pays no attention to it, it will just fade away to nothing. And Dante acts like this is some passing fashion I'm wearing this year but which I'll discard the moment something new comes along.

For heaven's sake, I've known I was gay since I was thirteen.

And what's more, I like it. Scratch that, I love it.

I just wish Dad and Dante would chill out about it.

15

Dante

When Dad finally came home, it took him three trips to the car to bring in all the stuff he'd just bought. I swear he came home with three-quarters of the contents of the baby store he'd been to. After ten minutes of unpacking the car, the sitting room was an obstacle course. Leaning against the wall adjacent to the door, a ready-to-assemble cot packed in a box took pride of place; there were enough disposable nappies to soak up all the water in the English Channel, a baby carrier thing that let you carry a baby against your chest arms-free, a bottle of baby bath, baby moisturizer, baby cream for nappy rash and other baby pharmaceuticals, baby cutlery, baby bottles to replace the one Mel had left, a bottle sterilizer, baby bedding, a highchair, a few toys like a soft ball and a teddy bear, a couple of picture books, a dress and other baby clothes, baby booties, baby wipes – baby, baby, baby.

Adam handed a now-waking Emma back to me and flitted around the room like it was Christmas and every new thing was for him. Blinking like a stunned owl, I looked from Emma to all the stuff such a tiny thing needed and back again. And that's when it hit me just how truly clueless I really was.

'This lot must've cost a fortune,' I said, still shocked by the amount Dad had bought.

'I was only going to get a cot, some nappies and a change of clothes,' said Dad ruefully.

I stared at him.

'They're for my granddaughter, OK?' said Dad. And if I didn't know any better, I'd swear he was embarrassed. 'Everything else after this is down to you.'

Down to me . . . ? I'd be broke inside a week. And all these things . . . Dad had bought this stuff like he thought Emma was staying for a while, a long while. She'd be here a day or two, maybe a week at the very longest – just until I got back the results of the DNA test.

Emma wriggled in my arms, reaching out with both arms for the stuff on the carpet. From the strange, impatient noises she was making, she was just as excited as Adam.

'She wants you to put her down,' said Dad. 'She wants to explore.'

'Is it safe?'

Dad smiled at me. 'Yeah, just be ready to pick her up if it looks like she's about to touch something she shouldn't.'

Frowning, I placed the baby on one of the few bare patches of carpet. Emma took off like a shot. I've never seen anyone move that fast on all fours! We all burst out laughing, then looked at each other in surprise. It wasn't often these days that we shared a laugh. I was the first to stop. I was about as far from being in a laughing mood as it was possible to get.

Emma crawled over to the sofa, then tried to pull herself up. She landed on her bottom twice but she didn't cry or protest in any way, she just kept trying. Finally she managed to stand, wobbling a bit but staying upright.

'She can walk?' I asked, amazed.

'Not yet. She can stand though, so walking isn't too far away,' said Dad.

Emma pulled a packet of baby wipes towards her then sat down with a thump, taking the wipes with her. She examined the packaging like it was truly riveting. Moments passed as we all watched her. She was fascinated by something as trivial as baby wipes.

'First things first,' said Dad after a few moments. 'We need to sort out the cot. Adam, you can help me make it whilst Dante looks after Emma.'

Adam's eyes widened. He pointed to himself. 'Me? Dad, these are not the hands of a manual labourer.'

'Well, I can't do it by myself.' Dad frowned.

'Fine. Then I'll look after Emma and Dante can help you with the lifting and shifting.'

Dad sighed. 'Adam, Dante needs to spend time with his daughter. He needs to get used to being with her and she needs to get to know him. That's why you're going to help me instead of him.'

'That's not fair,' Adam complained.

'Sucks to be you,' said Dad, one eyebrow raised. 'Now move your backside and help me carry this cot upstairs.'

Adam turned to scowl at me. I smiled. It made a change for him to be the one on the sharp side of Dad's tongue. I was loving that!

'Well, let me go and change out of these clothes at least,' said Adam. 'I'm not ruining one of my favourite T-shirts.'

Adam was out the door before Dad could stop him. Dad raised his eyes skywards and shook his head. 'That clean freak in him is your mother's gene, not mine,' he said. Then, 'Dante, don't let your daughter chew the plastic.'

I turned my head. Emma now had the corner of the baby-wipe packet in her mouth and was sucking on it.

I took it out of her hands. 'No, don't put that in your mouth.'

Emma looked up at me indignantly. Her lips pursed, her eyes scrunched up. Hell! I knew what was coming.

'Here, Emma. Look at this.' I grabbed the soft felt multi-coloured ball Dad had just bought and handed it to her. 'See the pretty ball?'

Emma took the ball from me and, after turning it in her hands, raised it up to her mouth and started chewing on it.

Phew! Disaster averted!

When I straightened up, Dad had a smile on his face.

'What?' I asked.

'Nothing,' Dad replied.

Well, it was clearly something but he wasn't prepared to share it.

Adam came back downstairs wearing different jeans and a different T-shirt. The colours had changed but otherwise the style was exactly the same. From his expression, Dad was thinking the same as me. He looked Adam up and down and raised an eyebrow but didn't say anything.

'Adam, grab hold of that end and we'll make a start,'

he said. 'Dante, you stay down here and start sorting this stuff out. And make sure you keep an eye on your daughter.'

'D'you really think she's mine?' The words made a bolt for it before I could rein them in.

Adam and Dad both turned to look at me.

'Never mind,' I mumbled.

' 'Course she's yours,' said Adam. 'She looks just like you for a start.'

'I thought all babies are supposed to look like Winston Churchill?' I said, eyeing Emma doubtfully.

He laughed. 'Yeah, for about one day after they're born. After that, they take on their own looks. And Adam is right. She looks just like you.'

I couldn't see it to be honest. But then, I'd only just started looking.

'Dad, when you're in my room, could you take down the poster of Beyoncé, please?' I asked.

Dad tried and failed to suppress a chuckle. 'Why?'

My face started to burn. I decided not to rise to the bait. Luckily Dad put me out of my misery by not pushing it.

'Yeah, no problem, son.'

I ignored the knowing smile on Dad's face.

Adam squatted down and placed the tips of his fingers under the box. 'I bet this gives me blisters,' he grumbled.

Dad rolled his eyes. 'This is going to be painful,' he sighed.

16

Adam

Well, that was deeply unpleasant. Remind me never to do that again.

Still, it was for a good cause. For my niece. I still can't get used to saying that. *My niece.* I like the sound of it, though. Strange as 'niece' might sound, I bet 'daughter' sounds even weirder to my brother. Poor Dante. He's been a nanosecond away from puking his petrified guts out ever since Dad and I got back from the 'D' word. Talk about a rabbit caught in headlights. Dad's being all efficient and organized in the hope that Dante will follow his lead and get on with things as he so obviously can't get out of it. But I don't think Dante quite sees it that way.

I still can't get over it.

Dante – Mr Boffin, Mr Truth, Justice and the Bridgeman way, Mr Every-second-of-my-life-planned-for-the-next-ten-years – has got a kid. A beautiful baby girl. He's a secretive little bunny, isn't he? Study freak by day. Stud by night. Ha! I can't wait to tease him about that. Shouldn't really kick him when he's down but it's the first time I can remember him really messing up.

Dante is supposed to be the sensible one, is he?

To be honest, I was a bit hurt when I heard Dad say that. Talk about eavesdroppers never hearing anything good about themselves. But Dante hasn't cornered the market in having brains. I think Emma downstairs proves that. And Mr Playboy never even told me he wasn't a virgin any more. Whatever he told Dad, I wonder how many girls he's really slept with? God help us if more women come knocking on the door, claiming he's a daddy.

It is a shame that he didn't love Melanie though.

Time to get out of this shower before I turn into a prune. But at least a shower has made me feel human again.

17

Dante

When Dad came back downstairs forty minutes later, he had a face like a handful of mince and his eyes were blazing.

'What's the matter?'

'Your brother didn't stop complaining from the moment he took hold of the box till the time I turned the last screw,' said Dad. '*I've* got a damned headache now.'

'Where is he?'

'Having a shower. Tightening a few bolts and using a screwdriver have apparently made him pigsty dirty.' Dad flopped down in the armchair and watched as Emma examined her new teddy bear, sticking her fingers in its ears. 'Haven't you picked her up since we went upstairs?' he asked me.

I shook my head. 'She's been fine playing with her toys.'

'Have you spoken to her?'

'To say what?'

Dad sighed. 'Dante, you've got to talk to her all the time. How d'you think she'll learn to speak if you don't talk to her?'

'What should I say?'

'Anything and everything,' said Dad, adding quickly, 'anything that's appropriate.'

'Yeah, Dad. I'm not completely stupid.' Though the evidence, now poking at the eyes of the teddy bear, might suggest otherwise.

'I never said you were,' sighed Dad. 'You've got to stop thinking that every word I say to you is a criticism.'

'Could've fooled me.' The words shot out of my mouth like bullets.

Dad sighed again. 'I know . . . sometimes I'm a bit hard on you . . .'

'Sometimes?' I scoffed. 'I can't even remember the last time you praised me for anything. When was the last time you said "Well done, Dante"?'

Hell, when was the first time?

'And what should I be praising you for? Knocking up some girl and having a kid at seventeen?'

'No, Dad. I'm not expecting praise for that,' I replied angrily. 'But once in a while, just once in a while, a word of praise or encouragement would be nice.'

'I praise you when you've done something to deserve it.'

'What? Four A-stars for my A levels wasn't enough? Getting the grades to go to university wasn't good enough?'

'Of course it's good enough. You did well,' said Dad.

Oh my God! 'Don't strain yourself,' I replied.

'I mean it. You got good results and I'm happy for you.'

'Yeah, and if I use the telescope at Jodrell Bank I just might be able to detect that. Nothing I do will ever be good enough for you, will it?'

'Now you're talking rubbish,' Dad dismissed.

'Am I? As far as you're concerned, I always have been – and I always will be – a total waste of space.'

'That's not true. But I had such high hopes for you. I wanted you to do something with your life, *be* someone.'

'Instead of what I am – which is a screw-up with a kid? Well, I'm sorry, Dad. Sorry, sorry, sorry.'

'Don't shout at me . . .'

Emma started bawling. Not just crying, but bawling.

'Emma has the right idea. The way you two were shouting at each other would make anyone weep,' Adam said from the door. 'What the hell is wrong with both of you?'

Dad stood up. Adam headed over to Emma but I got to her first and picked her up.

'It's OK, Emma,' I whispered. 'I'm sorry. It's OK.' I held her close, my hand moving slowly stroking her back, whispering words of apology into her ear. I turned to see Adam and Dad standing close behind me.

'D'you want me to take her?' asked Dad.

And prove to Dad that in this, as with everything else in my life, I was a failure? I shook my head. 'I don't need your help. I can manage.'

Emma kept moving her head, straining to look over my shoulder. It took a few seconds but I finally realized why.

'Emma, your mum isn't here. She's gone away and left you – with me. She's not here. And she's not coming back.'

'Dante, don't tell the child that,' Dad admonished.

'Why not? It's the truth, isn't it?' I said. 'Emma, you and I are in the same boat.'

I don't know if Emma understood me, probably not, but she quietened down a bit after that, resting her head on my shoulder. I was here, her mum wasn't. And at least for this moment, as far as Emma was concerned, I'd done something right.

18

Dante

I couldn't sleep that night. It wasn't that Emma kept me awake, she didn't. To my surprise she slept the whole night through, so that was an unexpected result. No, what kept me awake was something else. Fear, like a ravenous animal gnawing on me. Fear of the future. Fear of the unknown. Fear like I've never felt before. More than once I got up and stood at the side of the cot, just looking down at Emma. Once, twice at most, I stroked her cheek or her hair before I even realized what I was doing. But the more I looked at her, the more terrified I got – and not for me but for her. She deserved more than I could give her. She deserved more than to be dumped by her mum. Quite frankly she deserved better. But I guess no one gets to choose their parents. You were just lumbered with what you got.

It'd been a strange evening after Dad and I had our bust-up. After one of our mega arguments, I usually strode off to my bedroom, Dad would retreat into his and Adam would stay downstairs watching TV alone.

But not this time.

Dad assembled the highchair whilst Adam got down on

his knees and started pulling silly faces at Emma, making her chortle. I tried to make myself useful by sorting through all the things Dad had bought. But all I did was shift them from one spot on the sofa to another and back again. When Dad left the room to take the highchair into the kitchen, Adam rounded on me.

'What the hell, Dante? What is *wrong* with you?' he asked, moderating his tone after a swift glance at Emma.

'Huh?'

'Dad's doing his best. Can't you even meet him halfway?'

'Now wait just a minute—' I began. A mew from Emma and the scrunched look of anxiety on her face forced me to smile and change my tone as well. I took a deep breath. 'I'm more than willing to meet Dad halfway but he won't take a step in my direction.' I spoke softly so Emma wouldn't get alarmed. 'Did you hear him say congratulations or well done when I told him my exam results? 'Cause I didn't.'

'No, I didn't hear that,' my brother admitted, adopting the same sing-song sickly sweet tone for Emma's benefit. 'But I didn't hear a single thank you from you when you saw what Dad bought for Emma either.'

'I did say thanks.'

'No, you didn't,' Adam insisted. 'The trouble with you and Dad is you're too alike.'

'Are you nuts?' I was outraged. 'I'm nothing like him.'

'Yeah, you keep telling yourself that,' Adam dismissed. He turned back to Emma and started pulling more faces. Then he picked her up and put her on her feet. 'Go on,

Emma. Walk to your daddy. Go ahead. Walk to your daddy.'

That made me start. The word 'daddy' scratched at my skin like sharp fingernails. Dad came back into the room.

'Don't want to walk to your daddy? I don't blame you,' said Adam, thinking he was being funny. 'Walk to Grandad instead. Can you say "Grandad"?'

'Oh my God!' Dad exclaimed. 'Grandad? I'm not even forty yet.'

Dad made it sound like, at thirty-nine, he was eons away from forty.

As the evening wore on, Adam didn't let up. I swear he didn't pause for breath once. Dad and I were the opposite. We didn't say one hell of a lot. Dad and I ferried Emma's new things upstairs to my room and to the kitchen as necessary with barely a word spoken between us. I kept sneaking glances at him.

Dad . . .

Funny how, before today, that word meant just a person who was always there but in the background, like wallpaper. Funny how that one short word could now travel so far and go so deep. Once the sitting room was clear of all but Emma's toys and one or two of her new books, we stayed downstairs. I don't know why Dad and Adam stayed put, but I was relieved. I must admit, I was more than a little nervous about being alone with a baby.

Damn, I still couldn't get used to that word – baby.

Dad turned on the TV, pretending he was watching some quiz show or other, but he barely took his eyes off Emma. Adam lay on the carpet and chatted away to Emma about all her new toys and anything else that popped into his head. I sat in the armchair and just watched. The atmosphere only changed when Emma started to grizzle, which quickly turned into something more meaningful.

'You need to feed her, give her a bath and get her ready for bed,' Dad informed me.

At my stricken look, he said, 'At the risk of being handed my head, would you like some help?' He had adopted the same tone I had used earlier with Emma.

The room went quiet. No unintelligible burbles from Emma, no incessant chat from my brother. They were both watching me like they knew *exactly* what was going on. I turned back to Dad.

'Yes, please,' I mumbled.

'Pardon?' Dad cupped a hand round his ear. 'I didn't quite catch that.'

Adam, the git, started to laugh. Emma looked from me to Adam and began to giggle too. Dad's lips twitched. And then, just like that, we were all laughing. Laughing like we'd all just heard the best joke in the world, when it wasn't even that funny. I guess after the day each of us had had, we needed to let off some steam.

But what I really felt like doing wasn't on the menu.

Dad nuked a macaroni cheese in the microwave, then boiled some peas and carrots. He instructed and supervised as I mashed them up, mixed them all together and fed them to Emma. Dad told me to always take the first mouthful myself to test the temperature, but duh! I'd already figured that out for myself. To my surprise and slight revulsion, Emma loved it. I gave her the spoon to feed herself but more ended up covering the highchair and me than in her mouth, so I took over. After that, Dad told me what to do and watched whilst I gave Emma a bath and put her to bed. The bath was tiring – and nerve-racking. I got just as wet as Emma with all the splashing about she did. And I couldn't take my eyes off her for a single second. I had visions of her slipping down into the water if I even blinked for too long. By the time she had on her night-gro and was in her cot, I was knackered. It wasn't just all the physical stuff of feeding and bathing and nappy changes and trying to coax her into lying down and getting some sleep. It was the mental exhaustion of having to concentrate and pay attention every second.

And people did this voluntarily?

Trying to get her to go to sleep was the most exhaust-ing. Every time I lay her down, she'd pull herself upright and stand hanging onto the side of the cot. After the third or fourth time of doing this, she started to cry. Again.

'She's in a strange room and she's not used to you yet,' said Dad from my bedroom doorway.

'So what should I do?'

'Sit her on your lap and read to her or sing or some-thing,' Dad suggested.

'Sing?'

Dad smiled. 'That's what I used to do with you.'

'You did?' I asked, stunned.

'Yep.' Dad shuffled slightly and looked down, like he was sorry he'd shared.

'But your singing sucks.'

Dad looked at me, one eyebrow raised. 'Didn't seem to bother you when you were a baby.'

'That's because I couldn't protest and didn't know any better,' I replied.

'True!' Dad smiled. 'If I were you I'd make the most of Emma at this age. Before too long she'll be looking at you like you're a doddering old fart who knows absolutely nothing – if she even bothers to look at you at all.'

Dad's words echoed around the room.

'Is that how I treat you?'

'Most of the time – yeah,' said Dad. 'But that's what happens when your kids grow older. At least Adam still thinks there's a tiny bit of life in the old dog yet!'

Dad and I regarded each other.

I turned away first. 'I'll read to her. I think she's upset enough without having to listen to me sing.'

Picking her up, I went over to my bed and sat down, carefully placing Emma on my lap, her back to my chest. Leaning slightly to grab one of her bedtime books from the foot of my bed, I held the book in front of both of us and opened it. But it was damned awkward.

'If you let her lean against your arm, then you'll both be more comfortable and she'll probably fall asleep faster,' Dad advised.

Which I have to admit worked far better. I read the picture book through twice, explaining the pictures as I went before Emma finally fell asleep. Then I moved like an arthritic tortoise to carry her to her cot, praying every second that she wouldn't wake up. I even managed to lie her down without waking her up, after supporting her head the way Dad told me.

The day was finally over.

The fear wasn't.

When the house was still and dark and everyone was finally asleep, I switched on our computer, letting the light from the monitor wash over me. One typed-in web address, a few keystrokes and a couple of mouse clicks and I was at the desired page. I sat still for, I don't know how long, just staring at the screen. Damn it, I had to do this. I couldn't give up my future, I just couldn't. I confirmed that I would be taking up my place at the university.

Now I just had to make sure it happened.

Switching off the computer, I tip-toed upstairs and back to my room, before tumbling into bed.

When I finally felt sleep creep up on me, I closed my eyes, thinking, *When I wake up, things will be back to normal. I'll have my life back.*

I'd wake up from this strange dream where I'd been landed with a baby who was a terrifying stranger.

19

Dante

I woke up to the sound of plaintive mewing, like next door's cat was upset or something. Eyes closed, I mentally swatted away the noise. Then I remembered. When I managed to will my eyes open, Emma was standing up, holding onto the sides of her cot, watching me. Throwing back my duvet, I stumbled out of bed. The closer I got to her, the more the smell hit me. And the smell was appalling. I mean, really, *really* bad in a throat-catching, nose-blistering way. I didn't need to be a rocket scientist to know I was about to be hip-deep in baby poo.

Damn it, I didn't sign up for this.

There had to be some way out. I wasn't going to get saddled with a kid who might not even be mine. Kids were truly minging, smelly and relentlessly demanding. I didn't need that. My life was full already. There was no room for Emma. I wasn't going to play this game, putting my life on hold for the next eighteen years. No way. But for now, I'd do what I had to do. Just for now.

Ten minutes later and the assault on most of my senses was over. But Emma was still grizzling.

'What's wrong now?' I asked, irritation more than

evident in my voice. I'd changed her nappy, cleaned her, and she wasn't tired as she'd only just woken up – so what was the problem?

She must be hungry, I realized. Reluctantly picking her up, I headed downstairs. Dad was already dressed in his suit and tie and was sitting at the kitchen table with Adam.

'Hiya, Emma,' grinned Adam.

'Morning, angel,' said Dad. And he sure as hell wasn't talking to me!

And good morning to you guys too!

'I've made some porridge,' Dad told me. 'Yours is in the microwave. Emma's baby porridge is on the hob, cooling.'

I sat Emma in her highchair. 'I'm not hungry. Could you do it, please? I'm going back to my room,' I said to Dad.

'Not without your daughter you're not,' said Dad.

'What?'

'Where you go, she goes,' said Dad stonily. 'You don't get to palm her off whenever you feel like it.'

Dad and I exchanged a look of mutual antagonism. But I could read his expression like one of Emma's picture books. If I went back to my room, he'd make sure Emma joined me about five seconds later. With a sigh, I poured her porridge into one of the bowls Dad had bought her and got out the matching spoon. I tried a spoonful to check the temperature, but then really wished I hadn't. It was bland to the point of being totally tasteless.

'What's up with this?' I asked Dad.

'It's probably salt-free. Children Emma's age can't handle a lot of salt,' Dad told me.

My bowl of porridge sat in the microwave, beckoning me. I was ready to douse it in maple syrup and devour it. I was starving. Putting Emma's porridge on her high-chair, I handed her the plastic spoon and headed towards the microwave to get my breakfast.

'Watch out!' Dad yelled.

I turned and immediately made an intercepting dive that a Premiership goalie would've been proud of. Didn't work, though. Emma's porridge hit the floor, followed a nanosecond later by her bowl. Her spoon was then dropped on my head.

A moment's silence. Then the room erupted. Dad and Adam cracked up laughing. Emma burst out crying. My head was beginning to hurt – and not just from being walloped on the back of it by the spoon.

'Dante, that's what happens when you take your eye off the ball,' Dad told me when he managed to control himself.

Grabbing some kitchen towel, I started to clean up the mess on the floor. Dad got up and poured another helping of baby porridge and milk into the saucepan on the hob. Adam took Emma out of her highchair and started rocking her.

And all I could think was, *suppose I had to do this by myself?* Suppose I had to clean up the mess and make more breakfast and pacify Emma with no help and by myself? Is that what Melanie had had to cope with all alone, day in, day out?

'It's OK, sweetie. It's OK,' Adam soothed.

'D'you want to give her to me?' asked Dad, opening his arms.

'No, it's OK. I've got her,' said Adam.

Dad's hands dropped reluctantly to his sides. There it was again, that burning flame in the pit of my stomach as I took in all of them in the kitchen. I straightened up slowly. Half the porridge mess was still on the floor but I didn't care. What did Dad and Adam think they were doing? Eating breakfast, chatting, carrying on like nothing was different. I'd fallen down a rabbit hole.

'Why're you both acting like this?' I asked.

'Like what?'

'Like she's normal.' I pointed to Emma. 'Like having her here is the most normal thing in the world.'

'Dante . . .' Dad glared at me.

'What?' I didn't even begin to hide my bitterness. 'What is this? I've had a baby dumped on me, my life is being flushed down the loo and you guys are carrying on like it's no big deal. Thanks a lot.'

'Someone woke up on the wrong side of bed,' sniffed Adam.

I took a step towards him.

Dad stepped between us. 'Dante, calm down,' he warned.

'Dad, this is bull-crap. You're both behaving like nothing is wrong.'

'How would you like us to behave, Dante?' Dad asked evenly. 'Should we yell? Break things? Kick in all the doors? What?'

'She doesn't belong here!' I shouted.

'Dante, she belongs with you,' said Dad quietly.

He wasn't listening to me, but then he never did. Emma

98

was still crying. Her bottom lip was quivering and she was looking at me with trepidation, like she was scared of me or something. It was that look that got to me. Dad and I might not get on, we might have our disagreements, but I had never looked at him the way she was looking at me now. I closed my eyes and took a deep breath.

When I could trust myself to speak, I opened my eyes and said, 'Don't worry, Emma. I'll clean up this mess and your grandad will make you some more porridge. OK?'

She visibly relaxed at the changed note in my voice.

'*Grandad* . . . that's going to take some getting used to,' said Dad. 'Nothing like kids to make you feel decrepit.'

The anger inside was dying down. Now it just whispered around me like an acid breeze, choking and corrosive. I had to hang in there. A few more days at most and then I'd have my life back. I could hang on for a few more days.

Whilst cleaning up the rest of the mess on the floor, I kept a surreptitious eye on Dad to see what he was doing. Making porridge for myself meant pouring some out, adding some milk and nuking it, then drowning it in syrup. The baby version seemed more involved.

'Why have you bought goat's milk?' I asked as I noticed the carton in Dad's hand. 'No one in this house drinks that stuff.'

'Babies find it easier to digest than cow's milk,' Adam informed me before Dad could open his mouth. At my stunned look, he said, 'What? I looked it up last night.'

'Why?' I said.

'Just in case a tree falls on you and I have to take over

for a while,' Adam replied. 'You know how I always consider worst-case scenarios. I like to be prepared.'

I shook my head. 'Damn, Adam, but you're weird.' The worst-case scenarios he came out with weren't just off the scale, they were off the planet.

Take two.

This time Emma's breakfast was more successful. After testing the temperature myself, I fed her spoonful after bland spoonful. She seemed to be enjoying it at any rate. With each spoonful she took, the day ahead began to weigh on me.

'Dad, when will you be home?'

Dad shrugged. 'It's Louise's leaving-do tonight so we're all due to go to the pub to give her a proper send-off, so maybe around ten o'clock?'

'I see.'

'Why?'

'Nothing,' I replied.

But it wasn't nothing. It was a big something. I was going to be alone with Emma and I was clueless about what to do with her all day. Plus I was due to go out for a drink with my mates later. How was that going to work? For the life of me, I couldn't see how to fit the baby around all the other things I wanted to do with my day. My year. My life.

'I'm hitting the shopping centre with Ramona later,' said Adam.

'Oh dear God,' Dad sighed. 'What're you going to buy this time?'

'Just school stuff, Dad,' Adam replied like butter wouldn't melt.

'I'll believe that when I see it,' Dad huffed. 'Adam, don't go spending money I haven't got.'

'As if.'

'Yeah, right.' Dad wasn't the least bit convinced.

So even Adam was going out.

I regarded Emma, running my hands over my head.

What was I going to do?

Dad sighed. 'I can help you with Emma this weekend, Dante, but I really need to get back to work.'

'I know, Dad,' I replied.

Dad was studying me. He stood up and pulled off his tie with a sigh. 'OK, Dante, I'll phone in sick or something but this is the very last day I'm taking off.'

'Really? Really?' I glanced at Adam, before turning back to Dad. 'Thanks. I appreciate it.'

'Hmmm,' said Dad with ill grace. But I didn't care. He wasn't going to leave me alone.

'But I'm still going to Louise's leaving-do tonight. I'm not missing that,' Dad warned. 'You should be OK because Emma will be asleep for the night by the time I leave and I'll only be gone an hour or two. OK?'

'OK. No problem. Thanks, Dad.' At the moment, I'd settle for whatever help he could give.

The rest of the day wasn't anything spectacular. I had to change Emma's clothes 'cause she'd washed her current baby-gro in porridge. Then Dad helped me to set up a routine for both myself and the baby. Nappy change, breakfast, play time, nap, nappy change, lunch, play time, nappy change, dinner, play time, bath, nappy, bed.

'It's the only way we managed with you and your brother,' Dad told me. 'I set up a schedule so we'd know what we should be doing at any hour of the day.'

It sounded a bit regimented to me, but whatever worked. And at least I'd know where I was with a timetable. Josh and a number of my other friends phoned throughout the day to ask about my exam results and to chat about the forthcoming party. Much as I wanted to chat back, I couldn't. I had to tend to Emma. But I promised each one that phoned that I'd see them later. The party was my oasis, the sliver of normality that I so desperately needed.

In the afternoon, Dad suggested I take Emma out in her buggy, but I wasn't ready for that. The only good thing was that Emma was already getting used to my face, because she didn't wear that look of unease any more when I picked her up. So I'd woken up and opened my eyes that morning, and a blink later it was early evening and Dad was heading out the door to go to his friend's leaving-do.

'Are you sure you'll be OK?' he asked.

I nodded. 'Yeah, I'll be fine. Enjoy yourself. Say hello to Louise for me.' I'd met her twice and she was OK.

'Well, Emma's bathed and ready for bed, so all you have to do is read to her until she's sleepy, then put her in her cot. I'll be back soon, an hour or two at most. If you need me, phone me – OK?'

'Dad, I'll be fine,' I insisted.

I waited a few seconds after the front door closed before heading back into the sitting room. Adam was rolling Emma's ball to her, much to her delight.

'Adam, can you watch Emma for me? I need to get changed.'

'For what?' Adam frowned.

'The end-of-school party at the Bar Belle,' I reminded him. 'It starts in less than an hour.'

'Text Josh and the others and tell them you can't make it.'

'Are you nuts?' I said, aghast. 'This'll be my last chance to see half of them. And it's going to be a great night. I'm not missing this for anyone or anything.'

I glanced at an oblivious Emma, who was sitting on the carpet now playing with the assorted toy farm animals my dad had bought her.

'What about Emma?'

'What about her?'

'You're going to leave her here alone?' Adam was scandalized.

'Of course not. You're here. Can't you baby-sit for me?'

'Me? Sorry, but I'm meeting my friends at the BB in . . .' Adam glanced down at his watch, exclaiming, 'Forty minutes! I need to go and get ready.' He jumped to his feet.

'Hang on.' I had to pull him back as he was practically out of the room already. 'All right then, I'll pay you.'

Adam shook his head. 'I'm going out. I'm not the one with a kid and no life.'

I only just managed to stop myself from telling him where to go and what to do when he got there.

'Adam, she's your niece,' I said. I didn't want him to know how much his words stung.

'She's your daughter,' Adam pointed out. 'I think that comes first.'

'Oh, come on. You can meet your friends any time.' I wasn't ready to give up. 'But mine is an end-of-an-era, once-in-a-lifetime thing.'

'Dante, I'm not changing my plans.'

'Not even for your niece?'

Adam smiled down at Emma. 'Nice try. See you when I get back. Bye, Emma. Look after your daddy.'

And he was out the door.

But if he or Dad or anyone else thought I was going to stay home, then they were dead wrong. No way I was staying in tonight.

Emma would just have to come with me.

20

Dante

Second and third thoughts darted around my head as I stood outside Bar Belle. We'd eaten at this wine bar a number of times before and it had a great, lively atmosphere, but now that I thought about it, I'd never seen any really young kids or babies in there. Emma was asleep in her baby carrier, her face turned sideways against my chest, but I couldn't guarantee she'd stay that way once I went inside. It was only seven-thirty, but looking through the windows, I saw the place was already more than half full. I couldn't see Adam though, which was maybe just as well. Hopefully he wouldn't spot me either. A quick hello to my friends, maybe one drink and then I'd leave . . .

Checking that Emma was still asleep, I stepped inside. The smell of sour beer, sweet wine, faint perfume and sweaty armpits – both washed and otherwise – hit me first, quickly followed by chatter, laughter and some kind of old-style jazz music. Glasses clinking, a door slamming somewhere in the distance – every sound jarred. The trouble was, getting to the restaurant area meant walking through the noisy bar. I glanced down at Emma anxiously.

It was past her bedtime and she was sound asleep, but how long would that last?

'Dante! We're over here.' Collette's voice rang out over the general noise.

Turning, I saw her standing up and beckoning to me. Josh, Logan and at least seven or eight others were already taking over one corner of the restaurant. They sat at a long table which was already covered in drinks and snacks. Collette was looking good as always. She wore a blood-red T-shirt and black jeans. Her large, brown, almond-shaped eyes shone as she smiled at me. Her braids were tied back in a ponytail and long, thin, golden tear-drop earrings glinted against her skin. My mate Josh was sitting next to her. As usual, Josh's light brown hair had been gelled to within a millimetre of its life. He was holding his bottle of lager like it was a long-lost friend and from the glazed, happy look in his dark blue eyes, it wasn't his first.

I glanced down at Emma again. How was I going to explain her? My decision to bring her with me was beginning to whiff like one of her used nappies. This could turn out to be . . . complicated. I headed over towards Collette and the others.

'Hiya, mate.' Josh grinned as I approached.

'Hey.' I smiled.

'What the . . . ?' Josh wasn't the only one to exclaim, stare or do a double take when they realized what I was carrying.

'So, how is everyone?' I asked, like there wasn't a thing wrong.

Josh shuffled over so I could sit between him and Collette.

'Hiya, Collette.' I smiled, leaning forward.

She tried to meet me at the other end of the offered kiss, but the baby got in the way.

'What's that?' Josh pointed to the contents of the baby carrier strapped around my upper body.

'What does it look like? A potato?'

'You brought a baby along?' asked Logan.

Logan was thin and wiry. He ran at least ten kilometres every day before or after school and was super-fit – and hell, did he make sure everyone knew it.

'Are you supposed to be baby-sitting?'

'Did you get lumbered?'

'You brought a kid *here*?'

Questions flew around my head like flies around a carcass.

'Is it a boy or a girl?'

'Is it asleep?'

'He's not going to poo or puke or anything nasty at the dinner table, is he?'

'I think Josh has better table manners than that!' I replied to Amy's horrified question.

'Oi!' Josh exclaimed.

'Whose kid is it?'

That was the question I'd been dreading. And my girl Collette was the one asking it.

'It . . . er, she . . . she's a relative. That is, she's . . . well . . . a relative really. And yeah, I was supposed to be baby-sitting but I didn't want to miss this.' I was babbling.

'What's her name?'

'Why on earth did you bring her?'

'Isn't she cute!'

'How old is she?'

'Her name is Emma.' I picked the easiest question to answer.

'Hi, Dante.' Adam's voice rang out from behind me. My heart plummeted. 'Oh my God! You brought Emma?'

'Yeah. So?' I turned in my seat, challenging him to make a thing of it.

'How come Dante got stuck with looking after his relative and you didn't?' asked Collette.

I glared at him – my eyes narrowing with threat and meaning. Somehow the message must've got across because, even though he looked distinctly unimpressed, he didn't say anything. It's not that I was trying to hide the truth exactly. I just wanted to tell my friends about Emma in my own time, in my own way.

'What brings you over here?' I asked my brother. Not that I particularly cared about his answer. I just didn't want him to give the game away.

'My friends haven't arrived yet,' Adam replied, stroking Emma's cheek with one finger. 'Can I hang with you guys until they get here?'

'Hell, no,' Josh snapped. 'This is a private party. You aren't invited.'

Well, I didn't want my brother hanging around with us either, but there wasn't just vehemence in Josh's voice, there was venom.

'Dante, tell your brother to get lost,' Josh ordered. 'He's not wanted.'

My frown deepened.

'You heard him,' Logan joined in. 'Get lost.'

'Hang on . . .' I began.

'Hang on for what?' Josh challenged.

I opened my mouth to argue, only my brother got in first. 'Dante, never mind. It doesn't matter.' Adam put a hand on my shoulder. 'I'll see you later.'

I looked up at my brother but he wasn't looking at me. Instead, he and Josh were regarding each other, the same belligerent expression on both their faces.

Adam turned sharply and walked away. I turned to my mates. 'Josh, that's my brother you were talking to.'

'So?'

'So if anyone tells him to get lost, it should be me not you. And, Logan, that goes for you too,' I said.

'I'm sorry, but your brother gives me the creeps,' said Josh.

What the . . . ?

'Why would Adam creep you out?' I asked slowly.

Uncomfortable silence ricocheted around our group. Against my chest, Emma was beginning to stir.

'Well?' I persisted.

'He just does.' Josh tried to shrug away his comment. 'The way he's always hanging around you and staring at . . . everyone . . .'

Staring . . . ? 'What a load of—'

'Besides, Dante, we don't want some little kid dragging around with us,' Logan interrupted.

I looked from him to Josh and back again. Were they talking about some little kid in general or specifically about my little brother?

Why didn't I ask Josh that question straight out? Was I afraid of the answer?

Josh and I had been mates since we'd both started secondary school, me at ten and Josh at eleven. Logan joined our school at sixteen and had immediately latched on to us for some reason. And to my surprise, Josh had decided to let him. Logan had been a permanent fixture ever since. But there was something a bit off in the way neither he nor Josh could quite meet my gaze.

'OK, Josh, what's going on?' I asked.

Josh shrugged. 'Nothing. Come on, Dante. You don't want your brother with us any more than I do.'

'You guys need to chill. You'll wake the baby,' said Collette.

By the way Emma was beginning to wriggle against my chest, it was already too late to worry about that. Emma opened her eyes, took a second to check out her surroundings, looked up at me – and wailed.

Damn it.

I unstrapped the carrier and tried rocking Emma in my arms, but the music was suddenly too loud and the laughter too raucous and the lights were so bright and the smell of lager was nauseating. I looked down at Emma, feeling the world through every pore as maybe she was feeling it.

And it was horrible, like the shriek of twisting polystyrene.

And I hadn't brought out her baby bag so I had no food,

no nappies, no book, nothing. The realization of how unprepared I was rubbed against my skin like sandpaper.

'It's OK, Emma. I'll take you home,' I whispered to her as she clung on to my shirt. I should never have brought her here in the first place. Stupid, stupid idea.

'God, she's kinda ugly, isn't she?' Logan laughed as he watched her cry.

My blood stopped flowing, my heart stopped beating, my lungs stopped working – just for a second. But that was long enough. I looked down at Emma, her face pinched and closed in on itself, her eyes scrunched as she sobbed her misery.

Adam was right. She was . . . beautiful.

Really beautiful.

I stood up, placing Emma back into her carrier, gently turning her head so she'd be comfortable against my heart. 'First of all, Logan, no one looks at their ever-loving best when they cry. And second and more importantly, if you ever call my daughter ugly again, I'll punch your face in.'

Stunned silence.

I regarded Logan. I didn't need to stare or glare or raise my voice for him to know I meant every syllable. Look at him. He had a face like a weasel and a constant sneaky, sly look in his eyes. And he had the nerve to call Emma ugly? I glanced around. All eyes were on me.

Well, I'd told him and all of them about Emma now. When I'd decided I'd do it in my own time and in my own way, this wasn't quite what I'd had in mind.

'Your daughter?' Collette was the first to speak.

'That's right.'

'Your daughter?' Josh repeated.

My friends were looking at me like I'd just emerged from a spaceship. Then Josh started to laugh.

'Ha ha! Good one, Dan. You had us going there.'

Some of the others also started to laugh. Most didn't. They were watching me for their cue. One '*Gotcha*' from me and I'd have 'em rolling in the aisles – well, around the tables at any rate. One word and I'd be off the hook. Emma would be my secret, a family secret. A secret . . . I looked down at Emma. She was looking straight up at me, still crying. I kissed her forehead, before turning to look directly at Collette. So many things I'd wanted to say to her, so many things I'd wanted to explain before this moment arrived. Just once, couldn't my life run according to my schedule?

'Emma is my daughter and I'm taking her home. Have a great night, everyone.'

I turned round and headed for the door. Behind me, a chorus of exclamations and questions started up, but I didn't let that stop me.

'Hang on, Dante.' Collette was at my side before I'd barely set foot on the pavement. She looked from me to Emma and back again. 'You . . . you weren't joking?'

I said nothing. If there was a joke then it was on me, not by me.

'Who is its mother?'

Pause. 'Melanie Dyson.'

'Mel?' Collette's eyes drank me in and spat me out. 'All this time you've been carrying on with Melanie behind my back?'

'Collette, you should know me better than that. Mel and I split up after Rick's Christmas party. That was almost two years ago. And like the rest of you, I haven't . . . hadn't seen her since.'

'How old is that thing?' Collette pointed to Emma.

I raised an eyebrow. 'Emma is . . . eleven months. She's a year old next month. And she's not "that thing".'

'OK. I'm sorry. But I don't understand. How come you didn't tell me that you had a daughter?'

'I only found out yesterday. Mel came round and brought Emma with her.'

'Are you two back together again?'

'No.'

Collette wore her shock like a neon dress. Not that I could blame her. I should've been in the Bar Belle, knocking back an ice-cold lager and celebrating my A level results with my friends and Collette. My head was supposed to be buzzing with plans and schemes and dreams of university and beyond. Now my entire horizon was filled with Emma and nothing else. The laughter washing out of the BB mocked me. I wanted to get far away from it.

'Didn't you know Mel was pregnant?'

'No, I didn't.'

'Is that why she left school so abruptly?'

'I guess so.'

I really wasn't in the mood for twenty questions. And the laughter inside the Bar Belle was beginning to get to me.

'Where's Mel? Why didn't you bring her along tonight?'

'She's gone.'

'Gone?' Collette frowned.

'Yes, gone. She went to live with friends and dumped Emma on me. Mel didn't want Emma and neither do I, but I'm stuck with her,' I said. The moment the bitter words were out of my mouth, I wanted to call them back. I glanced down at Emma. Now that she was outside the restaurant, she'd stopped crying but was still awake. I closed my eyes. Damn it. I shouldn't have said what I did and I sure as hell shouldn't have said it in front of her.

Damn it.

Sorry, Emma . . .

There it was again, that hard, painful lump in my throat that made it hard to swallow, hard to breathe.

'I really do have to go now,' I said wearily. 'I'll phone you tomorrow, OK?'

'I can come round if you'd like?' Collette offered.

'Yeah, OK. Whatever. I'll see you.'

I turned round and walked away. I had to get Emma home.

I had to get my daughter home.

21

Adam

Josh is such a crap-head. If only the way people are inside was reflected in the way they look outside, then Josh would look like Dorian Gray's portrait. He really is a toxic little toad. I know exactly why he didn't want me to join Dante's group. Well, it wasn't hard to figure out.

I only had to walk past Josh's table for him to get stuck in the moment I was in his sights. Dante was nowhere around so Josh waded in with one of his usual stupid comments, spurred on by that shit-stirring weasel, Logan. Logan really thinks he's all that, with his designer fade and his designer attitude and his music-producer dad who had had a couple of chart hits back in the Stone Age. I mean, who cares – apart from Logan? Josh doled out the insults whilst Logan laughed longer and louder than was necessary. Moron! I gave Josh better than he was dishing out and moved on. Josh really wasn't worth my time or effort. I wasn't going to let him or anyone else spoil my evening.

Heading for the bar, I weaved in and out of people, making painfully slow progress. It was my round but the place was now heaving. Sharpening my elbows, I tried to attract the attention of one of the barkeepers. Dante must've been nuts to think he could bring Emma to this place. I couldn't help wondering where my brother had got to though. Maybe he'd stepped outside for a while? I'd already checked out the loos, thinking maybe Dante had gone to change Emma's nappy, but he wasn't in there. Maybe, just maybe, he had seen sense after all and gone home.

'Do they even serve your kind in here?' a voice whispered in my ear.

I spun round, knowing as I did so just who was behind me. And I wasn't wrong either – unfortunately.

'How d'you manage to stay upright without your knuckles dragging on the ground?' I asked with contempt.

'Huh?'

'Exactly.' I turned away, waving the cash in my hand as I tried to get served.

'You think you're smart, don't you?' hissed Josh in my ear.

'And good-looking and talented.' I turned my head slightly to inform him. 'Don't forget those.'

Silence.

Then to my intense surprise, Josh started to laugh. 'You think a lot of yourself, don't you?'

'Yes, but I'm not alone in that,' I told him.

He laughed even harder. I turned around, now suspicious. Oh my God. He was actually smiling at me. Why? Was he feeling all right?

He was up to something.

'What're you drinking?' asked Josh.

'Why?'

''Cause I'll buy it for you,' said Josh.

My eyes narrowed. 'By the pricking of my thumbs . . .'

'Huh? What's wrong with your fingers?'

'Nothing. It's just a quote from *Macbeth*.'

'Why're you spouting Shakespeare?' Josh frowned.

By the pricking of my thumbs, something wicked this way comes. I wasn't about to finish the quote out loud though. I wasn't that stupid. But I was instantly on my guard.

Josh was definitely up to something.

22

Dante

My bedroom door opened about two seconds before I was going to repeatedly bang my head off it. I sprang back, Emma in my arms. She was still screaming.

'What's going on?' Dad asked wearily.

'I was just coming to get you,' I admitted. The words came out almost slurred, I was so tired. 'I need your help, Dad. Emma won't stop crying. It's doing my head in.'

'Is she hungry?'

'No. I tried warming up some milk but she didn't want it. And her nappy is dry and I've checked her cot in case something in it was making her uncomfortable, but it's fine. Why is she constantly crying?'

'Dante, your daughter can't speak yet, so how else is she supposed to let you know that something is wrong?'

'Dad, you're missing the point. How on earth am I supposed to know what's wrong with her then. I'm not telepathic.'

'No, you're missing the point,' said Dad. 'You don't need to be telepathic, you just have to listen to her and respond. Your mum told me that you and your brother used to have different cries when you wanted different things.

Jenny said both of you had a higher-pitched wail when you were hungry and a more whiney low-pitched cry when your nappy needed changing. Maybe it's a woman thing or a mum thing 'cause I could never hear the difference.'

Dammit. The last thing I needed at two bloody thirty in the morning was a stroll down memory lane.

'How does that help? I still don't know what's wrong with her,' I snapped.

'What I did instead, as I didn't have your mum's expert ears, was check everything. I'd check your nappy, I'd try feeding you, I'd make sure you weren't too hot or too cold or too thirsty. Dante, you have to work by a process of elimination.'

'But that takes up more time,' I protested.

'And you're in a rush to do what exactly?' asked Dad, eyebrows raised.

'Sleep,' I said plaintively. At that moment I would've paid hard cash to be able to get some sleep.

'Well, unless you want to be marching up and down with Emma all night, I suggest you try to find out what's wrong with her,' said Dad. 'Pass her here.'

Gladly. I handed Emma over to him, my tired arms flopping to my sides. I watched as Dad placed a hand on Emma's forehead and then her cheeks.

'Hmmm . . .'

'What? Is she OK?' I asked, suddenly and inexplicably anxious.

'Well, she's slightly hot and she's dribbling like a water feature,' said Dad. 'Emma, sweet pea, I'm just going to look at your gums.'

Using the side of his index finger, Dad moved first Emma's top lip then her bottom lip out of the way.

'Does she need a doctor?' I asked. 'Should I call out a doctor?'

'No need. She's teething,' said Dad. He handed Emma back to me. 'Wait here. I'll be right back.' And he disappeared out of my room. He came back waving a tube of teething gel in his hand and grinning. 'Aren't you glad I did all that shopping?'

Glad? At that moment I just wanted to bow down and worship at his sweaty feet.

'Sit with her in your lap and then you can apply some of this to her gums.'

'Is it safe?' I asked.

Dad regarded me, distinctly unimpressed. 'I did check first, Dante. I have done this once or twice before.'

'OK. No need to jump down my throat,' I mumbled.

'It's safe for children over two months,' Dad informed me. 'Are your fingers clean?'

'Of course.' I frowned.

Dad squeezed some gel onto my index finger and watched as I applied it as gently as I could to Emma's gum where her two bottom teeth were beginning to show. Emma was chomping on my finger as I applied it but it didn't hurt. I guess she was as keen as I was to stop her gums from hurting.

Dad waited with me for another five minutes, until Emma settled down and finally fell asleep. Moving like a zombie I placed Emma in her cot, covering her up to her waist with her baby blanket. Then I fell onto my own bed, too tired to do anything else.

'Night, son.' I was only vaguely aware of Dad pulling my duvet up around my body.

'Night, Dad.' I muttered.

And I was out for the count.

'Come on, Emma, just a few more mouthfuls,' I pleaded.

Each of my eyelids felt like they were made of solid lead as I struggled to keep them open.

'Open up, Emma,' I said, waving the spoon around in front of her firmly closed lips. 'Here comes the airplane!'

But she wasn't having it and I couldn't say I blamed her. She was probably just as tired as I was, but if she didn't eat now, the whole day's feeding schedule would be history. I knew I was supposed to be flexible about these things with a young kid, but flexibility and tiredness didn't really go together. And it felt like I had only just closed my eyes to sleep before it was morning and time to open them again.

'Come on, Emma. Please eat some more of this yummy banana porridge.' I leaned forward and opened my mouth to show her how it should be done.

Emma reached out and her tiny fingers touched my cheek. I froze. We watched each other intently. Emma stroked my cheek and smiled. That's all it was, a smile. Slowly I drew away, feeling strange and not sure why.

I finally finished feeding Emma her breakfast and she was now drinking juice out of her non-spill toddler tumbler. I reckoned I had about one minute – two, if I was lucky – to wolf down my bowl of wheat flakes and a couple of mugs of coffee before she started agitating to be let out of her highchair.

Emma loved to explore and at the moment, of all the rooms in the house, the kitchen was her favourite. I looked around the room doubtfully. Two days ago it had been just a kitchen. Yes, the floor had been a little sticky and the work surfaces had needed a bit of a wipe, but it had been perfectly functional and I'd never given it a first thought, never mind a second one. Now it was a deathtrap, with hidden dangers lurking at every lethally sharp corner and in every perilous cupboard. I'd already used every anti-bacterial wipe we had in the house on cleaning the floor, the cupboard handles and all the work surfaces. The kitchen hadn't looked this good in years. Only then had I let Emma crawl around whilst I made her breakfast, but I must've broken some speed records a dozen times already to pull Emma away from potential dangers. It wasn't even nine o'clock yet and I felt like I'd run a half-marathon. I was bloody knackered.

Adam entered the room, spinning round to leave the moment he caught sight of me. But too late. I was on my feet in a second.

'Adam, what happened to your mouth?'

'Nothing.' Adam paused before heading back into the kitchen. 'Morning, Emma.' He smiled at her, only to wince, his hand flying to his mouth. His top lip was swollen and his bottom lip was split, red and angry-looking.

'"Nothing" doesn't cut your lip.' I frowned. 'What happened?'

'I fell over.'

'And landed on your face?'

'It was an accident,' said Adam. 'And I'll live, so leave it alone. Besides, why should you care?'

'Huh? Of course I care. You're my brother.'

'When it suits you.'

'What's that supposed to mean?'

No answer.

'What is your problem?' I asked, exasperated.

'You didn't exactly leap to my defence last night,' said Adam, his voice edged with resentment.

'I did, actually,' I replied, knowing instantly what he was talking about. 'I told Josh not to talk to you like that. That's my job.'

My attempt at a joke failed miserably. Adam regarded me, stony-faced.

'Wait a minute, did Josh do that to you?' I asked.

'I've already told you, I fell over.'

I scrutinized my brother but he looked me right in the eye and didn't look away. If Josh had been responsible for splitting his lip, my brother would tell me.

Wouldn't he . . . ?

'What would you do if Josh *had* done this?' asked Adam, pointing to his lip.

'I don't know, but I would do something.'

'Against Josh?'

'Against Wolverine himself,' I assured him. 'No one does that to my brother.'

Adam smiled faintly. 'Well, you don't need to take on Wolverine – or Josh. Though I'll never understand why you hang around with that loser. For a start, he's got a face like prosciutto ham stretched over a toad.'

I burst out laughing. 'D'you mind? He's my mate.'

'Why?'

'Huh?'

'Why are you friends with him? And that Logan is even worse. Why d'you let Josh get away with saying and doing whatever he wants?'

'Like what?' What was Adam driving at?

'Never mind.' Adam sighed.

But I did mind.

OK, sometimes Josh came out with things that made me . . . cringe, but he didn't mean them, not really. Besides, when I first started at Mayfield Manor Secondary, I was a weed. Yeah, I admit it. Reluctantly. And like sharks sensing blood in the water, a couple of boys in the year above started focusing their attention on me. Little-big things like knocking my books out of my hands, pulling my bag off my shoulder and using it as a football, stuff like that. Well, it was Josh who stood by my side and stood up to them.

'You don't want to do that,' Josh told them. 'I mean, you *really* don't want to do that.'

And there must've been something in the way he said it because they backed down and backed off and never troubled me after that. And from that day Josh and I had started hanging out together. He didn't like the books I read, the films I watched, the music I listened to, but that was OK 'cause I learned to like his.

'He's my mate,' I said again.

'Dante, you only see what you want to see,' sighed Adam. 'That's always been your trouble.'

'Oh yeah? So tell me what it is you think I'm missing.'

Adam looked at me but didn't reply. My eyes narrowed.

'Did something happen at the Bar Belle after I left last night?' I asked.

'Nothing happened,' Adam said faintly, turning away from me.

He was hiding something. I could always tell when he was hiding something.

'Adam?'

Adam turned to me and smiled. 'Stop fussing. You worry too much.'

Probably true. After Mum died, it seemed like stressing over Adam had passed to me instead, which kind of sucked with a cherry on top.

'So did your friends turn up at the BB?' I asked.

'Yeah – eventually.'

'Who?'

'Anne-cubed.'

'Pardon?'

'Roxanne, Leanne and Diane.' Adam smiled. 'So everyone calls them Anne-cubed.'

'A name you created, no doubt?'

'Of course,' preened Adam.

Naturally.

Why were most of Adam's closest friends girls?

'So what did you do?' I asked.

'Had a laugh mostly.'

'What did you talk about?'

'Films and fit actors we all fancy, mostly.'

'Bloody hell, Adam.'

'What? I'm going to be an actor so I need to keep up-to-date with all things theatrical,' said Adam. 'And don't swear in front of your daughter.'

A quick glance at Emma established that she wasn't paying attention to our conversation, but I'd have to watch that in future.

'Weren't there any guys in your group last night?' I asked.

'Nah. Dylan and Zach didn't turn up, which was fine by me. It was just me and three girls hanging on my every word.'

'Yeah, right,' I scoffed.

'It's true. It was my chance to shine,' grinned Adam.

Oh my God.

'Why can't you be more like . . . ?'

'You?'

'Other guys,' I said.

'I'm a leader, not a follower,' Adam informed me loftily. 'Unlike some I could mention.'

'Meaning?'

'Meaning I'm not afraid to be different.'

'Different is going to get your arse kicked.'

'Not with you to look out for me,' smiled Adam. 'And watch your language – sewer-mouth.'

If Emma hadn't been present, he would've been treated to a full-blown, five-act, sewer-mouth extravaganza.

'Have you decided what you're going to do about your place at university?' Adam asked before tucking into his yoghurt mixed with oatmeal and grapes (very good for the skin apparently).

'No,' I admitted. 'Not yet.'

'Waiting for divine inspiration?'

'No. Waiting for the postman,' I replied.

'Pardon?'

'Never mind.' I wasn't prepared to tell Adam or Dad about taking a DNA test. Not yet. They wouldn't understand. They'd think I was trying to get out of something.

Dad rolled into the kitchen, scratching his bum and yawning, his boxers slung low on his hips. Thank God I'd already had my breakfast.

'Dad, d'you mind?' I asked, putting my hand in front of Emma's eyes.

'Setting up your granddaughter for years of therapy there, Dad,' said Adam.

'Oh. I'll be right back,' said Dad. He was already turning when he finally took in Adam's face. 'What the hell happened to you?'

'I tripped and fell,' said Adam.

Dad frowned. 'Don't your bloody eyes work?'

'Dad, d'you mind not swearing in front of Emma, please?' I said. 'I don't want her to inherit your pottymouth.'

'Cheeky bugger.'

'Dad!'

'OK, OK. Sorry, Emma. And Adam, be more careful.' Dad muttered to himself all the way back up the stairs. Adam and I exchanged a smile. Emma pulled down my hand and giggled.

Dad returned wearing the dark green dressing gown I'd bought him for his birthday about three years ago. I'd seen him in it precisely twice, the day I gave it to him and today. 'Happy now?' he asked as he entered the kitchen.

'I'm sure Emma is.' I spoke for her.

'Hello, angel.' Dad headed straight over to Emma and lifted her out of her highchair. He raised her high above his head, beaming up at her. 'How is my precious?'

'You sound like Gollum,' laughed Adam.

'Your uncle is a cheeky sod. Oh, yes he is. Oh, yes he is,' said Dad.

'Dad, not in front of Emma, please,' I sighed.

'Sorry. Your grandad is very sorry, Emma. Damn! Grandad! I still can't get used to how that word makes me feel so bloody old.'

'Dad!' Adam and I said in unison.

'Oh yeah, sorry,' said Dad ruefully. 'Emma, you're such a good baby, aren't you? Aren't you a good baby?'

'Good baby? You do remember that I was up most of last night with her, don't you?' I said sourly.

Dad turned to me. 'Dante, count yourself lucky that she's not a newborn. Newborn babies wake up about every two hours throughout the night, wanting to be fed. At least, you guys did. You see these wrinkles around my eyes? They're thanks to you two.'

'You've got those because you don't moisturize,' said Adam.

'I'd rather have the wrinkles,' said Dad. 'So how have Emma's teeth been this morning?'

'Well, she's not crying any more but she's still drooling

all over me,' I said, remembering how soggy my T-shirt was by the time I'd carried Emma downstairs for her breakfast.

'No female would drool over you for any other reason,' said Adam.

My brother really thought he was funny.

The metallic click of the letterbox heralded the arrival of the postman. I headed for the front door before anyone else could move.

It had arrived.

My DNA kit had arrived.

23

Dante

Dumping the other two letters on the hall table, I called out, 'I'll be right back,' before racing upstairs. I needed to be alone whilst I figured out what needed to be done. Tearing open the packet, I carefully placed its contents on my bed. There were three different-coloured collection envelopes; one blue, one pink and one yellow. Blue for the dad, pink for the mum and yellow for the baby. How very stereotypical. Luckily for me this test didn't require a swab from Melanie to establish paternity. Each collection envelope had details on it that needed to be completed before the swab was put into it. As well as the collection envelopes, there were two pages of instructions, a reply envelope and three plastic packets each containing two cotton swabs. According to the instructions, I wasn't allowed to drink coffee or tea for at least four hours before taking my cheek swab and I had to wait at least two hours after Emma had eaten before I could swab her cheek. I could still taste the cup of coffee I'd just finished so now I'd have to wait. Damn it.

Each swab was wrapped in sterile plastic packaging which should only be opened just before being used, and the instructions dictated in capital letters that I couldn't touch the swab end at any time. They'd provided two swabs per person, and each swab had to be allowed to air dry for at least half an hour before being placed in the appropriate collection envelope. I could choose to have the results either posted or emailed back to me. I thought long and hard about that. Email was faster, but we all shared the one computer and I sure as hell didn't want Adam or my dad getting the results before me. I didn't want them to even know what I was doing, not yet. So snail-mail it was then.

Now that the test was here, I just wanted to get on with it. Instead I'd have to cool my heels until just before lunch time. Then I'd have to wait between four to seven days for the results. I thought back to the early hours of the morning, pacing up and down, up and down and trying to rock Emma to sleep. Not even my nights were my own any more. The funny thing was though, when she was awake, I couldn't stop watching her, looking at her.

My daughter, Emma . . .

My daughter, Emma?

'I just need to know the truth,' I whispered into the silence in my room.

That's all I wanted, the truth.

So how come I still felt so guilty about doubting that Emma was mine?

After tidying up the stuff on my bed and hiding it away in my bottom drawer, I retrieved my mobile which I'd left off and recharging all night. It was a reflex to switch it on and stuff it in my pocket but the moment I put in my pass code and SIM code, the thing started beeping. Seven missed calls from a number of my friends and twice that number of missed texts. The word had really got around. I pushed the phone into my trouser pocket before heading back downstairs. I'd only just reached the bottom of the stairs when the doorbell rang. I opened the door. It was Collette. Well, she hadn't wasted much time.

'Can I come in?'

I stood aside to let her pass, shutting the front door once she'd walked past me. We stood facing each other, awkward embarrassment flapping like some captured bird between us. She leaned forward. A brief kiss followed, more to get it out of the way than for any other reason.

'Dante, how're you? You OK?' asked Collette.

'Fine.' I shrugged, though it had to be obvious that I wasn't.

'How's . . . er . . . ?'

'Emma? She's fine. She's in the kitchen.'

I led the way, feeling really uncomfortable. Yesterday, I'd been so pissed with Logan that there hadn't been room for anything else. But now, I felt hot with something beyond embarrassment, something a little too close to mortification. Collette was my girlfriend. We'd exchanged loads of kisses and the odd grope or two or twenty, but nothing more. And here I was with a kid.

'Hi, Adam. Hello, Mr Bridgeman,' said Collette as we entered the kitchen.

'Oh, hi, Collette. Excuse my dressing gown,' said Dad, looking daggers at me.

Adam nodded in Collette's direction before continuing

with his breakfast. Collette looked at Emma but didn't say anything.

'I'll just go and get changed,' said Dad, drawing his dressing gown further around himself. He scooted past us, still glaring at me. That'd teach him!

'Aren't you going to say hello to Emma then?' asked Adam.

Funny, but I'd been thinking the same thing myself.

Collette was momentarily taken aback. 'Oh yes. Of course. Hi, Emma.'

Collette walked over to the baby and awkwardly patted her head. Adam raised an eyebrow. Frowning, Emma looked up at Collette. I hurried over and took Emma out of her highchair before she could protest at Collette's treatment the only way she knew how.

'So this is your daughter?' said Collette. I could see she was struggling to find something appropriate to say.

'No flies on you,' said Adam.

Collette shot him an impatient look. Emma wrapped an arm round my neck and looked Collette up and down like she wasn't terribly impressed. I had to bite my lip but Adam wasn't as discreet.

'Dante, your daughter is a smart one,' said Adam as he stood up and headed for the dishwasher. 'She must get her brains from her mum.'

Emma began to chortle.

Collette frowned. 'Adam, you're not funny.'

'Emma thinks I am,' replied Adam.

Which made me bite my lip even harder. There was something about Emma's laughter that was infectious.

Though judging by Collette's stony expression she was immune.

'Dante, she looks like you,' said Collette.

'No one is that unlucky,' Adam quipped.

'Dante, can we go for a walk or something?' said Collette, exasperated. 'I'd like to talk to you in private.'

'Adam, I don't suppose you could . . . ?'

'No, I couldn't baby-sit,' interrupted Adam.

'We could take Emma with us,' suggested Collette. 'Maybe to the park?'

Take Emma out? In daylight?

'We could take Emma in her buggy,' said Collette.

Oh God. Pushing a buggy . . . I took a deep breath. I mean, it wasn't that I was . . . ashamed of Emma. I wasn't. It was just . . . People were bound to gawp at me. I glanced out of the kitchen window. It was a beautiful day with a blue sky and not a cloud in sight, so I couldn't even use the weather as an excuse to stay put.

'Would you like to go for a walk?' I asked Emma. She smiled at me. I took that as a yes. 'I'll be right back,' I told Collette. 'Help yourself to a drink from the fridge if you want one.'

I headed upstairs with Emma and changed her out of her baby-gro and into one of the new dresses Dad had bought her. Her legs kicked out constantly like she was riding a bike in a triathlon. It was only my super-fast reflexes that stopped her kicking seven bells out of my arms. I put some fabric booties on her feet and we were ready to go. I hit the landing just as Dad came out of the bathroom.

134

'You might've told me that Collette was coming round this early,' he admonished.

'I didn't know she was,' I replied.

'Hmmm.' Dad was only slightly placated. 'Are you going out then?'

'Yeah, we thought we'd take Emma to the park.'

'Er, not without a hat on her head,' frowned Dad. 'It's baking out there. D'you want the girl to get heatstroke? Where's the pink cotton bonnet I bought her?'

'In my drawer,' I replied.

'Well, it'll do more good on her head,' said Dad, adding with a sly smile, 'I remember you had the sweetest little yellow bonnet and you used to cry your eyes out whenever your mum or I took it off you.'

'Ha ha, Dad.'

'I'm sure I've got a few photos of you in your sweet little hat if you'd like to show them to Collette.' Dad's grin broadened.

'Oh, my splitting sides,' I said sourly before heading back into my room to get Emma's hat. Behind me, Dad chuckled.

Emma now had one of the three drawers in my chest of drawers. All my stuff that used to be in there had been chucked into the bottom of my wardrobe. I put Emma in her cot and rooted around in the drawer until I found her hat. The moment I put it on her head, she raised her hand to try and pull it off.

'I don't blame you,' I told her. 'But we're going out now and it'll protect you from the sun.'

'Nnuuh, nnuuhg . . .' Emma told me.

'I hear you,' I replied. 'But it's for your own good.'

We headed downstairs. Collette followed me into the sitting room and watched as I put Emma in her buggy. I checked Emma's baby bag to make sure I had spare nappies and we were ready to go.

'See you later, Dad,' I called out.

He appeared at the top of the stairs, fully dressed in jeans and a blue T-shirt, thank goodness. 'Enjoy your walk.'

Collette opened the front door and we walked out into the sunshine.

I'd never pushed a buggy before, and to be honest it felt a bit strange. Different. Unfamiliar.

'D'you want me to push her?' Collette asked from beside me.

'No, it's OK. I've got it,' I told her.

We walked in silence for a while. I honestly couldn't think of anything to say – something that had never happened between me and Collette before.

'I'm sorry,' said Collette finally.

'For what?'

'That you've got stuck with a kid you don't want.' Collette was only repeating what I'd said the night before, so why did it jar with me?

'I was stupid, that's all.'

'Did Melanie say when she's coming back?'

'No. It could be next week or next year. Or never.'

'What're you going to do?'

'I'm not sure. I'm thinking about my options,' I said.

'What about university?'

'I'm still hoping to go, but . . .' I shrugged. I didn't need to say anything else. Silence.

'What will you do if Melanie doesn't come back before you're due to start at uni?'

I shrugged again. 'I'm trying to sort it out so that I can still go to uni, but it'll take a week or two before I know one way or another what my options are.'

'What're you planning?'

'I don't want to say yet.' I forced a smile. 'I don't want to jinx it.'

Pinning all my hopes on a DNA test was clutching at straws the size of quarks but it was all I had. If Emma . . . if she wasn't my daughter, then I could hand her over to social services with a clear conscience.

But if it turned out that she was my daughter . . .

'Nnuuu . . . wwunn . . .' said Emma.

I peered over the buggy. 'What's the matter?'

Emma was kicking out and waving her hands and didn't look at all happy.

'What's wrong?' asked Collette.

'I think she's thirsty,' I replied.

Well, it was a hot one. The sun was beating down like it was in a bad mood. Emma was grizzling, and quite frankly I couldn't blame her. It hadn't been my idea to come out in the first place. We were only halfway to the park and I was already feeling like a wilting lettuce leaf.

'We could all do with something to drink,' I decided. A few shops further along the high street was a newspaper shop that sold groceries as well. I swung the buggy round and we all headed inside. Heading straight for the fridge,

I grabbed a carton of orange juice for Emma, a can of ice-cold ginger beer for me and a strawberry and banana smoothie for Collette 'cause I knew it was her favourite. Then we went over to join the queue of people who'd had exactly the same idea.

A blonde middle-aged woman in the queue directly ahead of us turned round, to check out who was behind her, I guess. She looked fed-up and bored, but the moment she caught sight of Emma she was all smiles.

'Hello, petal,' said the woman, bending down to beam in poor Emma's face. I pulled Emma's buggy back slightly. I mean! 'She's gorgeous.' The woman smiled at me. 'And doesn't she look like you.'

How I wished people would stop saying that. 'Hmm . . .' I replied noncommittally.

'How old is your sister?' asked the woman.

'Er . . .'

'It's not his sister, it's his daughter,' Collette provided.

Why on earth did Collette volunteer information the woman hadn't even asked for?

The expression on the woman's face changed dramatically. Her eyes were wide, her mouth open in shock. 'She's your *daughter*?' she asked, scandalized. She didn't say it quietly either. More people in the queue turned round. My face began to burn. 'She's your daughter?' the woman repeated, even louder than before just in case there was someone in the country who hadn't heard her the first time. 'How old are you?' she continued, her eyes narrowing.

None of your business, that's how old I am, I thought

belligerently. I glanced at Collette. She was looking down, embarrassed.

'Well?' the woman persisted.

'Seventeen,' I said reluctantly.

Instant facelift. Her eyebrows almost hit her dyed blonde hairline. 'Seventeen?'

Oh my God. The echo in this shop was truly astounding. The woman looked Collette up and down like Collette wasn't much.

'Don't look at me. It's not my baby,' Collette proclaimed. 'I'm just a friend. It has nothing to do with me.'

I looked at Collette, taking in the indignation lining her face. Her lips resembled an umbrella in the pouring rain.

One glance revealed only too clearly that the blonde didn't believe her. 'Kids having kids,' the woman sniffed. 'And no doubt you're not working and living off benefits.'

'It's none of your business what I'm living off.' That last comment made me snap like a ginger biscuit.

'It is my business when it's my tax money that's providing your child benefit and Jobseeker's Allowance and whatever else it is that wasters like you get from the state.'

'Excuse me?' She wasn't really saying what I thought she was saying, was she?

'Seventeen and with a kid.' The woman shook her head.

'For your information, I don't get a damned penny off the state,' I said furiously.

'Dante, just leave it.' Collette tried to place a placating hand on my arm but I was so bloody angry, I vigorously shrugged her off.

'You don't know a thing about me, so where d'you get off talking to me like that?'

'Look, I don't want any trouble in my shop,' the shopkeeper called out from behind his counter.

'Leave him alone,' piped up a woman behind me. I spun round to see who was speaking. A brunette with a tired, sagging body to match her tired, sagging face was holding onto the hand of a small boy about six or seven years old. 'At least he's in his child's life. At least he hasn't done a runner like a lot of men do.' The brunette put an arm around her boy to pull him closer as she spoke.

Her words should've made me feel better, but they didn't.

The blonde woman who was giving me a hard time pursed her lips and favoured me with one last filthy look before she turned away. Others in the queue ahead of her were regarding me with varying degrees of disapproval.

'What?' I asked, spitting out the word with intense resentment.

They all made a great show of turning to face the front.

And all I wanted to do was punch the living daylights out of something. Or someone. And all I wanted to do was hop on the first train, destination: Anywhere, with just the clothes I was wearing and nothing else. And all I wanted to do was sink into a super massive black hole and hide.

It hit me like a ton of bricks. I was in a lose–lose situation.

Ironic that when I'd saved up and bought my phone, it'd come with all kinds of information.

When Dad had bought our family computer, it had been packaged up with all kinds of instructions.

When Melanie dumped Emma on me, there was nothing. No manual, no briefing, no crash course, nothing.

I was doing my best, but if Emma stayed with me, every person I met would feel they could comment or condemn or criticize. And if Emma . . . went away, it would be the same deal.

No matter what I did, no matter how hard I tried, it would never be enough.

24

Adam

Some days memories wrap around me and keep me cocooned and warm and safe. And some days memories wrap around me, spiky and sharp as rusty barbed wire. How can the same memories bring two such completely different feelings?

Today I'm thinking of my mum.

And it hurts.

25

Dante

In spite of every instinct telling me to go back home, I didn't. Was I really going to let some ignorant old biddy ruin my day? The verdict was already in on that one. Three streets and not much chat later, we reached the park, which made pushing the buggy a lot easier. On the way there, I'd had to wheel it out into the road at least three or four times because inconsiderate gits had parked their cars more on than off the pavement, making it impossible for a buggy to get past. Before Emma, I wouldn't have even noticed. Now I wanted to key each car barring my way.

Once we reached the children's playground, I put Emma in a baby swing after checking it carefully to make sure there was no way she could slip out. Then I pushed her gently back and forth. She loved it, laughing with pure abandon. I smiled as I listened to her pure joy at a little thing like a baby swing. As Emma's laugh washed over me, the storm still raging inside began to fade and die. I looked around the playground, noticing all the other kids having fun. It'd been quite some time since I'd even been here. Listening to the laughter and shouting brought back memories of how much I used to love this place. Strange that I should've forgotten that.

It wasn't that I hadn't considered having a wife and children of my own some day. To be honest, it was one of those things I considered inevitable, like a mortgage and paying taxes. If only this were ten or fifteen years in the future, then I'd have no trouble doing it. No trouble at all. It wasn't Emma who was wrong. It was just the timing. Just my lousy timing.

'This feels strange,' said Collette.

'Yeah, I know,' I agreed.

We stood together yet apart. I carried on pushing Emma.

'So how was the Bar Belle last night?' I asked at last.

'To be honest, I left about thirty minutes after you did. I didn't really feel in the mood to celebrate much,' said Collette.

We exchanged a look, full of meaning. I smiled apologetically.

'Was anything said about me while you were there?'

'Not much.' At my wry smile, Collette laughed. 'OK, you were . . . mentioned.'

'I bet.'

'One or two were surprised you had a kid and reckoned you were a bit of a dark horse. Logan said at least it showed you weren't firing blanks, just duds – but then he would say something like that. Lucy thought it had to be a wind-up and Josh . . . never mind.'

'No, tell me. What did Josh say?'

Collette shifted from foot to foot, unable and unwilling to meet my gaze.

'Collette, what did he say?'

'It was no big deal. He just made some comment about your kid and your brother.'

'What kind of comment?' It was like trying to get blood out of a stone.

It was only when Emma mewed in protest that I realized I had stopped pushing her. I resumed at once.

Collette sighed. 'He said that living with Emma was probably the closest Adam would ever get to the opposite sex. But don't worry, Adam told him where to go.'

'Josh said that to Adam?' I asked sharply.

'Adam was walking past our group and Josh started up. You know what he's like when Logan's around goading him. But Adam gave as good as he got.'

Damn it. That's what I was afraid of.

'Stop worrying. Adam is more than capable of taking care of himself.'

'Yes, I know,' I said.

Adam had a tongue like a razor, so my money was on him to win any argument. But not all arguments were fought with sentences. I needed to have a word with my brother. I really didn't understand this antipathy between my brother and Josh. They both had a similar sense of humour, the same degree of self-confidence and they both lived their lives at least fifteen minutes ahead of the rest of us. So why all the hostility?

I remembered a school trip to Paris when we were fourteen. On our way back to our hotel from some museum or other, Mrs Caper, our teacher, told us that there was something really weird about the next street we were going down. It was a well-known fact that for some unexplainable, inexplicable reason, travelling down that particular street made everyone's toes change colour. Well, of course, everyone wanted to see that. There was a real buzz of excitement in the coach as everyone started pulling off their shoes and socks, me included, and started examining their feet.

All except Josh.

'Ooh, it's true. My toes are orange!' said someone – I think it was Ben.

'You plank!' Josh nudged me from where I was bent over, still examining my big toe.

'Huh?'

'Look out the window,' said Josh.

Puzzled, I sat up and did that. The next moment, my eyeballs were on stalks and staring. Sex shops galore! The things I saw in those windows were the best education I received throughout the whole Paris trip. I looked around the coach. Everyone except me and Josh – and the teachers – was checking out their toes.

'Mrs Caper only said that so we wouldn't look out the window and see all the sex shops,' said Josh, confirming what I'd only just realised.

'My toe is blue! My toe is blue! It really works!' exclaimed Paul.

Josh and I laughed ourselves hoarse at that one. Even now, just thinking about it brought a grin to my face. And when I told Adam that night, he figured out the punch line long before I reached it. He guessed it'd been Mrs Caper's ploy to stop us from looking out of the window. Like I said, fifteen minutes ahead of everyone else.

'Dante, what happens if . . .' Collette's voice snapped me back to the present.

'Yes?'

'If Melanie doesn't come back at all?'

'I really don't know,' I replied.

Silence.

'Dante, what's wrong with me?' Collette asked quietly.

Huh? 'What d'you mean?'

Collette took a deep breath. 'How come you had a kid with Melanie, but you've never wanted more than a kiss and cuddle from me?'

I stared at her. Was she serious? Where Collette had had trouble meeting my eyes before, she was looking straight at me now.

'You never said you wanted to take things further,' I said.

'That's 'cause you never asked.'

'Would you . . .?' A quick glance down at Emma. 'Would you have wanted to, if I had asked?'

Collette shrugged. 'I honestly don't know. But I was never given the opportunity to make that choice, was I? So what's wrong with me, Dante?'

'Nothing. I promise.'

'Then how come you wanted Mel, but not me?'

I sighed. 'It's not that simple.'

'Explain it to me then.'

Oh God. This was beyond uncomfortable.

I took a moment to frame the right words. 'Collette,

d'you remember Rick's party a couple of years ago, the day after Boxing Day?'

Collette nodded.

'Well, that's when it happened between Mel and me. But we were both drunk and we were both anxious that someone would burst into the room at any moment so it was . . . well, it wasn't the best of circumstances.' Cheeks flaming, I really didn't want to say much more than that. Collette nodded again to show she understood. 'That was the one and only time,' I said. 'And it was nothing to email home about either. But you and me . . . well, I've been thinking a lot about the two of us together recently, before Mel turned up with Emma. But you live at home and so do I and I wanted the first time with you to be different to what it was with Mel.'

'Different how?'

'I wanted it to be somewhere where we could both take our time and not have to worry about being interrupted. I thought that maybe at uni when we both had our own rooms . . .'

'Oh, I see.'

I smiled faintly. 'Like I said, I've been giving it a lot of thought. But now there's Emma . . .'

'Yeah.' Collette regarded Emma thoughtfully.

'So what are your plans now?' I asked Collette.

'My plans haven't changed. I still want to get my degree and make something of my life.'

'And if I can't join you?' It was really unfair of me to ask but I needed to know.

'Dante, I like you, I really do, but I'm going to

university. I'm going to have a career. I've got plans. I want to have a life. All this . . .' Collette's gesture was open-handed, but she might as well have pointed directly at Emma. 'All this is a bit . . . overwhelming.'

For me too. Didn't anyone recognize that? But I got the message. This was not what Collette had signed up for.

'I understand,' I said. And I did. My lousy timing had struck again.

'It's not fair that you should have to give up on all your dreams for something that wasn't planned or wanted,' said Collette, anger lending an edge to her voice.

It wasn't that simple. The 'something' she was referring to was a 'someone'. A someone I was currently pushing in a swing. A someone who had kept me up most of the night, but a someone who only had to laugh once to make me smile. A real, living, breathing person – and that made all the difference.

'There must be something we can do.' Collette shook her head.

'I don't see what,' I replied. 'Emma doesn't come with an on-off switch that I can use for the next three years while I get my degree.'

'I'm not giving up,' said Collette.

But she had to know there was nothing she or I could do.

We spent another half an hour at the playground. I held Emma upright all the way down the baby slide and we did that a few times. Next, I placed her on the baby seesaw, holding her whilst Collette pushed the other end up and down. And the whole time Collette and I discussed uni, school, friends, politics, even the weather – but not Emma.

And there was no more talk about the two of us.

We headed home after that. I invited Collette inside but she declined.

'I have a lot of stuff to sort out before I leave for university,' she said.

That should've been my cue to say, 'So do I.'

I said nothing.

'I'll phone you soon, OK?' said Collette.

'OK.'

'Don't worry, Dante. We'll sort something out,' said Collette, before leaning in for a kiss. And as I kissed her, I couldn't help wondering if this would be the last time ever. She and I would soon occupy different worlds.

I went indoors. The cool quiet of the hall was more than welcome. Unfastening the buggy straps, I took Emma straight upstairs, closing my bedroom door firmly behind me. I swabbed her cheek. I swabbed my own. I left the swabs balanced two-thirds on, one-third off my desk so that they could air dry. Emma sat on the carpet, exploring rather than reading one of her picture books. I sat on my bed and watched her as I waited for my old life to return.

Emma looked up at me and smiled, before returning to her book. I looked down at her and tried to figure out exactly what I was feeling, but I had to give up. The cocktail of thoughts and feelings coursing through me was far too mixed up to decipher.

Once the swabs were dry, I placed them in the proper collection envelopes and sealed them before placing them in the reply envelope. Time to head out again. I'd just wash my hands, then we'd get this done.

In the bathroom, I stared at myself in the mirror above the sink. Was it my imagination or was my face thinner? I wasn't eating regularly. I just snatched a snack here and there when Emma was taking a nap. And by the time she was in bed, I was too knackered to bother eating. Looking after a kid was a twenty-four/seven deal. There wasn't a hell of a lot of room for anything else. I was just drying my hands when a strange, hollow sensation crept over me. My bedroom door . . . I had shut my bedroom door, hadn't I? I stepped out onto the landing. Emma was crawling along the landing, a second away from the top stair and still moving.

'*Emma!*'

Emma turned towards me but her hands were past the top stair now. Her momentum was going to pitch her forward.

'EMMA!' I've never yelled so hard or moved so fast.

Emma cried out, her body tilting forward. I snatched her up – but only just in time. And it was only sheer luck that I didn't tip over and plummet down the stairs with her in my arms. Emma was wailing now – and God knows I knew how she felt.

'EMMA, DON'T EVER DO THAT AGAIN!'

She bawled even louder at that. I wasn't helping matters, but I'd had to shout over the sound of my own heart roaring. I felt sick. My blood had been replaced by adrenalin to get to her in time, but now I actually felt physically sick. My head was filled with images of what might have happened – and all because I'd left my bedroom door ajar. I half collapsed, half sat down on the landing, Emma still gripped in my arms. I rocked back and forth slowly whilst dragging air back into my lungs.

'I'm sorry, Emma. I'm sorry.' The words were softly spoken and heartfelt. It wasn't her fault. I was the one who'd left my bedroom door open. I hugged her even more tightly. 'I'm sorry.'

And I was, and for more than just my bedroom door.

That was five years off my life, right there.

Dad used to say that, whenever Adam or I got up to some mischief which he then had to bail us out of: '*That's another five years off my life,*' was what he always said after he'd finished shouting at us.

For the very first time, I knew exactly what he meant.

'What's going on? What's all the shouting about?' Dad emerged from the kitchen.

'Nothing, Dad.' I stood up, my legs still wobbling.

Dad frowned at me. 'Are you OK?'

'Yeah, I'm fine.'

Still clutching Emma to me, I headed back to my room. I needed to buy a gate for the top of the stairs as soon as possible. The cost would put a considerable dent in what was left of my money, but no way was I going to go through that again. The envelope containing the swabs lay on the bed, mocking me. I sat down next to it and rocked Emma in my arms until she quietened down. Snatching up the envelope, I made tracks whilst holding Emma firmly.

There would be no more accidents or incidents.

Less than a minute later, Emma was back in her buggy

and I was wheeling her towards the nearest postbox. But when I stood in front of it, for some reason I couldn't fathom, I hesitated. I looked down at Emma, who was trying to eat her own toes. I looked down at the brown A5 stamped envelope in my hand.

And still I hesitated.

What the hell was wrong with me?

'This isn't about her or me,' I told myself. 'This is about the truth.'

And I'd already paid a whole heap of money for this so I couldn't afford to bottle out now. Forcing myself to focus on what was in my hand rather than what was in the buggy, I thrust the envelope into the postbox.

I was doing the right thing.

Wasn't I?

26

Dante

That evening, Emma just wouldn't settle. I guess her teeth were still giving her grief, which meant her teeth gave everyone grief. I rubbed some baby tooth ointment on her gums and the hard shell of her emerging two bottom teeth but it didn't seem to make much difference. I rocked her, I paced up and down, I lifted her high, I even tried playing my favourite songs on low volume to try and get her to fall asleep – but nothing, and I mean *nothing* worked. Plus the phone wouldn't stop ringing. I hadn't replied to any of the messages or texts on my mobile so my friends had resorted to using our landline. By the time Dad had taken the fifth message, he was getting pretty pissed off.

'Dante, I'm not your social secretary,' he told me. 'Next time, you answer it.'

Then, on top of everything else, the doorbell rang. As I was already on my feet rocking Emma, I headed for the door before Dad or Adam had the chance to stand up.

It was Aunt Jackie.

Damn! The family grapevine was working overtime. The moment I opened the door and saw her, my heart didn't so much sink as dive-bomb. Emma took one look at my aunt and cried louder. She was very perceptive.

Looking at my aunt always made me feel . . . wistful, I guess. She and my mum had been twins, though not identical, but close enough in looks for me to see Mum every time I looked at Aunt Jackie. But their looks had been the start and the end of their similarities. Mum had been honey, whereas my aunt was vinegar. Mum always had a ready smile. It needed an Act of Parliament for my aunt's lips to turn upwards. And from the look on her face, I was about to get it – both barrels.

Aunt Jackie gave Emma a significant look. 'I see the news is correct. You've been a busy boy.' She launched straight in with this verbal uppercut to the chin. Then she tapped her cheek. I reluctantly gave her a kiss, following our usual ritual. I stepped away from her pretty damned sharpish the moment the kiss was planted. Emma was squirming in my arms. Terrified I was going to drop her, I tried putting her down on the ground, but she just cried harder at that. With a sigh, I placed her against my shoulder again. Aunt Jackie gave Emma a long, hard look before turning her attention back to me.

Here it comes, I thought, bracing myself.

'Can you say the word "contraception" or is that too many syllables for you to handle?'

Right hook to the temple.

'Hello, Aunt Jackie,' I said faintly. I doubt she even heard me over the sound of Emma's crying, which was probably just as well. The tone of my voice would've given far too much away.

'I seriously thought you had more sense,' said my aunt.

155

Left jab to the stomach.

'But like ninety-nine per cent of men, you don't have enough blood in your body for your brain and your willy to function simultaneously.'

My blood turned to lava and not just my face but my whole body was now burning hot with embarrassment.

Knockout blow – and down for the count.

'Hhmm, give her to me.' Aunt Jackie held out her hands.

I wasn't keen on handing Emma over to Aunt Jackie's tender mercies, but my aunt wasn't a woman who took no for any kind of an answer. Aunt Jackie gently touched Emma's hair and stroked her cheek, before resting my daughter against her shoulder and gently jiggling her. But Emma was still crying.

'What's wrong with her?' asked my aunt.

'She's teething.'

'Ah! Teeth giving you gyp, love?' she said to Emma. 'Well, I'm over . . . er . . . twenty and my teeth still give me gyp. If they weren't so useful, I'd have them all taken out.'

I didn't know whether to laugh or snatch back my daughter.

My daughter . . .

'Dante, you look tired.'

'I am,' I admitted.

'Get used to it.'

Stupid me. For one brief second there, I'd actually thought that some sympathy might be heading my way. Aunt Jackie placed her free hand under my chin and gave it a squeeze.

'Honey, don't beat yourself up. Yes, you were careless, but you were also damned unlucky.'

I waited for the tripwire. None appeared, so I tried to smile but it wobbled on my face.

'You hang in there, OK?' said my aunt. 'All this must be totally overwhelming but for now just take one day at a time.'

'I'm trying, Aunt Jackie, but it's hard.' I couldn't speak above a whisper. Any louder and the words would make me choke.

'And Emma has everyone's attention?' asked Aunt Jackie with a smile.

Her words made me start with surprise. 'Something like that,' I admitted.

'Honey, just hang in there.'

'I'm hanging on by my fingertips as it is,' I told her.

'You hang on by your fingerprints if you have to,' said Aunt Jackie.

'What if I muck up?'

'Don't you think every parent worries about exactly the same thing?'

'Do they? Even when they're old and in their thirties?'

Aunt Jackie smiled. 'Yes, even when they're that old.'

'But, Aunt Jackie, what if I fail? Emma is a real, live person. I muck this up and someone else suffers.'

'D'you want some advice?'

I nodded warily.

'Do your best, love. That's all any of us can do. If you can look at yourself in the mirror and know you did your best then you're ahead of the game.'

'Aunt Jackie, how come you never had any kids?' I asked.

My aunt looked at me thoughtfully as if she were trying to decide something. Then she sighed. 'I was desperate to be a mum actually. I managed to get pregnant four times, but each time I had a miscarriage.'

'Oh, I didn't know,' I replied, not quite sure what to say next. 'Did you decide to stop trying after that?'

'After my fourth miscarriage, I was told I'd never be able to have children. That's when my ex walked.'

'That's why you and Uncle Peter got divorced?' I said, shocked.

Aunt Jackie nodded.

'What a bastard.'

Aunt Jackie smiled sadly, shaking her head. 'No, he wasn't. He was just as desperate to be a dad as I was to be a mum. But he could walk away from the situation, and I couldn't. That's just the way it is, Dante. Some get to walk away. Some don't.'

Aunt Jackie and I looked at each other, and in that one moment, we understood each other perfectly.

'Jackie? You should've warned me that you were coming round.' Dad emerged from the sitting room.

Aunt Jackie pursed her lips. 'Oh, so you need a warning now?'

'I didn't mean that the way it came out,' sighed Dad.

There was something odd about the way Dad and Aunt Jackie acted around each other. There was a strange watchfulness between them, like two animals circling each other. Even when Mum was alive, I can't remember my aunt and Dad ever having much to say to each other.

'Why are you still out in the hall?' asked Dad.

'I'm talking to my nephew.'

'Jackie, the boy doesn't need one of your lectures,' said Dad.

'No, but maybe the truth would help him instead?'

'What d'you mean?' I asked.

'Yes, Jackie,' said Dad, drawing himself up to his full height, a muscle pulsing in his jaw. 'Why don't you tell us all what you mean?'

And I didn't need super-vision to see the look that passed between them. The temperature in the hall was rapidly approaching absolute zero.

'Aunt Jackie, what's going on?'

'Tyler, don't be so sensitive,' Aunt Jackie told Dad. 'All I meant was that you can help Dante, if he gives you a chance, 'cause you've had to bring up him and his brother alone for the last few years.'

It took a couple of seconds but Dad relaxed slightly and Aunt Jackie did the same, taking her cue from him.

'Oh, I see.'

He might. I didn't. There was definitely something not quite right going on.

'Look, you two, we do have chairs. Why don't you chat sitting down?' said Dad. 'Jackie, d'you want a cup of tea?'

'I'd love one,' said my aunt.

Dad headed off towards the kitchen.

'Have you and your dad had a heart-to-heart about all this?' Aunt Jackie lowered her voice to ask.

'About all what?'

'About how you're feeling? How you're coping?'

'Of course not. Besides, girls do that – not guys.'

Aunt Jackie shook her head. 'Dante, you are so like your dad.'

'No, I am not,' I denied. Adam had said the same thing and I didn't appreciate it then either.

Aunt Jackie gave me a knowing smile. 'Here, I think your daughter would rather be held by you.'

She handed Emma back to me. To my surprise, Emma settled against my shoulder and did indeed quieten down. Making sure she was secure in my arms, I leaned my head against hers briefly. Aunt Jackie gave me a significant look. I straightened up, moving my head away from Emma's.

'What?' I asked.

'Dante, don't . . . underestimate yourself,' my aunt told me.

'What d'you mean?'

Aunt Jackie sighed. 'I remember how . . . withdrawn you became when your mum died. I think Jenny's death made you . . . wary of change.'

'I'm still not with you.' I frowned.

'All I'm saying is, don't let the past make you afraid of getting to know your daughter.'

Is that what she thought was going on? If so, then she had it all wrong. But I wasn't about to argue with her.

We headed into the sitting room.

'Hi, Aunt Jackie.' Adam sprang up and gave our aunt a hug. Adam did that kind of stuff so much more easily than I did.

'Hey, Adam, how's life treating you?' asked Aunt Jackie,

her eyes narrowing as she noticed his cut lip.

'Don't worry about this.' Adam laughed it off. 'I fell, that's all.'

'Any other injuries?'

'No.'

'Hhmm . . . Funny-peculiar fall that cut your lip and nothing else . . .' Aunt Jackie was no more convinced than I was.

Adam shrugged but remained noncommittal.

'So how are you?' Aunt Jackie asked my brother.

'Got a bit of a headache, but apart from that I'm fine,' said Adam.

I only half listened as Aunt Jackie and my brother chatted about her shoes and some musical Aunt Jackie had recently seen at the theatre and other world-shattering stuff. My aunt's words kept playing in my head. I held Emma on my lap until she wriggled to be free. Aunt Jackie watched as Emma crawled here, there and every-where, exploring every corner of the room. At the first sign of potential danger, I was on my feet but nothing happened. Mind you, I was bobbing up and down like a yo-yo, just in case. Emma used the armchair to pull herself upright. She looked around the room, taking in me, my brother and my aunt.

'Walk to Daddy,' said Aunt Jackie. 'Go on, honey, walk to Daddy.'

Emma turned her head towards me straightaway. Already she knew who I was. Just that one action made my heart hiccup inside me. Was there more to family than biology? Was there some instinct at work as well? I mentally shook my head. What the hell? All kinds of strange thoughts seemed to have taken over – thoughts of Emma at five, and fifteen and thirty-five. Thoughts of playing football with her, going on holiday, taking her to school, discussing art and politics and music and truth, teaching her stuff . . .

Fantasies of her staying . . .

Emma's hands came away from the armchair. I squatted down and opened my arms.

'Come on, Emma. Walk to . . . me.' I smiled.

She took two, then three steps before falling straight into my arms.

But she had walked.

And to me.

Adam started clapping excitedly. Aunt Jackie was ooh-ing and aah-ing all over the place. I scooped up Emma and held her above my head. She smiled down at me. I grinned up at her.

'Clever girl,' I told her. 'That's my gene!' There was no explaining the pride I felt at that moment. I hugged her to me. 'Aren't you a clever girl?' I said softly.

I was about to kiss her on the forehead, but then I remembered the letter I'd dropped in the postbox earlier. I put Emma down on the carpet again. She immediately crawled away to play with one of her toys. When I looked up, Aunt Jackie and Adam were watching me.

Without saying a word, I headed up to my bedroom.

I needed to be alone – just for a while.

In spite of all I'd promised myself, Emma was affecting my thinking.

27

Adam

I turned to the left. I rolled to the right. I lay on my back. I twisted round to lie on my stomach. I picked up my pillow and buried my head under it. It was no good. I could still hear Emma wailing. At this rate, by morning the bags under my eyes would be the size of holiday suitcases. I couldn't stand it any more. Hopping out of bed, I headed next door to Dante's room. I mean, what was he doing? Just letting her cry in her cot? Not bothering to knock, I flung open his bedroom door. Dante was holding Emma and pacing up and down.

'How much longer does this go on for then?' I demanded.

Dante's stunned stare rapidly morphed into a blood-freezing glare. 'Are you kidding me?' he asked, his voice clipped and staccato.

I pulled a face, beginning to think that I might've been just a bit hasty. 'Well, I'm sorry, but how am I supposed to get to sleep with that racket going on?'

'And how are you supposed to sit down ever again once I've finished kicking your arse?' Dante asked. And his expression told me as words couldn't that he was mere nanoseconds away from carrying out his threat.

'D'you want some help?' I offered by way of apology.

'Make her stop crying and I'll give you anything you want,' said Dante.

'You look completely frazzled,' I told him.

'You try marching up and down with a crying baby for two hours. See how you look at the end of it,' Dante snapped.

'Maybe you're holding her the wrong way?' I suggested. I didn't have a clue what I was talking about, but it sounded reasonable.

'Why don't you come over here and show me how it should be done?' said Dante.

'Because Mr Bridgeman only raised one stupid son, not two,' I told him.

I only just made it out of the room in time before his pillow smacked me in the head.

Dante had the last laugh though. Emma's crying kept me awake for at least another hour. By the time the house was quiet, I was beyond exhausted. Half-awake, half-asleep, I promised myself that the next time I passed a pharmacy, I would pop in to buy Dante a dozen boxes of condoms. Though it was sort of locking the stable door after the horse inside had been well and truly fertilized.

28

Dante

Over the next few days I tripped and fell into a strange domesticity. My days, nights and thoughts all seemed to revolve around Emma. The daily schedule Dad had written out for me was a life-saver. At least with that I could kid myself that I sort of knew what I was doing.

Sort of.

To be honest, compared to everything I'd heard – and feared – about looking after babies, Emma wasn't too bad. I guess it was because she wasn't a newborn. I'm not saying she wasn't hard work, 'cause she sure as hell was. She demanded constant attention and concentration. Melanie hadn't just dumped Emma on me, she'd dumped a strait-jacket of anxiety on me which I couldn't remove. Was I overfeeding Emma or underfeeding her? Was I feeding her the right stuff? Was she getting enough exercise? Was she warm enough? Cool enough? Enough sleep? Enough attention?

Enough?

And yet, in spite of feeling like I was messing up at every second, Emma kept smiling at me and when I picked her up she clung to my neck like . . . like I mattered to her. And when I blew raspberries against her stomach, she would laugh like it was the funniest thing in the world.

Now that she had found her feet, she toddled here, there and everywhere. And I mean, everywhere. She got hold of one of Dad's slippers and started banging it against the DVD player which was on the floor in the sitting room whilst I was otherwise occupied in the loo. When the DVD tray sprang out, Emma decided that what the slipper really wanted was to go through the hole in the centre of the DVD tray and all it needed was a little brute-force persuasion. When I entered the room, the tray was creaking ominously. One more shove and it would've broken off completely.

'No, Emma. That's naughty. You mustn't do that,' I told her, snatching the slipper away from her.

One brief look of surprise, then she scrunched up her eyes, opened her mouth and wailed.

'Emma, you can't put your slipper in there. It wasn't designed for that. You wear slippers on your feet like this.' And I proceeded to demonstrate. 'Or you can use the slipper as a football and head it, or you can wear the slipper as a hat.' I put the slipper on my head and started strolling up and down the room like a model on a catwalk. Emma started giggling, thank God. Major tantrum averted. So I did it some more, really getting into it now.

'*Dante is wearing the latest in designer slippers. This slipper is made from the finest er . . . synthetic material and the lining is pure er . . . synthetic material.*'

'Something you want to tell me?' Adam quipped from the door.

I spun round. The slipper flew off my head. Adam gave me a round of applause. Chortling, Emma joined in. I bowed low to my adoring fans.

Not a day passed without me having to fix something Emma had 'redesigned'. Like when she managed to pull two of the hob control knobs off the cooker before I could stop her. I pushed them back on, hoping no one would notice. That same night when Dad was heating up some soup for his dinner, one of the knobs came right off in his hand.

'DANTE!'

Emma's fixation with slippers continued. I caught her dipping one of Dad's slippers in the downstairs loo. After telling Emma what she was doing was wrong and naughty, I rinsed off the slipper and put it back in the hall, hoping that by the time Dad came home it would dry out and he wouldn't notice. No such luck.

'DANTE!'

One time, I was in the sitting room with Emma and telling her more about each of her toy-farm animals. The morning was reasonably bright, though it was more cloudy than otherwise. Emma was banging the heads of a cow and a goat together when a ray of light suddenly hit the empty crystal vase on the windowsill and a whole host of rainbow colours began to dance across the cream-coloured wall in front of us. The animals in Emma's hands hit the carpet and she took off on her hands and knees like a shot. Using her hands against the wall, she pushed against it to rise to her feet. Bracing herself with one hand, she tried to snatch the dancing colours off the wall with her other hand, chuckling with glee as she did so. And in spite of myself, I couldn't help laughing with her. How amazing that she could find so much joy in *colours*.

And as I watched, I realized that Emma's antics weren't so much getting to me as she was. I had to catch myself from laughing too hard with her, or smiling at her for too long, or letting her get inside my head too much.

I didn't want her inside my head.

My life was already spinning around so fast that I had no idea which way was up any more. My thoughts and feelings were all over the place, and with each passing day it grew worse, not better.

And on top of all that, Adam was up to something. I didn't need to be a rocket scientist to figure that one out. His new routine quickly became predictable. Shower at six-thirty each evening for at least twenty minutes, take at least another thirty minutes to get dressed, spend around ten minutes on his hair, leave the house between seven thirty and seven forty-five. And he didn't get home till about ten each night. Once or twice and I probably wouldn't have noticed. But he started going out every night, which was rare for my brother. Dad had to work late to make up for the couple of days he'd taken off when Emma first arrived, so he wasn't around to question my brother the way I would've liked. So it was down to me.

'Where're you off to? Again?'

'Out,' Adam replied.

'I gathered that. Out where?'

'Out out.'

My brother was being even more annoying than usual. 'Adam, where are you going?'

'How is it any of your business?' Adam frowned.

'In case something happens to you,' I argued.

'And how will knowing where I'm going stop anything happening to me?' asked Adam.

Like I said, bloody annoying.

'So you're not going to tell me?'

'Dante, Emma is your child, not me,' said Adam. 'I'll see you later.'

And he was out the door.

Why was he being so secretive? I shook my head; Adam was right. Emma was the one who needed looking after, not my brother, and if he wanted to play Man of Mystery that was his business.

The days when I was home alone with Emma were the most nerve-racking. Dad phoned on the hour every hour to make sure everything was OK. I didn't know whether I should resent his regular check-ups or be grateful for them. I settled for somewhere in-between.

But this constant not knowing what to do next was doing my head in. I had to make some hard decisions. I couldn't afford to waste any more time dithering. It wasn't fair on Emma for a start. And even though I now had a kid, that didn't stop me from trying to hold onto some of my old life, but it didn't seem to be working. I phoned Collette – more than once – but all I got was her voice-mail or her answering machine. I tried phoning Josh but he had plans every night of the week so he couldn't come round. A few of my other mates like Ricky, Ben and Darren dropped by to see me, but Emma demanded and got most of my attention so they didn't stay long. My other friends were busy during the day and I couldn't go out at night, not without Dad being able to guarantee he'd be home in time to baby-sit.

Saturday morning brought drizzle, the postman and the DNA results – in that order.

One glance at the white envelope and I instantly knew what it was. One deep breath after another as I tried to steady my racing heart. This was what I wanted – proof positive. And it had arrived at last. I stared down at it.

'Dante, open the damned envelope,' I told myself.

And yet it remained unopened in my hands.

'Annggg . . . annggg.' Emma was calling me from her high-chair in the kitchen. Taking my letter and three for Dad back to the kitchen, I dumped them on the work surface as I went to see what was wrong with Emma. She'd dropped her spoon on the floor. Not that giving her a spoon was that effective. It usually ended up on her lap or on the floor but Dad said it didn't hurt to start early so she'd get used to the feel of it.

'Morning, angel. Morning, Dan,' yawned Dad as he entered the kitchen.

'Hey, Dad,' I replied.

'Nnyaang,' said Emma.

Dad walked over to the baby and kissed the top of her head. He doted on her already. I took Emma's spoon over to the sink to give it a quick wash before handing it back to her. It was another warm, sunny day outside.

Maybe later we'd go to the park. Emma enjoyed it there. Plus I got kudos for not being too full of myself to take out my baby 'sister'. On two separate occasions, different girls had struck up a conversation with me when they saw me pushing Emma on a swing. So having a baby around had some perks after all!

'Dante, what's this?'

Dad was looking down at the semi-unfolded piece of paper in his hand. One glance at the other opened letters on the work surface told the whole story.

'You opened my letter?' I accused.

'It said *Mr Bridgeman* on the envelope. I thought it was for me.'

'It said Mr D. Bridgeman.'

'I was opening them on autopilot and only registered Bridgeman,' said Dad. 'What is this?'

I closed my eyes briefly. So much for not getting the result via email in case it got intercepted. Any chance of bluffing my way out of this one? From the look on Dad's face, there wasn't much hope of that. And how ironic that he should read the results before I'd even had a chance.

'Dante?'

'You know what it is. You've read it,' I said.

'Not all of it,' Dad denied. 'I read enough to know it's not mine, but not the whole thing.' He'd obviously read enough to get the gist of it though.

I straightened up and looked directly at my dad. 'I sent off for a DNA test. Those are the results.'

'You did what?' Dad asked me, astounded.

'I needed to know for sure.'

Dad stared at me. 'Dante, anyone with half an eye could see Emma is yours.'

'I needed to know for sure,' I repeated.

'Still trying to wriggle away from your responsibilities? Is that what this is all about?' Dad's tone was scathing. 'And if this test says Emma is your daughter, will you have another test done, and another, and another after that till you get the answer you want?'

'No, Dad.'

I doubt he even heard me. I'd seen him angry with me before, but never anything like this. His body was held rigid and his lips were clamped together so tightly they had practically disappeared.

'I'm not trying to get out of anything, Dad,' I said quietly. 'I just wanted to know the truth.'

'The truth? Here's a newsflash. The truth isn't going to bend itself to suit you.'

'I know that.'

'I don't think you do,' Dad shot back. 'What are you doing about your offered university place, or have you already accepted because you reckon Emma – my granddaughter – will no longer be a problem by the time term starts?'

We regarded each other with varying degrees of dislike.

'Dad, you really don't think much of me, do you?' I said.

'I'm not the one trying to find an excuse to get rid of my own child.'

'Neither am I,' I told him.

'What's this then?' Dad waved the DNA results under my nose.

'I haven't even read that yet,' I reminded him. 'You opened it, not me.' Dad's narrowed eyes shouted condemnation. 'And for your information,' I continued, 'I've already withdrawn my university confirmation. I did that two days ago. And I cancelled my student loan.'

That surprised him. 'You did?'

I nodded. 'And if you don't believe me you can phone the university or check my application online. My application status doesn't say accepted, it says *withdrawn*.'

Dad's hand dropped to his side as he regarded me. At last he'd stopped waving the sheet of paper around. 'Why?'

'Because I realized I can't go to uni and look after my daughter at the same time.' I shrugged. 'I looked into crèches and nursery places for Emma whilst I attend uni but I don't have that kind of money. And if I went to university and got a job in the evenings and at weekends to pay for a nursery place, who'd look after Emma whilst I was working? I think she's been moved around enough in her life already.'

'You really gave up your university place?'

'That's right.'

'You knew what the DNA result was going to be?' asked Dad.

'I'm not clairvoyant, Dad.' I smiled faintly. 'But everyone says Emma looks like me and she laughs like Adam and she's stubborn like you, so she's definitely a Bridgeman. I don't need a piece of paper to tell me that.'

Dad frowned down at the DNA results in his hand. 'Maybe you should read this?' He held out the sheet of paper.

173

I pulled Emma out of the highchair and cradled her, kissing her on the forehead. 'You tell me what it says,' I said, holding Emma fractionally tighter.

A watchful silence descended over the kitchen. The only sound was my heart thumping fitfully. Emma was a Bridgeman. I was ninety-nine per cent sure of that. But the remaining one per cent of doubt kept gnawing away at me. And now, as I stood in the kitchen, my heart pounding, sweat beading on my forehead, I realized I was afraid. But which result was I more afraid of – that Emma was my daughter or that she wasn't? Dad raised the sheet of paper to read it properly. His lips started moving. Why couldn't I hear what he was saying?

'Pardon?' I said.

'Emma is your daughter,' grinned Dad. 'It's confirmed. But I could've told you that. In fact, I believe I did!'

'Nnggghh . . .' Emma mewed.

I relaxed my grip around her. I didn't need to hold onto her quite so tightly. I smiled at her, kissing her cheek. Dad was still blathering on about how I'd wasted my money and how I should've just listened to him.

Emma . . .

My daughter . . .

My daughter, Emma.

'Hello, Emma,' I said softly. 'Say "Daddy". Can you say "Daddy"?'

29

Dante

Emma wasn't quite so heavy to carry and I smiled a lot more readily at her after that. I could wear the truth like a bespoke suit and make proper decisions now. There really was no need for me to analyse why I gave up my university place before I knew the DNA result. The reason was obvious: Emma needed looking after, no matter what. That was all there was to it. And giving up my place at university didn't mean I couldn't go next year or the year after that or sometime in the future.

Just one problem.

How was this supposed to work money-wise?

Now that I had Emma in my life, I needed to look after her. With university no longer on the horizon, that meant a job. But how was I supposed to get a job, never mind keep one, with a kid in tow? I could just see it now, turning up to job interviews with Emma in her baby carrier strapped to my chest. That would go down like a dozen lead balloons. I couldn't afford a private nursery – a couple of phone calls to check out the prices had quickly confirmed that – and Emma was apparently still too young for a state nursery place. Plus I was told I should've put her name down on the waiting list from the moment she was conceived to stand any chance of her getting a place before she had kids of her own.

So how exactly was this supposed to work? How did other parents do it? I didn't have a clue. Was I missing something crucial? Was there some secret that only got told to parents in their twenties and thirties to show them how to manage?

A couple of Saturdays after I got the DNA results, I decided to take Emma for a walk.

'You want to go for a walk, don't you?' I asked Emma as I opened the child gate at the top of the stairs and carried her down to the hall. Placing her in her buggy, I fastened the safety buckle.

'I'll come with you,' said Adam as he came downstairs behind us.

I was honoured – and my eyebrows told him as much.

'Yeah, yeah,' said Adam, reading my expression. 'I know I haven't been around much lately.'

'Much? Try – you haven't been around at all.'

'Well, I'm here now.'

'No headache today?' I asked.

'Nope.'

I placed the back of one hand against my forehead. 'What? No "Oh, my poor head. I must take to my bed"?' I asked, adopting a girly voice.

Pause.

'Sod off and die, Dante,' said Adam sourly.

'Please remember that there are young ears present,' I reminded him with a grin.

Adam squatted down in front of Emma in her buggy. 'Sorry, Emma, but I was provoked!'

'So are you going to tell me what you've been up to?' I asked.

'No.'

'You're not doing anything . . . stupid, are you?'

'Like what?'

'You tell me,' I said.

'No, you tell me.'

'You tell me,' I insisted.

'Why don't you tell me?'

'How 'bout you tell me?'

'You tell me as you obviously have a scenario or two in mind.'

'Oh, for God's sake! Both of you tell each other something or give it a rest,' said Dad, emerging from the kitchen. 'You're giving *me* a headache. And Adam, no more late nights, please, not when you've got school the next day. And Dante, try to remember you should be setting a mature example to your younger brother and Emma.'

Adam started it!

'Where're you all off to?' Dad asked.

'To the park, probably,' I replied. 'It'll give Emma a chance to stretch her legs.' She was toddling all over the place now. It was keeping me fit just trying to keep up with her.

'Want me to come with you?'

Stunned didn't even begin to describe my reaction to Dad's question. Dad had stopped taking us to the park when I was around eleven or twelve.

'That'd be great, Dad,' said Adam, before I could scrape my jaw off the hall floor.

So off we went.

'I'll push her,' said Dad before we even reached the pavement. I stepped aside to let him, walking to his right between the buggy and road.

It felt kinda strange all of us walking along together. We hadn't gone to the park or the cinema together in not just months but years.

'How come we haven't done anything like this in a while?' I asked.

'You started going out with your friends and you didn't want a bumbling old relic like me tagging along,' smiled Dad. 'And Adam followed your lead, so I was pretty much redundant. The joys of fatherhood.'

I regarded him. Was that true? Was I the one who'd made him feel surplus to requirements? I hated to admit it, but I probably was.

'What about our holiday last year?' said Adam. 'We were together then.'

Dad had booked us into a cheapo holiday resort near the coast. It was one of those forced-smiles-with-every-sentence and chips-with-every-meal places, but at least it was a holiday away from home. Our first in quite some time.

'Pfft! I paid for the holiday and drove us there and back – and that was it. From the time we hit the resort you two

178

went off and did your own thing and I couldn't see you for dust,' said Dad. 'And Dante, you didn't even want me near you at the swimming pool in case the girls you were chatting up should take one look at me and run a mile. You made me feel like Quasimodo!'

I looked from Dad to Emma and back again. 'I'm really sorry, Dad,' I said quietly. 'And I never properly thanked you for all the stuff you bought Emma and for helping me with her. I'm sorry about that too.'

Dad started in surprise. 'I wasn't recriminating, I was just saying.'

'I know. But I really am sorry.'

'Apology accepted. And you're welcome.' Dad smiled at me.

I smiled back at him.

'Guys, please. You're embarrassing me,' said my brother.

We all laughed – including Emma – and carried on walking.

'Hi!'

'Morning.'

'Hiya.'

'Lovely day.'

'Hey.'

'Hello.'

'For God's sake, Adam,' I said exasperated. 'Why the sudden need to hail every person we see?' Adam was greeting each person who passed within two metres of us as if they were long-lost friends.

'Don't be such a grumpy, anti-social git,' said my brother. 'Leave that for Dad.'

'Oi!' Dad exclaimed.

'Can't I say hi to people if I want to?' my brother said, ignoring Dad's indignation.

'Yes, but your permanently cheerful mood is getting on my nerves. Plus it's kinda creepy,' I told him.

'Get over yourself, Dante,' said Adam.

'Dannhg ... Dannhg...' burbled Emma, her legs kicking out every which way.

'Did you hear that?' I beamed at Dad and my brother. 'She said "Dad"!' I squatted down in front of the buggy. 'Emma, you said "Dad"! Aren't you clever. Say it again.'

'She said "Dad", my left buttock,' Adam dismissed.

'Dante, I think she was just bringing up wind to be honest,' Dad teased.

'You two obviously have serious ear-wax problems,' I said sourly. 'Want to stop off at a pharmacy to get that checked out?'

'Dannhg ...'

'See! Emma agrees with me.'

'So "Dannhggg" means not just "Dad", but "Grandad and Uncle Adam, get thee to a pharmacy"?' asked Dad.

I hadn't heard Dad misquoting bits of Shakespeare in quite some time. His favourite saying was: '*How sharper than a serpent's tooth are two ungrateful brats*'. He was fond of that one.

'Dad, Emma is a bit young to have your version of Shakespeare inflicted on her,' said Adam.

'No, she isn't. Dad's right. She's very advanced. She takes after me.' I grinned.

'Dante, move out the way.' Dad waved me to one side. 'I'm not Mary Poppins, I can't fly over you.'

I did as he asked and we all carried on walking.

'Hi!'

'How're you?'

Adam got out two greetings to total strangers before I clamped my hand over his mouth. He struggled to pull my hand away but it wasn't going to happen, not without some assurances first.

'I'll let you go when you promise to stop being so cheerful!' I told him.

Adam finally nodded whilst Dad just shook his head. The moment I let him go however, my brother took off like a bat out of hell. At a safe distance, Adam turned round to face us.

'Hello, world!' he shouted at the top of his voice.

I creased up.

'Dante, it's good to hear you laugh again,' said Dad.

It felt good too.

'Dannhg . . .' Emma agreed.

30

Adam

How is it possible to be so happy and so miserable at the same time? I've met someone. And when we're alone, he's great. He's sharp and smart and he makes me laugh so much. But that's when we're alone.

When others are around, it's a different story.

I wish . . . I wish he wasn't quite so ashamed of me.

And if he could stop feeling so ashamed of himself, then maybe we might stand a chance.

31

Dante

Dad had left for work and Adam had gone to school and it was just me and Emma left in the house. The autumn morning was overcast but still warm.

'D'you want to go to the park, Emma?' I asked.

Emma waddled over to her buggy. I had my answer! Sitting Emma in my lap, I gently coaxed her booties onto her feet. I figured we'd walk to the park and she'd have a run around once we got there. That way she'd be good and tired after lunch and have a proper nap. It wasn't quite so nerve-racking looking after her any more, at least not in the same way as before. I mean, when she started crying for something and I couldn't figure out what it was, it did require whole ocean depths of patience I didn't know I possessed. But on top of that, there was something I hadn't expected. It was lonely. Some of my friends came round to see me, but once the novelty had worn off and their curiosity had been satisfied, they stopped calling. Most days it was just me and Emma until Dad and Adam came home. Walks around the shopping centre or to the park served to get us both out of the house, otherwise I would've gone bat-crap crazy. But even so, life was something that was happening to other people. Mine had been put on hold.

But I had Emma.

Buggy in one hand and Emma's hand held firmly in the other, we headed out the house.

'The park here we come,' I told Emma.

She looked up at me and smiled. But we were less than halfway there when the sky tore and the rain started chucking down. We were both drenched in less than a minute. In my head I was cursing up a blue streak. I mean, even my underwear was getting soggy! Emma, however, loved it. She walked through a puddle and laughed like a drain. It obviously felt so good that she pulled her hand out of mine and splashed through it again – and again, laughing her head off. Who would've thought a puddle could be so entertaining?

'You're a bit of a water baby, aren't you?' I grinned. I hadn't realized that before, although Emma did enjoy her evening baths, but I just thought that was a baby thing. Maybe I should take her swimming at the local pool? She'd love that. 'Come on, Emma. Time to go home,' I told her, lifting her up and putting her in the buggy.

Once she was securely fastened, I headed home as fast as possible. When we were at last indoors, I dried Emma off and changed her clothes. The last thing either of us needed was for her to catch a chill. I changed my T-shirt and pulled off my damp socks, then we headed downstairs. After a kiss on the top of her head and making sure that she was safe in the sitting room, I headed to the kitchen to start the laundry. I was turning into a domestic god and to be honest, that bit I hated. But at least it wasn't all the time – just ninety-five per cent of the time! I was just pushing some of Emma's dirty clothes into the washing machine when the doorbell rang. Straightening up, I frowned. I wasn't expecting anyone. Maybe it was the postman. Nah, far too early for the post. Anyone other than an axe murderer and I'd be happy to stand and chat! I headed for the front door.

'Hello, Dante.'

I regarded the woman on my doorstep. She looked vaguely familiar. A few centimetres shorter than me, her black hair was tied back in a ponytail and she wore a grey skirt suit with a pink blouse. Her face was expertly made-up and she carried an outsized bag over her shoulder. It took a few seconds to place her.

'Er . . .Veronica, isn't it?' I said. It was her eyes that helped me to identify her. She had the same almond-shaped eyes as Collette, her sister.

'That's right,' she smiled. 'May I come in?'

What on earth was Veronica doing here? 'Is something wrong with Collette? Has she had an accident or something?' I asked, concerned.

'No, no. Nothing like that,' Veronica rushed to reassure me. 'May I come in?'

Even more puzzled, I stepped aside. 'First door on the left,' I indicated the sitting room.

She entered the room, stopping momentarily when she saw Emma playing with her toy animals. And there was a distinctly pongy whiff wafting up from her. Her nappy needed changing.

'How is she?' Veronica asked. 'Emma, isn't it?'

'Yes, that's right. And she's fine,' I replied.

Should I change Emma's nappy now or wait until Veronica left? I decided to wait until Veronica left. I didn't want to appear rude by vanishing with Emma the moment she sat down. Collette's sister sat down on the sofa. Slowly I sat down in the armchair opposite. Emma played on the carpet between us. I waited for Veronica to get to the point.

'So how are you?' she asked.

My frown deepened. 'Fine, thanks. I'm not being funny but I'm sure you didn't come all this way just to ask about my health.'

'Well, I did actually – indirectly.'

I had a bad feeling about this . . .

'I don't know if Collette told you, but I'm a social worker.'

Every cell in my body was on red alert. 'Yeah, she told me,' I replied carefully, wondering where all this was leading.

'Collette also told me that your ex-girlfriend turned up with a child and . . .' A swift glance at Emma. 'Now you find yourself having to cope with that child alone?'

'I'm not alone. My dad and brother are here to help,' I said. What was all this about? 'Why're you here?'

'Don't worry, this is an unofficial visit. I've just come to see how you're managing,' said Veronica. 'Collette said that you were deeply unhappy.'

'I got over it.' *I'm getting over it* would've been more accurate but she didn't need to know that.

'But it can't be easy?'Veronica suggested.

I shrugged, saying nothing.

'As I said, I'm here in an unofficial capacity, but I do have a duty of care to make sure that Emma is in a stable, nurturing, safe environment.'

My blood ran ice-cold in my veins. 'What're you implying?' I asked slowly. 'What did Collette say?'

'Collette didn't say anything specific. But having a child can be a daunting prospect for any new parent – even when the child is wanted. You're only seventeen and Emma wasn't . . .' Another swift look at my daughter. 'Well, she wasn't a life choice you deliberately made, now was she?'

I said nothing. I was only too aware of the land mines suddenly scattered all around me, just waiting for a word out of place to set them off.

'I understand that you're trying to find a way out of your current situation?' Veronica continued.

'You've been misinformed,' I replied. 'Emma is my daughter and my responsibility. I'm not trying to find a way out of anything.'

Veronica looked puzzled. 'But you're going to university.'

'I withdrew my application.'

'So what d'you intend to do now?'

'Find a job so I can support my daughter.'

'And who will be looking after your daughter whilst you work?'

How was any of this her business? I bit back what I really wanted to say with great difficulty. I was only too aware that this woman had the power to make it her business, but with each passing second I resented her presence more and more.

'I'm looking for an evening or night-time job so that my dad can look after Emma whilst I'm working.'

'What kind of evening job?'

'I don't know. I'm still looking.'

'And what happens when your dad isn't available to baby-sit?'

'I'd only work on a part-time basis initially, maybe three or four evenings a week. Dad and I plan to organise a schedule of nights when I can look after Emma myself.'

'Hhmm . . .' Veronica didn't sound convinced. 'And what happens when Emma is sick or needs you at home and you're at work?'

'The same thing that happens to any parent in a similar situation,' I replied. 'I come home to look after my daughter.'

'Hhmm . . . I'm not being funny, Dante, but are you even close to coping?'

'What d'you mean?'

'I can smell that Emma's nappy needs changing but I don't see you making any moves to do anything about it,' said Veronica.

Calm down, Dante. Don't let her get to you.

'I know her nappy needs changing but I didn't realize you'd be staying so long, otherwise I would've changed her before now.'

'Don't let me stop you,' Veronica said.

Was this a test?

After a moment's hesitation, I took Emma's baby bag off the handles of her folded-up buggy which was leaning against the wall and I set about changing Emma's nappy without saying a word to Veronica. The burning resentment I felt must have been scorching her skin though. As I fastened Emma's clean nappy, she said, 'Dante, I'm on your side.'

It didn't feel like it.

'So you've decided to keep Emma with you?'

'She's my daughter,' I replied. That said it all.

'Have you really thought this through?'

Was she serious?

'I've thought of nothing else. I've only had Emma for a few weeks now. I'm still learning, I'm still adjusting. But I know I could be a good dad if I'm given the chance.'

'You're seventeen, Dante. You can't be expected to have the patience or aptitude for this that an older parent would have.'

I wasn't having that. 'There are plenty of older parents who abuse their kids. There are plenty of older parents who don't give a damn about their children and let them fend for themselves. I know I'm only seventeen. I can't help that. But I'm eighteen in two weeks' time and all my family, not just me, are determined to make this work.'

'I'm glad to hear it,' said Veronica, 'because if I feel this is not the best environment for Emma, there are a number of steps I can take.'

I stood up. 'Are you talking about taking my daughter into care?'

'That would be a last resort. There are quite a number of intermediate steps before we ever get to that point . . .'

But I hardly heard her. I bent to pick up Emma, hugging her to me. She rested her head on my shoulder and started sucking her thumb. I wanted to tell Emma not to do that as it would make her teeth grow outwards, but if I removed her thumb from her mouth, would Veronica think I was being cruel? Would that be a mark against me?

'Tell me something,' I asked bitterly. 'Would we be having this conversation if I was Emma's mum instead of her dad?'

Veronica frowned. 'I don't see how that's relevant.'

'Isn't it? You're automatically assuming that because I'm Emma's dad, not her mum, I'm failing. Well, let's talk about her mum. Melanie was the one who didn't even tell me she was pregnant. Nor did she bother to let me know I had a daughter when Emma was born. Melanie arrived here, told me she didn't trust herself with Emma and was afraid of what she might do, she gave Emma to me and did a runner. She's the one who has disappeared somewhere up north with no forwarding address. And yet you're here ready to condemn me?'

I didn't shout, though God knows all I wanted to do was yell at the bitch and chuck her out the nearest window. How dare she? And Collette had a damned nerve.

'I can see I'm upsetting you.' Veronica stood up.

'Of course I'm upset. You're threatening to take my daughter away from me for no other reason than my age and my gender.'

Veronica scrutinized me. 'Dante, believe it or not, I am

on your side. This really isn't an official visit. And I can see that you've already bonded with your daughter. And I'm here to do whatever I can to help. But this requires a commitment from you for at least another eighteen years. Think about it.'

'I have. And like I said, I'm already looking for a job.'

'I'm not just talking about your employment,' said Veronica.

'What then?'

'There are a number of other factors to consider.'

'Like what?'

'Like, where does Emma sleep?'

'In a cot at the foot of my bed,' I informed her.

'And in five years time, where will she be sleeping?'

Huh? 'I have no idea.'

'My point is, she'll soon be needing her own room,' said Veronica. 'I understand from Collette that this is a three-bedroom house. You, your dad and your brother each have your own bedroom. So where does that leave Emma?'

'I can share my brother's room and Emma can have mine when she's old enough,' I said. 'My aim is to have my own flat at some point for me and Emma.'

I was aiming at a lot of things – my own flat, a good job, prospects and a good life for me and my daughter, but it'd be pointless to tell her all those things.

'It's not just that,' said Veronica. 'Have you taken her to your GP for a check-up? Have you even registered her at your doctor's surgery? There are a number of things that need to be sorted out if you plan on having your daughter stay with you for any length of time . . .'

'Well, I wasn't going to make an appointment for Emma to see a doctor until she was actually sick with something, but OK, I'll sort out a check-up at the doctor's first thing in the morning. I'll do whatever is necessary. But Emma's staying with me. I'm not letting you or anyone else take my daughter away from me,' I told her straight.

Emma must've picked up on the tension in me because she started mewing. Another few seconds and she'd be crying.

'It's to your credit that you feel that way.' Veronica smiled. 'Look, I'm going to leave my number. If you need advice or help, just give me a call.' She dug into her handbag and produced a business card. I watched as she scribbled her mobile number on the back. She held out the card to me. I hesitated, but I took it. 'I have another appointment now, but let me stress, we do everything in our power to keep families together. I really am on your side.'

Yeah, right.

'Your daughter is beautiful.' Veronica smiled at me. 'And doesn't she look like you.'

I said nothing.

'Bye, Emma.' Veronica put out a hand to stroke Emma's cheek, but I moved us both away from her and led the way to the front door. Opening it, I stood aside so Veronica would have no trouble leaving. She held out her hand. I was holding Emma, so couldn't reciprocate.

'Take care of yourself, and your daughter,' said Veronica, her hand falling to her side.

'I intend to.'

'I or one of my colleagues may be back within the next

few weeks for a chat with you and your dad, just to see how you're all doing.'

She headed off, her last comment ringing in my ears.

Was that a threat or a promise?

Either way, I was in trouble.

32

Dante

'Stop panicking.'

'That's easy for you to say, Dad.' I was practically shouting down the phone at him.

'Dante, it wasn't even an official visit,' said Dad.

'But Veronica still came here. She still questioned me. What if she tries to take Emma away from me?'

'You're getting way ahead of yourself,' said Dad. 'You said the social worker called that a last resort. The authorities wouldn't take Emma away from you unless she was in danger, which she obviously isn't. So calm down.'

All kinds of phrases I'd only heard on TV sprinted through my head wearing spiked shoes. Phrases like 'on the at-risk register' and 'family court' and 'foster care'. The Dante who only a few weeks ago had sat at the computer looking up the procedures for putting a child into foster care wasn't me. I looked back and I didn't even recognize that person. What was that saying? Be careful what you wish for 'cause you might get it? I took a deep breath, trying to follow Dad's advice.

'Dad, I'm . . . worried,' I admitted.

'Look, d'you want me to come home?'

'Why? Veronica has already left.'

'I know. But I'll come home if you need me.'

'You would do that?' I asked.

'Of course I would,' said Dad impatiently. 'You're my son, Dante. If you need me, I'm home in a heartbeat. Well, maybe two heartbeats depending on how the trains are running.'

'No, that's OK, Dad,' I said, feeling a little less ruffled. 'But thanks for the offer.'

'Well if you change your mind, just phone me. OK?'

'Yes, Dad.'

'And I'm not working late tonight so I'll be home around six thirty.'

'OK. Thanks.'

'Dante, don't let this Veronica woman rattle you. Emma is with her family now and that's how it'll stay. See you later, son.' Dad put down the phone.

It felt good . . . no, it felt great to know that Dad had my back. For the first time I thought about what all this must be like for him. It couldn't have been easy bringing up me and my brother after Mum died, coping on his own with the two of us, plus a mortgage and bills. And now instead of two, there were three that Dad had to provide for. I needed to find a job in a hurry. I had to make this work, now more than ever.

But first things first. I had a phone call to make.

'Hello?'

'Collette?'

'Speaking.'

I took a deep breath, trying to quell the anger that flared at the sound of her voice.

'Hello?' she prompted.

'I've just had a visit from your sister,' I said quietly.

'Dante? Hi. How're you?'

'I've just had a visit from Veronica,' I repeated.

'Oh, good. She promised she'd go and see you.'

Another deep breath. It wasn't working. 'You told your sister about Emma and me?'

'Well, yes,' said Collette, surprised I even had to ask. 'I told her how you weren't coping.'

'Why would you do something like that?' The words were coming out faster and harder.

Another deep breath. Chillax, Dante. Don't lose it.

'I was trying to help. This way the baby can be taken into care or looked after by a foster parent and you can get your life back,' said Collette. 'I've only seen you three times since she arrived on the scene. She's stopping you from doing all the things we'd planned and I miss the way things used to be.'

Collette spoke of my daughter like Emma was a fence which needed to be knocked down and trampled underfoot.

'Collette, *she* has a name – Emma. And Emma happens to be my daughter.'

'Not from choice.'

I had to restrain myself from answering for a few seconds.

'What exactly did you tell your sister?' I asked when I could trust myself to speak.

'Only what you told me,' Collette replied. 'That Emma had been dumped on you and you didn't want her.'

'You had no right!' I shouted.

'Excuse me?'

'You had no right to poke your nose in and interfere. You had no right to set your sister on me like some pit bull just 'cause you were feeling neglected,' I said with scorn.

'That's not why I did it. I was trying to help you . . .'

'By letting your sister take Emma away from me?'

'But you don't want her . . .'

'Collette, get this into your head because I'm only going to say it once. Emma is my daughter and she belongs with me. She's staying with me. If you don't like that, then tough. Tell your sister I'm coping just fine and both of you can keep your bloody noses out of my business. Enjoy university.' I hung up. Within seconds the phone was ringing. I accepted the call, then immediately hung up again. Hopefully now she'd get the message.

I headed back into the sitting room.

'Come with Daddy, Emma.' I held out my hand. 'Let's get you a drink.'

Emma waddled over to me and took my hand without hesitation. Her hand was warm in mine and so tiny. We shared a smile as I led the way to the kitchen. Popping her in her highchair, I poured out some diluted blackcurrant juice into her beaker. I stood and watched as she drank it thirstily. Grit or dirt or something was making my eyes smart. And I must've tried swallowing down my breakfast too quickly because it felt like there was a ball of concrete stuck in my throat.

'You're staying with Daddy,' I told Emma softly. 'I promise I won't let anything or anyone change that.'

33

Adam

I can't do this any more.

What I am isn't wrong. How I feel is nothing to be ashamed of. But that's how he's making me feel. Why did he even ask me out? It was his idea for the two of us to get together, not mine. But I think he sees me as some kind of spotlight, shining down on him mercilessly and drawing too much attention.

I want to live my life out loud. He wants me to whisper my way through life like him. He wants to keep his true self hidden away in the shadows, hoping no one will notice him.

I can't live my life like that.

I won't.

I really like him but I think . . . I think it's time to call it a day. I never realized it before now but he's my worst-case scenario.

This is never going to work until he learns to be happy with who and what he truly is. I'm beginning to think that's never going to happen. One thing I know for sure, it's beyond anything I can say or do to make him accept himself.

And I'm getting fed up waiting.

34

Dante

The next morning found me third in the queue outside the doctor's surgery, waiting for them to open. A sign on the door said that buggies had to be left in the porch area and couldn't be taken past reception so I took Emma out of her buggy and held her with one hand, whilst folding up the buggy with the other. What was up with this nationwide hatred of buggies? Luckily I didn't have to wait too long before the doors opened. The two people ahead of me made their appointments at the reception desk and headed straight into the waiting room.

'Can I help you?' asked the receptionist when I reached her.

'Hi, yes. I'd like to register Emma here with a doctor, please.'

Emma was watching the receptionist with avid interest.

'Are you already registered here?' asked the receptionist.

'Yes, I am.' I gave her my name and address, watching as she stared myopically at the screen to her left. 'And how old is . . . er . . . Emma?'

'She's one next Monday,' I informed her.

The receptionist frowned at the screen before turning

her frown on me. 'Do you have her NHS card, her birth certificate and her red book on you?'

'Huh? Er . . . no. What's her red book?'

'The book of her medical details to date.' At my blank look, the receptionist elaborated. 'It has information in it like all the vaccinations she's had to date, her birth details, that kind of thing. And I'll also need photo ID and proof of address from the person registering her.'

'Photo ID?'

'A passport or driving licence and a current utility bill showing your address.'

Damn! I thought I'd be in and out in about a minute flat. 'I don't have any of that stuff.' I shook my head. 'I thought you'd only need her name, address and date of birth and that would be it.'

The woman behind the desk gave me a pitying smile. 'I'm afraid not. Maybe you could get your mum to come in and register her once she's got all the appropriate documents together?'

'My mum is dead,' I replied.

'Oh.' The woman looked embarrassed. 'Well, how about your dad? Would he be able to come in and register your sister?'

Oh God.

'Emma is my daughter. My dad is her grandad,' I said, trying to keep my tone even.

'Your daughter?'

Here we go again, I sighed inwardly. 'Yes, my daughter.'

'And you're . . .' The receptionist turned back to her screen. 'You're seventeen.'

'I'm eighteen in two weeks.'

'Ah, I see. Maybe her mother could come in with the necessary documents and—'

'Are males barred from doing this kind of thing then?' I asked impatiently.

'No. No. Of course not. I just meant that maybe her mother has access to the necessary documents and she could come in and—'

'Emma's mother isn't around any more,' I explained, resenting the hell out of the fact that I had to. 'I look after my daughter and all I want to do is register her with a doctor.'

'If you could come back with all the things I mentioned then there should be no problem,' said the receptionist.

By which time all I wanted to do was repeatedly bang my head off the reception desk.

'OK,' I said, hanging onto my patience by a single thread. 'I'll be back soon.'

I turned and headed out, ignoring the curious and speculative glances from those who'd been eavesdropping behind me in the queue.

'Well, Emma, this is going to be a right p.i.t.a.' I told her as I reassembled her buggy and placed her in it. 'That stands for "pain in the buttocks",' I explained.

'Rannggghh . . . flluuuufff . . .' Emma agreed.

Once I got back home, I sifted through all the documents Melanie had left behind. I should've done it sooner. And now I thought about it, I remembered Dad telling me to do just that. There was indeed a red book with gold writing on the front which read 'Personal Child Health

Record'. Inside were a number of pages as well as various unattached sheets of folded paper. One sheet gave baby delivery details. I learned that Melanie had been in labour for seven hours and eleven minutes and she'd suffered a second-degree tear and blood loss. God . . . It sounded horrific. Who had been with Melanie when she gave birth? Her mum? Her aunt? Or had she been alone? No one should have to go through something like that alone. She should've told me, given me a chance to wrap my head around the idea and step up. I should've been there. Not just for Emma's sake and Melanie's, but for my own as well. Why hadn't Melanie told me?

Was it that she thought I'd hit the ground running?

Would I have tried to persuade her to have an abortion?

Would I have washed my hands of the whole deal?

I didn't know. I looked down at Emma, sitting on the carpet, playing with her teddy and I honestly didn't know.

There was a whole heap of other stuff on the same sheet of paper that I was clueless about. Things like 'Apgar scores' and 'Presentation: *Occipito – Anterior*'. Was that even English? I vowed to look up each and every word and phrase I didn't understand. Flicking further through the book I saw all the immunizations Emma had already had. She was due for another one between twelve- and fifteen-months-old, which I hadn't realized. There were developmental charts, weight and height graphs, pages of help and advice and a couple of pages of comments at the back of the book which I assumed were made by a nurse or maybe a health visitor or something. It wasn't much when you got right down to it, but at least it filled in some gaps.

Immunizations, work, a place at a state nursery, checking out the local schools, developmental milestones – I had
to get my act together and sort all of those out and more
besides. I couldn't afford to slack off, not if I wanted to
keep my daughter.

And I did.

But I needed to find a way to make that happen.

35

Adam

Oh God! I wish he'd stop phoning me and texting me and bombarding me with emails and messages. It's driving me nuts. It's got to the stage where I'm afraid to even turn on my phone any more.

It's over.

Why doesn't he get that? Does he think any of this is easy for me? This isn't what I hoped would happen. I thought that maybe . . .

I was stupid.

Why can't he understand that I'm just giving him what he wants – an uncomplicated, straight-as-a-ruler, boring-as-hell life?

Why can't he just leave me alone?

36

Dante

Emma had her first birthday, complete with a cake and one candle. We sang 'Happy birthday' to her and helped her blow it out. She loved that. And she loved the toys and clothes she got as presents from my dad, my aunt and my brother; yet more farm animals and an alphabet-block toy from Dad, a yellow dress with matching booties from Adam, and money from Aunt Jackie. Dad broke out his camera, the case of which was covered in dust, and took enough pictures to fill a dozen photo albums. It was just like old times. It made me smile to watch him at work with his camera again. We were all posed holding Emma, walking Emma, lifting her above our heads, rocking her, with Emma sitting on our shoulders (she really liked that one). You name it, Dad wanted a photo of it. And Adam loved it, of course. Turn a camera on him and he sparkled like champagne. But even he stepped aside when needed so that Emma could take centre stage. We all buzzed around her like bees – and she loved it.

It was a good first birthday.

A week later it was my turn. My eighteenth birthday

arrived but I sure as hell didn't need a cake and I didn't want presents.

'If you want to spend money, buy Emma something,' I told Dad and Adam.

Dad didn't need to be told twice.

I had no plans to go anywhere or do anything for my birthday, but Dad put his foot down: 'Dante, you and your brother go out and enjoy yourselves. It's your birthday, for God's sake. Go and have a meal or see a film – my treat.'

'What about Emma?' I frowned.

Dad raised an eyebrow. 'I'll baby-sit.'

'Er . . . I don't think that would look too good if Veronica turns up,' I said.

There had been no further word from Collette's sister Veronica, but I didn't doubt for a second that she'd be back. She hung over me like the sword of Damocles.

'Stuff Veronica,' Dad dismissed. 'It's your birthday. You're only eighteen once and it doesn't make you a bad parent to have an evening out without your kid once in a while. Go and enjoy yourself. Adam, take your brother out and remind him what a good time feels like.' He dug into his pocket, pulling out a few notes. 'Go on, you two. Off you go and have some fun,' he insisted.

I wasn't sure about this. I picked up Emma to explain. 'Daddy is going out but only for a little while. I'll be back before you know it.'

'Oh. Dear. God!' Dad exclaimed. 'You're going out for a couple of hours, not leaving for an expedition to the Antarctic. Emma will be perfectly fine with me. Go.'

To be honest, it felt kinda good to leave the house and not be pushing a buggy!

Dad walked Emma to the door to see us off. 'Say bye to Daddy,' he told Emma. 'Wave to Daddy.'

'Dannggghh,' said Emma, waving at me.

'Bye, Emma. See you soon.' I waved back. I really wasn't sure about this. I was just about to head back to her when Adam grabbed my arm, dragging me away.

'Dante, stop being so pathetically sad,' he told me.

'OK, OK,' I conceded.

With one final wave goodbye to Emma, Adam and I set off down the road.

'Where d'you fancy going?' I asked my brother.

He shrugged. 'The Bar Belle?'

'We always go there.' I pulled a face, remembering the last time I'd been in that place. 'Don't you want to go somewhere different for a change?'

'The Bar Belle will be great,' enthused Adam.

'No, the Bar Belle will be the same as always.'

'That's what I said. Oh, go on. Please?' Adam pleaded.

'Oh, OK,' I agreed reluctantly.

'Yes!' Adam leaped up, punching the air. He turned to me, a huge smile on his face, a mischievous glint in his eyes.

'What?' I was instantly on my guard. 'What're you up to?'

'Nothing,' replied Adam like butter wouldn't melt.

'Hhmm . . .' I said, eyeing him suspiciously. 'Whatever you've got planned, just don't embarrass me – OK?'

'As if,' said my brother, his eyes — his whole body — fizzing with excitement.

The Bar Belle was insanely busy for a Wednesday. After being told that there'd be a thirty-minute wait for a table, I was more than ready and willing to try somewhere else.

'We're here now,' my brother insisted.

So we parked it at the bar. Adam tried to order a Pina Colada — like that was going to happen! Dad would kill me. I was legal now but decided I'd rather have a ginger beer than anything alcoholic. Adam sat with his virgin colada, sulking that I hadn't let him have one with rum in it, but he had about as much chance of drinking rum or any other alcohol as Emma did with me around.

'I just need to talk to one of the waiters,' said Adam, hopping off his bar stool. 'I'll be right back.'

That's when I clicked.

'Adam, no.'

'No what?'

'You're not going to tell the waiters it's my birthday. I don't want a bowl of ice cream with a sparkler in it, thank you very much. And I sure as hell don't want all the staff singing 'Happy birthday' to me.'

'But Dante . . .'

'Read my lips — hell, no!'

'You're so bloody miserable,' said Adam, sitting back down on his chair.

My brother must be nuts if he ever thought that idea would fly. I shook my head and changed the subject. I tried talking about football but Adam didn't know a football from a bowling ball so I soon gave up on that one. Tennis, cricket and athletics were the only sports Adam knew anything about. As far as I was concerned, tennis was a dead loss – all the really good players ever did was serve aces, which was great for them but boring as hell to watch. Watching cricket was like watching my toenails grow and there wasn't enough physical contact in athletics. Adam started discussing some designer or other but that was knocked on the head when he saw my eyes begin to glaze over. We moved on to rugby, some house-buying pro-gramme, motor racing and the exploits of some Hollywood superstar or other with as little success. It struck me as I struggled to find a subject we were both interested in, that we hadn't sat and chatted, just the two of us, in quite some time. We'd drifted apart to the extent that now we seemed to have very little in common.

We finally settled on music. At last a subject where we had some overlap. Not much, but some – and I would take what I could get.

'Hey, Dante.'

I swivelled round on my seat. Josh, Paul and Logan were behind us, waiting in the queue to be seen and seated. I was surprised to see Logan. He'd applied to do Politics and Economics at university and as far as I was aware had achieved good enough grades to get in. So what was he doing around here? Paul had found a job at a car dealership. I wasn't sure about Josh.

'Hey, guys,' I said.

'Hi, Josh,' said Adam.

Josh didn't even look at my brother, let alone answer

him. 'Dante, I haven't seen you in a while,' he said to me.

Adam turned back to his virgin colada, looking . . . troubled.

'Josh, my brother said hello to you.' I frowned.

'I know. I heard him,' said Josh.

'Then don't bloody ignore him,' I said.

'Dante, leave it. It's OK. Really,' said Adam.

But it wasn't. 'Adam, I'm sick of Josh treating you like a window,' I told my brother.

'Oh, for God's sake. Hello, Adam. How's it going? Happy now, Dante?'

'Ecstatic.' Josh's attitude towards my brother was really pissing me off. I wouldn't let anyone treat my daughter like that, and no way was anyone going to treat my brother like that either.

'Guys, chill,' said Paul. 'Jeez.'

'So, Paul, how's the car-dealership business?' I asked. 'And what the hell have you done to your hair?'

Paul's mousy-brown hair was now the exact same colour as orange juice.

'I fancied a change,' shrugged Paul, running his fingers through his yellow-orange locks. 'What d'you think?'

'Er . . . d'you want me to be honest?'

Paul rolled his eyes. 'Never mind.'

'How's the car-dealership business?' I repeated.

'Fine.'

'Do you work shifts?' I asked, wondering if they might have a job for me.

'Are you kidding? I wouldn't take a job where I had to

work shifts,' scoffed Paul. 'I'm like a vampire. I only come alive when the sun goes down.'

Get him! Like he was all that. But no job for me then.

'What about you, Logan?' I asked. 'I thought you were off to uni?'

'Not for another week,' Logan replied.

'Oh, I see.'

I turned back to Josh. He was staring a hole through my brother. Adam was studiously ignoring him.

'Josh, are you OK?' I asked.

Josh's attention snapped back to me. 'Yeah, I'm fine. What've you been up to?'

'Looking after my daughter, Emma.'

'What else apart from that?' said Josh.

How ironic. I once asked Melanie what she'd been doing apart from looking after Emma. I remembered the knowing little smile she gave me. I realized what that meant now. Looking after a kid was a full-time, full-on, full-term deal. No wonder Melanie didn't reply to my ignorance. I'm lucky she didn't head-butt me in the stomach. I shrugged again. There was no point in putting Josh straight.

'So what're you guys doing here?' asked Logan.

'We're celebrating Dante's birthday,' Adam replied before I could stop him.

I groaned inwardly.

'Oh yeah, I meant to text you,' said Josh. 'Happy birthday.'

'Thanks.' I turned back to my ginger beer. Hopefully

Josh and the others would take the hint and head back to their place in the queue.

'D'you guys want to join us?' Adam astounded me by asking.

I glared at Adam, then turned to see their response. Paul was grinning like it was the best idea since the invention of the wheel. Logan was watching Josh, who in turn looked just as uncomfortable as I felt. Josh didn't want us to group up any more than I did.

'Yeah, OK,' said Logan before either Josh or I could find an excuse.

What the hell was Adam playing at? Why on earth had he invited them to join us? He didn't even like Josh.

We had to wait ten minutes longer as there were now five of us instead of two but at last we were shown to a table, which was actually two square tables pushed together. I sat with Adam on one side of me and Logan on the other. Josh was seated opposite Adam, with Paul next to him. The conversation began tentatively at first, but before long we were having a laugh and a joke, just like old times. And it wasn't too bad, at first. The only trouble was, my mates were knocking back lager like it was water, so by the time our starters made it to the table they were feeling no pain. More drinks with the starters and after the starters so that by the time our main courses arrived, chips were flying around the table like insults. Embarrassed, I looked around. We were the focus of all attention and if looks could kill we'd all be embalmed by now. The wait-ers and waitresses were giving us dirty looks too. If the others kept this up we'd be booted out.

212

'Guys, it's my birthday. I don't want to be chucked out of the Bar Belle on my birthday,' I tried to reason with them.

I could've been talking to the cutlery for all the good it did.

Adam was tucking into a plate of rabbit food – I think it was called a Caesar salad on the menu – whilst grinning at the antics of the others, like chucking food around was the funniest joke he'd heard in a while. Me? I was just annoyed.

'Josh, can I try one of your chips?' Adam asked, his hand already on Josh's plate.

Josh grabbed Adam's wrist, twisting it viciously. 'I don't want your hand in my food, you queer son-of-a-bitch.'

'Josh . . .' Adam gasped out.

Silence descended on our table like a ton of bricks. I was having trouble drawing breath. Adam's whole body slumped. He bent his head. Instinctively I knew he was mere moments away from tears.

I pushed back my chair. 'Josh, let go of my brother. *Now*.'

Josh was scowling at Adam with such intense hatred it flowed over everyone at the table like lava. I was on my feet. Josh let go of Adam's wrist. Adam pulled back his arm, rubbing his left wrist with his right hand, his head still bent.

'Sorry, Dante, but I don't want your brother touching my food,' said Josh, adding viciously, 'God knows what I might catch.'

I moved towards Josh, ready to smash his head off the table, but Adam jumped up and barred my way.

'Adam, move,' I ordered.

'Dan, no. Don't. He's not worth it,' Adam told me. 'He's just a coward, a scared little kid afraid of everything and everyone.'

But I barely heard my brother. I wanted to do my talking with my fists. If only Adam would move out of the damned way.

'Don't you ever talk to my brother like that again,' I hissed at Josh.

'Josh, what did Adam mean?' Logan asked. 'Is there something you want to tell us?'

Nostrils flaring, Josh was on his feet. Now if my bloody brother would only move.

'If you gentlemen can't behave, I'm afraid I must ask you to leave.' The manager appeared from nowhere to stand at our table. Behind her were three burly waiters who looked as if they'd like nothing better than to toss us all out on our ears.

'Come on, guys,' said Josh, pushing his plate of steak and chips away in disgust. 'I've lost my appetite anyway.'

I looked around the table. Paul wore an expression of consternation, no doubt wondering how he could be having a laugh and a food fight one minute and be on the verge of a real fight the next. Josh's lips were clamped together, his fists clenched at his side. And I was more than ready for him. But it was Logan who made me pause. He was smiling. Not laughing at me and Adam, and the effect Josh's words had had on us.

No, he was *smiling*.

A slight, secret smile that was directed solely at Josh.

Paul was already on his feet. Logan was the last to stand. He and I exchanged a look of mutual loathing as he headed out of the restaurant after Josh and Paul.

Adam sat back down at the table, his head bent. I placed a hand on my brother's shoulder. He was shaking and trying his best to hide it.

Good riddance, I thought, as I watched the others swagger out.

Until I realized they'd stuck me with the damned bill.

Bastards.

37

Dante

'You should've let me pummel him.' I was still fuming as Adam and I walked home.

Paying the bill had wiped me out. Even with the money Dad had given me for our night out, being stuck with the bill for three extra meals meant I had to break out my plastic. My bank account was now empty and I had no idea where my next penny was coming from. But that was nothing compared to the rage I still felt at all the things Josh had said to my brother. Even now Josh's words burned holes in my head. Adam hadn't said much since the others walked out of the Bar Belle. Scratch that – he'd barely said anything at all. Mind you, I wasn't in a particularly chatty mood myself. I wanted . . . no, I *needed* to get home. Thankfully we were almost there. A couple more minutes and we'd be indoors. At that moment, all I wanted was to hold my daughter and to try and make sense of the world – in that order. All I wanted was to . . .

Time stopped.

Darkness. Then crashing lights behind my eyes.

I was lying on the pavement, my head pounding, giant bells pealing relentlessly in my ears. I struggled to stand up, only to be knocked flat again. The pain in my head was screaming at me.

It took a moment or two to realize why I couldn't move. Someone was kneeling on my legs and my arms were being pulled back.

I raised my head. Josh was standing directly in front of my brother, pushing him backwards until Adam's back was against the brick wall that made up the side of the house at the end of our road. And still Josh kept pushing my brother, keeping him off balance.

'Josh, stop it. Leave him alone!' I yelled desperately.

Josh turned to laugh at me, which just made Logan and Paul pull even harder on my arms. A fiery shriek of pain kept shooting up and down my arms and across my back. They were going to pull my arms out of their sockets. If I could just get one arm free . . . One hand, that was all I needed. But the pain in my arms was nothing compared to what was going on inside me as I watched Josh and my brother.

Every time Adam tried to straighten up, Josh pushed him back against the wall. But that didn't stop my brother from still trying to straighten up. And Adam never took his eyes off Josh. Not once.

'You're disgusting, you little fairy. You're a filthy little queer. You make my skin crawl,' Josh hissed.

Each word hurt me like a vicious punch. I flinched from every insult.

But Adam didn't say a word.

'Poof. Queer. Shirt-lifter.' Josh went through every derogatory name he could think of to chuck at my brother and each name was punctuated with another shove. Each word roared inside my head like some savage beast. I bucked and heaved but Paul and Logan didn't loosen their grip for a second.

'Josh, leave him alone, you shit-head . . .'

And then Adam did something that made the world stop in its tracks. He pushed Josh's hand aside and, leaning forward, he kissed him.

Adam kissed Josh full on the lips.

Paul and Logan forgot to yank at my arms. I forgot to struggle. Josh forgot to speak, forgot how to move. But only for a moment.

Just a moment.

Then hell erupted.

Josh lost it.

There was no other way to describe it. He cried out before lunging at my brother. His hands morphed into fists and he battered at my brother, punching Adam's face over and over. Adam put his arms up to try and protect himself but it was no use. Josh was beating the crap out of him. Adam fell to the ground, curling into a ball, his arms still up by his head. And Josh was punching and kicking him with not even a second's pause between blows. I struggled like a madman to get free to help my brother, but I was still on the ground, being pinned down. Logan was kneeling on my back. Paul shifted to kneel on my legs. They were going to snap my spine or my legs or both. They were both getting in the odd punch or two or three whilst I lay there, struggling and helpless. Josh was upright now, kicking my brother's head, stomping on it, over and over.

'You always thought you were better than us. Gonna go to university, gonna be a journalist and write about the truth,' Logan hissed in my ear. 'Look at you. The truth is you're a no-life, low-life with a kid and no job and a queer for a brother.'

I bucked and heaved and tried to kick out but I was down and out. All I could do was turn my head. All I could see was Josh and my brother.

'GET OFF HIM. JOSH, YOU BASTARD, GET OFF HIM. STOP. FOR GOD'S SAKE. YOU'RE KILLING HIM!'

All I had were words but they weren't getting through . . . Josh was still beating on my brother. Blood dripped off Josh's fists.

And Adam wasn't moving.

Paul jumped to his feet. 'Josh, stop. He's had enough.' Paul tried to pull Josh away but he wasn't strong enough.

'Logan, for God's sake, help me,' Paul cried out.

Logan jumped to his feet but he didn't move.

Twisting like a snake, I sprung up, fists ready, and caught Logan on the side of his head. He fell away from me with a grunt of pain. I lashed out again, punching him to the ground and then, as he was so super-fit, kicking him a couple of times to make sure he stayed down. I pounced on Josh. My arm around his neck, I dragged him back so hard and fast that only his heels were touching the ground. Dropping him without a second thought, I ran back to Adam, falling to my knees beside my brother who lay on his side. I couldn't make out any of Adam's features. His entire face was covered in blood.

'Adam . . . ?' I whispered.

I put my ear down towards his mouth and nose. Was that his breath against my face, or just a night breeze?

'Josh, we've got to get out of here. Now!' Paul shouted at Josh, still trying to pull him away.

'What on earth is going on out here?' A stocky man wearing trousers and nothing else emerged from the nearest house. 'Zoe, call the police,' he called over his shoulder.

I leaped up to look Josh in the eye. 'Leave now or I'll go to prison for you, I swear I will.'

The words were quietly spoken but I meant every single one of them. Fists clenched, I waited. The only way any of them would get to my brother again was over my dead body.

'Josh, for God's sake. Let's go,' Paul pleaded.

Logan and Paul took off, dragging Josh behind them.

I dropped back down to my knees.

Adam's face was a mess of blood and bone and hanging flesh.

I didn't know what to do.

Turn him? Leave him? What?

'Adam?' I stroked his head, whispering in his ear, 'Adam, don't die. Please, please don't die.'

38

Dante

Time obviously ran at a different rate in hospital. The seconds crawled by with mocking apathy. I sat in the waiting room which was more than half-full, feeling totally alone.

Two women, one with locks tied back in a ponytail, the other with short-cut brunette hair parted at one side walked through the automatic doors and headed for the reception desk. I watched without curiosity as they struck up a brief conversation with the receptionist behind the desk, that is until the receptionist pointed straight at me. Police officers. I should've expected it but it still made my heart bump as the two women headed my way. They both wore trouser suits, the first in navy-blue, the brunette in black. I stood when they got near, deciding that it would be better to face them rather than looking up at them as I'd have to do if I remained seated.

'You're the one who came in with the victim of the assault?' asked the woman in navy-blue.

I nodded.

'I'm Detective Sergeant Ramona Crystal. This is my colleague, Detective Constable Samantha Kay. Would you mind telling us your name?'

'Dante. Dante Bridgeman.'

'So, Dante, what can you tell us?'

Silence.

I didn't have a clue where to begin. I watched as the sergeant broke out a notepad and pen.

'D'you know the name of the victim?'

'Yeah, he's my brother, Adam. Adam Bridgeman. He's sixteen,' I replied.

'What happened?' asked DC Kay.

'We . . . we were jumped.'

'How many were there?'

'Three.'

'Look, why don't we all sit down,' said the detective sergeant. She sat on the chair to the left of the one I'd just vacated. The constable remained on her feet until I sat down, then she sat on my right. 'I can see you're still in a state of shock but anything you can tell us now will help us catch the ones who did this that much faster,' said DS Crystal. 'Take your time and tell us exactly what took place.'

'Adam and I went out to . . . to celebrate my b-birthday . . .'

Oh God, it was still my birthday . . . The word tasted like bile in my mouth. The sergeant and DC Kay exchanged a look.

'Go on,' urged DS Crystal.

'We were walking home and we'd just turned into our road when we got jumped.'

'Did you know or recognize the ones who attacked you?'

Pause.

'Dante?' the sergeant prompted, her pen poised.

Why was I even hesitating? Why should I display loyalty to a scumbag like Josh? Why did I even have to think about it?

'Josh Davies, Logan Pane and Paul Anders,' I said quickly before I could change my mind. 'Logan and Paul held me down on the ground. Josh was the one who beat up my brother. He kept punching and kicking Adam in the head. He wouldn't stop.'

I started coughing. My stomach was heaving. I was mere seconds away from being physically sick. Tilting back my head, I took rapid deep breaths in a desperate effort to control myself. The officers gave me a few moments for which I was grateful. I finally lowered my head as the feeling slowly began to fade.

'Where did you go to celebrate your birthday?' asked DC Kay.

'The Bar Belle.' I didn't miss the look that passed between them at that either. 'Adam and I weren't drinking, if that's what you're thinking. 'Adam had two virgin coladas and I was drinking ginger beer all night, the non-alcoholic kind. Josh, Logan and Paul were drinking though. They were drinking lager all night.'

'So they were with you in the Bar Belle?' asked the DS, her voice sharp.

'Adam and I met up with them there but it wasn't planned. We shared a table but got into an argument, so the three of them left before us.'

The police questioned me for another twenty minutes, noting down every word I said, and I mean, every word.

By the time they finally left me in peace, I was exhausted. Even now I struggled to make sense not of what had happened, but why. I thought it had all been done and dusted and forgotten in the Bar Belle. Josh and I were friends, surely – even after everything that had happened at the restaurant. I had some vague notion that in the morning, when the lager buzz had gone and Josh's hangover kicked in and when I'd managed to calm down, Josh would phone me to laugh off his comments made to my brother. He'd apologize, I'd accept it and we'd all move on.

So why was I now sitting in hospital, wondering if my brother would live or die?

All the way to the hospital in the ambulance, I couldn't stop shivering. The paramedic inside the ambulance hadn't stopped monitoring my brother for a second. Before they even got him into the ambulance, the two medics had battled to clear Adam's airway and stabilize him, desperately trying to save my brother's life. A drip went into one arm, his face was wiped off and an oxygen mask put over his nose and mouth. His face was swollen and distorted. Nothing was in the right place. After they got him into the ambulance, the medic driving had taken off with full lights and sirens. I watched my brother lying there unconscious on the way to the hospital and I was unable to take my eyes off him. I didn't dare. I had the feeling that if I looked away, even for an instant, I would lose him for good.

Once we reached the hospital, Adam was immediately whisked away to be x-rayed and operated on. I phoned

Dad, with no clear idea of what I was going to say. The phone was answered within a couple of rings.

'Hiya, Dante. I hope you guys are on your way home. It's getting late. Did you have a good time?' Dad's cheerful tone jarred. 'And don't worry about Emma. She's fast asleep.'

'Dad, I . . . I'm at the hospital.'

'What? Why? What's happened?' The change in his tone was immediate.

'Adam . . . Adam was beaten up. Dad, he's really badly hurt . . .'

A male doctor who was bald and built like a brick house appeared from nowhere to stand in front of me. I'm tall, but I still had to look up to this guy. Dante, I need to check you over and you really shouldn't be using a mobile phone in here.'

'I'm talking to my dad.'

'Talk to him once I've made sure you're all right,' the doctor insisted. 'OK?'

Maybe Dad heard the doctor harrassing me. Maybe the sound of my voice was enough. Either way Dad didn't linger to get any more details.

'I'm on my way,' he said grimly before hanging up the phone.

'I don't need to be examined. I want to stay with my brother,' I insisted, pushing my phone back in my trouser pocket.

'He's in good hands,' the doctor attempted to reassure me. 'Let us do our job. But in the meantime we need to check you over.'

I had minor cuts and grazes and severe bruising down my back and on my legs. It didn't hurt though, not too much. I didn't have the time or the right to feel pain. I needed to focus on my brother. Dad arrived at the hospital about thirty or forty minutes after I did, carrying a sleeping Emma. The moment I saw her, I reached out to take her.

'No, it's OK,' said Dad. 'I've got her. No point in waking her up.'

So we sat in intense quiet after the raging storm. I'd done more praying in the last couple of hours than I'd ever done in my life before. Adam couldn't die. He just couldn't. I couldn't imagine life without him.

I didn't want to.

The waiting area we'd been directed to after Dad arrived was just an open-plan space off a corridor with about five grey plastic chairs and a vending machine. A youngish brunette man in his late twenties was already there when we arrived, but after a while he got up and left without a nurse or doctor coming to see him. Dad and I sat in silence, with Emma still fast asleep in Dad's arms.

'What happened?' Dad asked at last. I was so lost in my own thoughts that the sound of his voice made me start.

'We got jumped,' I replied.

'By who?'

'Some guys from my old school,' I said.

'You know the ones who did this? Look at me, Dante.'

'Yeah, I know them,' I replied, looking directly at him, not wanting to hide anything.

'Tell me everything that happened,' said Dad.

So I told him.

Everything.

'And this is the same Josh who used to come round our house? The one who was supposed to be your friend?' asked Dad.

I nodded.

Dad closed his eyes and leaned his head back against the wall behind our chairs.

'This is what I've always been afraid of,' he said quietly.

And what could I say to that? Nothing.

We sat in silence for a long, long time.

'Did you tell the police what you just told me?' said Dad at last.

I nodded.

'All of it?'

'Yes, Dad.'

'Dante!' Aunt Jackie called out to me the moment she turned the corner and saw us. She bustled straight over. I stood up. She gave me a hug which made me wince with the pain in my arms.

'Tyler.'

'Jackie.'

Dad and my aunt exchanged greetings but that was it. I guess we were all too worried to hold any kind of conversation. Aunt Jackie sat down next to me.

'How is he? How's Adam?' she asked.

'We don't know yet,' Dad replied. 'They're still operating on him.'

'What happened? asked my aunt.

'Adam was beaten up,' said Dad.

'What? Why? By who?' asked my aunt, her tone sharp.

I looked down at the ground, up at the ceiling, anywhere but at my dad and aunt.

'For being gay,' Dad provided, his voice bitter. 'I thought this gay-bashing bullshit was a thing of the past. This is the twenty-first century – or at least it's supposed to be.'

'Oh God . . .'

'God had nothing to do with it,' said Dad harshly. 'Just some homophobic scumbags who didn't even have the guts to make it a fair fight.'

'D'you know who they were?' asked Aunt Jackie.

'Some guys that used to be in my class,' I said.

'Why did you let them use your brother as a punch bag?' asked Dad.

I turned to Dad. 'I told you, they had me pinned down. I tried to stop them, but I couldn't move.'

'You're supposed to look out for your younger brother. You're supposed to protect him,' Dad snapped.

Did he think I didn't know that?

'I tried, Dad. They came out of nowhere.'

'You should've tried harder.'

'Tyler, that's not helping,' said my aunt.

'Keep out of this, Jackie. It's my son who's being operated on. It's my son who is fighting for his life.'

'And it's your son who's sitting next to you needing a kind word from his dad,' said Aunt Jackie.

I jumped up. 'Excuse me.'

'Where're you going?' Dad frowned.

I needed to get out of there. 'To wash my hands.' I headed for the men's room before Dad or Aunt Jackie could say another word. No matter how much Dad blamed me, it couldn't begin to compare with how much I blamed myself. But his words still hurt. Very much.

Once there, I splashed water on my face and washed my hands. The skin on a couple of my knuckles was grazed from where I'd punched Logan. I straightened up, catching sight of my reflection in the wide mirror above the three sinks. My eyes shimmered with unshed tears, my teeth were clenched together so hard that a muscle was pulsing overtime in my jaw. I couldn't stand to look at myself any more but I didn't turn away.

This was all my fault.

Adam had asked me, more than once, why I let Josh get away with the things he did. Staring at myself in the mirror, I now asked myself the same question. Why hadn't I slapped Josh down when he started spouting his ignorant crap? Josh was an equal-opportunity hater. Everyone got it in the neck: travellers, Muslims, Jews, gays, and God only knew what Josh said about me and other black people behind my back – but gays got vilified the most. Anything I wore that didn't consist of jeans and a T-shirt was gay. The music I liked was extra-gay. The books I read were super-gay. And I'd never challenged him about it, not once.

'It's just a word. It doesn't mean anything,' I'd tried to convince myself.

Never mind that words hurt. Never mind that sometimes the impact of words lasted far longer than physical pain. But I wasn't gay so where was the harm? It was like the way Josh called me a retard if I did anything he thought was moronic. The word jarred but I never called him on that one either.

It doesn't mean anything . . .

Yeah, right.

Adam had called Josh a coward, but Josh wasn't the only one. I turned away from the mirror, unable and unwilling to look at myself a moment longer. I headed back along the corridor to the small waiting area, where we'd been left to wait for the worst and hope for the best.

'I'm just saying, you've always been too hard on the boy, Ty. You're blaming him for things that weren't his fault,' said Aunt Jackie.

'You don't know what you're talking about,' Dad dismissed.

I didn't turn the corner to enter the waiting area. Aunt Jackie and Dad were talking about me. I stopped and listened.

'Don't I? You think me and my sister didn't talk? You think she didn't confide in me?' my aunt challenged. 'You think she didn't know how much you resented her and Dante for what happened?'

'What're you talking about? I didn't resent her. I married her, didn't I?' said Dad.

'Yeah, but you didn't want to, not at first and you made sure that Jenny knew it.'

'That's not fair. I was young and scared out of my mind, but I did the right thing,' said Dad.

'With precious little grace.'

'Jackie, give me a break. I was only twenty, for God's sake. It wasn't an ideal way to start a marriage.'

'The only reason you put a ring on my sister's finger was because she was pregnant with Dante. D'you think Jenny didn't know how much you resented her and your son? She knew you didn't love her—'

'That's a damned lie,' Dad denied emphatically. 'When she died, I wanted to die too. Only two things got me out of bed each morning – Dante and Adam.'

'Ty, all my sister ever wanted was for you to love her.'

'What the hell are you talking about?' Dad shouted. 'I did love her. She was my whole life.'

'Then why didn't you ever tell her that? Not once did you ever tell her you loved her,' said Aunt Jackie.

'I . . . I . . . I loved her,' Dad replied, his voice now so quiet that I had to strain to hear him. 'Jenny knew that. I've just never been good with those kinds of words. But Jenny knew how much she meant to me.'

'The way your boys know it?' asked Aunt Jackie. 'The way you show Dante you love him every time you put him down or dismiss him? The way you show Adam you love him by not even acknowledging the fact that he's gay? Is that how your boys know it?'

'Of course I know Adam is gay. I've come to terms with that,' said Dad angrily. 'Don't make me the bad guy here, Jackie. Just because I don't agree with this navel-gazing, talk-about-our-feelings-every-two-seconds crap that seems to be the vogue at the moment.'

'No one's asking you to talk about it every two seconds, Tyler, but you won't talk about it at all.'

'Jackie, what should I have said to Adam? Go on, enlighten me.'

A deep silence and then a sigh from my aunt. 'Tyler, I'm not here to argue with you. This is neither the time nor the place.'

'I'm glad you realize that,' said Dad. 'Nice to see your opinion of me hasn't changed one bit from the day I married your sister.'

'That's not true,' said Aunt Jackie. 'All I've ever wanted was what was best for you, my sister and my nephews.'

'And you don't think that's what I want too?'

'Then why didn't you tell Dante the truth about—?'

I walked round the corner. Aunt Jackie's stream of words ground to an abrupt halt. Dad and my aunt both stared at me with varying degrees of shock. Each of us knew I'd heard every word. The silence between us sliced into me.

But knowing the truth hurt even worse.

'You . . . you only married Mum because she was pregnant . . . with me.' For ever passed before I could get out the whispered words.

That one fact alone explained so much. Too much.

'All this time, all these years I wondered why you never looked at me or treated me the same as Adam,' I said.

The answer was simple. Adam was wanted. I wasn't.

And suddenly so many things began to make sense. Like when I'd told Dad my A level results. I remembered his comment: '*If I had your chances I'd be a millionaire by now . . .*'

'That's why nothing I ever did was good enough,' I realized aloud. 'You blame me for ruining your life, for stopping you from doing all the things you wanted to do.'

Dad handed Emma to Aunt Jackie before swiftly walking over to me. 'Now listen to me, Dante. You are wrong,' he said urgently. 'Yes, your mum and I probably wouldn't have got married when we did if she hadn't been pregnant with you, but I cared very much about you and your mum. I still do.'

'But Adam was born with love – and I wasn't,' I said, my thoughts whirling inside my head like autumn leaves in a hurricane.

Should've been made with love . . .

'Dante, you're not listening to me. If I've ever made you feel like I didn't love you, then I'm sorry. Because it's never, *never* been true. And if I pushed you too hard, it's because I didn't want you to make my mistakes.'

'And I was your biggest mistake . . .' I tried to turn away but Dad placed his hands on my shoulders to stop me.

'No, son, you weren't,' Dad insisted. 'Sometimes the things you're convinced you don't want turn out to be the things you need the most in this world. You have Emma, so you know exactly what I mean. You and your mum and Adam are the only things in my life I've ever cared about. Yeah, I had plans before your mum got pregnant. I was going to finish university, I was going to work in films, maybe as an editor. It didn't happen. But if I could go back and live my life all over again, I wouldn't change a thing. Not one single thing. D'you understand?'

I searched Dad's face for something, though I had no idea what.

'D'you believe me, Dante? It's really important that you believe me,' said Dad urgently.

'Mr Bridgeman?' The surgeon appeared to stand before all of us, saving me from having to reply.

'How is Adam? Is he OK?' Dad stepped forward.

I couldn't breathe. My heart had moved up to my throat and I couldn't breathe.

Please . . .

'Adam sustained a number of very serious injuries. His jaw and his nose were broken and his eye socket was shattered but we managed to save his eye. Plus he has two broken ribs and severe bruising over most of his body. But he's out of theatre now and stable.'

'Can we see him?' asked Dad sombrely.

'Just for a moment. I have to warn you that his face is going to take a long time to heal and he'll probably have one or two permanent scars. We had to wire his jaw, realign his nasal bones and the surrounding tissue and we had to use metal plates and screws to hold his right cheek-bone in place. I just need to prepare you for what you're about to see.'

I turned to Aunt Jackie and held out my hands for my daughter. Aunt Jackie looked like she might argue, but then thought better of it. She handed Emma over to me. I lifted Emma up so that her head was resting on my shoulder. She barely stirred, still fast asleep. My daughter smelled fresh and clean and new. She smelled of hope. The only thing keeping me in the same postcode as rational at the moment lay asleep in my arms. We followed the surgeon as he led the way. It was way past midnight and I

234

was about ready to drop, but I kept going – one foot in front of the other.

'Oh my God . . .' Dad breathed.

Aunt Jackie's horrified gasp as we approached said it all and didn't begin to say enough. The surgeon had tried to prepare us for what we were about to see, but this was far, far worse. All I could do was stare. I wanted to turn away, but I couldn't. Adam's face was unrecognizable. He had a bandage wrapped around his jaw, under his chin and running round the top of his head. And his face was even more swollen, misshapen and discoloured than before. He looked like his face had been shoved into a mincing machine. The transparent oxygen mask over his mouth and nose did nothing to mask his injuries. He had a drip of colourless solution running into one arm and a bag of blood running into the other.

'Our immediate concern is his breathing,' the surgeon informed us. 'Adam suffered displaced rib fractures, and what with that and his facial injuries, we have to monitor his breathing very carefully. And though we managed to save his right eye, it's very likely that his vision will be impaired as a result of his injuries. He's not out of the woods yet.'

Next to me, Aunt Jackie started to cry. Quiet, heartfelt tears which she tried but failed to control. Dad put an awkward arm around her, trying to offer comfort where there was none. Dad kept gulping, like there was something stuck in his throat.

'Adam is young and strong and with time and patience, there's no reason why he shouldn't make an excellent recovery,' the surgeon tried to reassure us.

Adam . . .

My beautiful brother, Adam . . .

And somewhere, out there, Josh was having a good laugh about what he'd done.

No matter. Once I found him, his laughter would stop.

39

Dante

Two days later when Dad, Emma and I arrived at the post-operative ward to see my brother, his bed was empty . . . Dad sprinted to the nurses' station whilst I ran, pushing Emma in her buggy close behind him.

'Where's my son? Adam Bridgeman?' Dad demanded of the two nurses at the station. One was a black guy in his late twenties, early thirties. The other was a middle-aged woman with a wrinkled forehead and red hair swept up in a high ponytail.

'Oh, Mr Bridgeman, I'm sorry. I meant to catch you before you got to his bed,' said the redhead. 'Would you come with me, please?'

'Where's my son?' Dad asked again, his voice a husky whisper.

Adam . . .

My whole body suddenly went cold. So cold that my blood instantly froze inside me.

Don't think . . .

Don't assume the worst . . .

The nurse led the way into a small waiting room, ushering us in before shutting the door quietly behind us.

'Mr Bridgeman, we had to take Adam back to theatre,' she said. 'A CT scan revealed a temporal bone fracture with an underlying chronic subdural haematoma. He's been taken back to theatre to have the haematoma drained.'

Dad collapsed down into the nearest chair. 'Oh God.'

'We're not sure the temporal fracture was a result of the recent attack. Has Adam been complaining of headaches recently?'

'Well, yes.' Dad looked thoughtful. 'And his headaches were beginning to get so bad that I took him to see our GP a few weeks ago. We were still waiting to be sent an appointment for his scan.'

'Ah,' said the nurse. 'Did he suffer any kind of injury or blow to his head that might've caused his headaches?'

Dad glanced at me. 'You said he was playing in a school football match when the ball hit him in the head. But I don't see how a football—'

'Dad, it wasn't a football match,' I interrupted, horrified. 'It was a cricket match.'

'What?' Dad stared at me. 'But Adam said he headed the ball when he should've ducked . . . Oh my God . . . I thought he was talking about a football. If I'd known he was talk-ing about a cricket ball, he would've been straight down the hospital, no matter how much he protested.'

'I'm sorry, I thought you knew,' I said. But the truth was I didn't think much about it at the time, or at any time.

'Well, that explains a lot,' said the nurse. 'But luckily for your son, very luckily, he was in the right place at the right time to get it attended to straightaway.'

'Why? What happened?' I asked. 'Did he pass out or something?'

The nurse smiled at me. 'The point is, we were on hand to take him straight into theatre. That's the fact you need to hold on to.'

'Is he . . . is he going to make it?' I couldn't help asking.

'Don't say that, Dan. Of course he is,' Dad replied vehemently.

'Draining a subdural haematoma is actually quite a straightforward procedure,' said the nurse. 'Don't worry, Adam is in very good hands. If you'd like to wait here, I promise I'll let you know the moment I have any more news.'

'Thank you,' said Dad.

I sat next to Dad, slowly pushing Emma back and forth in her buggy. After about ten minutes, Emma started agitating to get out. I unclipped the safety buckle and sat her on my knee. She was still restless.

'Dad, would you mind holding her for a second?' I handed Emma over, then dug into the baby bag hanging on the handles of the buggy. 'D'you want this, Emma?' I lifted up her teddy. 'Or your book?' I held up her favourite baby board book with well-chewed corners.

Emma reached for her teddy. Putting the book away, I sat down and put Emma back on my lap before handing over her teddy. The only sound in the room after that for quite some time was Emma burbling away to her toy in baby-speak. I absent-mindedly stroked her hair.

'Dad, d'you think all this will get back to Veronica and

the social services?' I asked the question that'd been gnawing away at me over the last couple of days.

'You mean about Adam getting beaten up?' Dad frowned.

'No, about me being involved in a street fight?'

'I don't see how or why. And even if it does, so what? You were ambushed and your brother is the victim here. You weren't the instigator.'

'D'you think she'll see it that way?'

'Dante, stop worrying about Veronica,' said Dad, looking me straight in the eye. 'Emma isn't going anywhere, I promise you. OK?'

'OK, Dad.'

We sat watching Emma for a while. I lifted her up and kissed her cheek, before resting my forehead against hers.

'Dante, I want you to know something.'

When I turned to Dad, I instinctively knew he'd been watching me. 'Yes, Dad?'

'I want you to know how proud I am of you,' said Dad.

Huh? I blinked like a faulty lamp at him.

'I don't think I've told you that, but I am. I'm proud of how you knuckled down and did so well in your exams. And I'm proud of the way you've become a real father to Emma.'

I didn't know quite what to say. This was a first.

'Thanks, Dad,' I said quietly.

'And I want you to know something else.'

'Yes?'

'I love you, son. Very much.'

Dad was looking straight ahead, not at me, but I didn't

doubt for a second the sincerity of his words. He'd never told me that before, but then I'd never said those words before either. I guess Dad and I were alike after all. I swallowed hard.

'I . . . I love you too, Dad.'

40

Dante

'Where is he, Paul?'

'I don't know. I swear I don't know. Let me go.' Paul struggled to get out of my grasp but he wasn't going anywhere. Not until I had some answers.

It'd been over a month since Adam had had his second operation and I was sick and tired of waiting for justice to be served on the ones who had put my brother in hospital. Adam had been in hospital for eight days and even though he was now home, he still had to take all his meals through a straw – when he could be persuaded to eat at all. His jaw had to stay wired shut for another two weeks at least. And he was in constant pain. My brother only left his bedroom to go the bathroom and that was only after he made Dad take down the bathroom mirror. He had given up trying to speak, using a notepad to communicate.

And his face . . .

He had a crisscross pattern of scars down the right side of his face and his right eye drooped noticeably, the result of facial nerve paralysis due to his fractured temporal bone. The doctors said that given time and effort on Adam's part it might improve. But Adam lost the will to make the effort. He didn't fizz any more. Not even close. And he never smiled. He didn't even attempt it.

And the ones who did that to him were out here somewhere having a good laugh and joke about their handiwork.

Well, if the police weren't going to do their job, then I'd do it for them. Starting with this little weasel, Paul. He'd been the easiest to track down. He'd been the easiest to track down. It'd only taken three phone calls to find out where he worked. Dad had stopped working overtime since Adam came out of hospital, so it was easy to ask him to baby-sit with the excuse that I needed to go for a walk for a little while to clear my head. I waited outside the dealership where Paul worked, far enough away to not get spotted but close enough to see him the moment he came out. Then it was just a question of following him until he was in a secluded-enough place for the two of us to have a little 'chat'. Ironic that it should be the park.

He didn't know what hit him.

And now he was on the ground, wriggling and slippery as a hooked fish, but I had him and I wasn't letting go.

'Paul, I'm not playing. Where's Josh?'

'At his house probably.'

'I've been there. His mum said he's staying with you for a few days. So this is the last time I'm going to ask: *where is Josh?*'

Paul stared at me like a rabbit stunned by headlights. 'He . . . he . . .'

I slammed the flat of my hand into the ground right

next to his head. And it bloody hurt, but if he thought I was mucking around, he was going to be painfully put right.

'The next one won't miss,' I warned him.

'He's at Logan's. He's staying at Logan's house for a few days,' said Paul, his words tripping over themselves to be heard. 'I'm just covering for him 'cause Josh's mum doesn't like Logan.'

'Logan is at university.' I scowled. 'He told me at the restaurant that he was off to uni the following week, so stop lying.'

'I'm not. I'm not,' Paul said quickly, his eyes wide with panic as I raised my fist. 'He didn't get the necessary grades. He's still at home. I swear he is. Logan was the one who lied. You've got to believe me.'

'Hhmm . . .' In spite of everything, I did believe him. I got to my feet, my eyes narrowing as I considered what to do next.

Paul struggled to sit up. 'I . . . I'm sorry about your brother . . .'

I stamped him back down against the ground just as hard as I could. 'Don't you dare talk about my brother,' I spat at him. 'Don't you dare.'

'I'm s-sorry . . .' Paul coughed.

I straightened up, asking icily, 'Are you going to phone Josh to warn him that I'm after him?'

Paul shook his head. 'But he already knows. That's why he very rarely stays at his own home or any place for too long.'

My eyes were like slits as I considered Paul, remembering

the way he'd knelt on me whilst Josh kicked the crap out of my brother. At that moment, I wanted to hurt him so badly – but I wanted to catch up to Josh more. So Paul would just have to wait his turn. He was further down my list of priorities. What I wanted to know was why they were all still on the streets after what they'd done to Adam? Why hadn't the police arrested them?

'Did the police come and see you?' I asked.

Paul lowered his gaze. 'Yeah. I had to go to the police station with my mum and dad. I was released pending further enquiries but they warned me that I'll probably be charged with affray and end up in court. They did the same to Logan.'

Affray? Was that it?

'And Josh?'

'The police haven't caught up with him yet,' said Paul. 'But my dad says Josh will be charged with GBH for sure.'

Grievous bodily harm? Not good enough. Not even on the same planet as good enough.

'He should've turned himself in,' I told Paul. 'He would've been safer than he will be when I get hold of him.' I straightened up. 'If you do phone Josh to warn him, tell him not to bother running because I'll hunt him through hell itself if I have to.' I turned to walk away.

'It wasn't Josh . . .' Paul called out after me.

I turned back with a frown.

'I mean, Josh . . . Josh hurt your brother, but it wasn't . . . wasn't him . . .'

What was he talking about?

'I mean . . . it wasn't Josh's fault,' said Paul.

245

I marched back to him. He'd just moved up my priority list. Paul drew back, shrinking into himself when he saw the murderous expression on my face.

'Whose fault was it then?' I asked softly. 'My brother's?'

'No. No,' Paul replied quickly. 'I just meant that we'd all been drinking and Logan was the one . . . Logan . . .'

'Spit it out,' I ordered impatiently.

'W-when we left the Bar Belle that night, Logan wouldn't leave Josh alone. He k-kept teasing Josh about being a . . . being the same as Adam. And Josh was just getting madder and madder. I tried to tell Logan to back off, but he wouldn't stop and then Josh said he'd prove how much he hated queers. And even then Logan wouldn't stop provoking him. So it was Logan's and Josh's idea to wait for you guys to head home and then Josh would prove once and for all that he wasn't one of . . . he wasn't a . . .'

'I get the picture,' I told him stonily.

'I didn't know it would go as far as it did, I swear. I've never seen Josh lose it like that, but he never would've done it if Logan hadn't kept provoking him.'

A conversation I'd had with Collette in the park crept into my head. What was it she'd said?

'You know what Josh is like when Logan is goading him . . .'

I ran a hand over my head, like I was trying to straighten out my thoughts. Had I got it wrong? Was Logan the one I should really be after? Was he really there in the background pulling everyone's strings like some malevolent puppet master? I shook my head. I couldn't afford to let doubts and second thoughts into my head. Not now. I'd spent the last few weeks thinking about what I needed to do. And I'd finally reached a conclusion. This was not the time for uncertainty. Josh first, then Logan.

'Paul, here's some advice. Stay away from me and mine if you know what's good for you. If you see me on the street, you'd better cross the road because the next time I see you, it's on.'

I spun round and walked away.

Time to find Josh.

41

Dante

It turned out to be easier than I thought it would be. I only had to watch Logan's house for one night without success. On the second night, I turned into Logan's street and there was Josh walking towards me, his head down, a bulging rucksack across his shoulder.

I stopped walking as I watched him approach. He wore denim jeans, a grubby grey T-shirt and the brown leather jacket he'd got for his sixteenth birthday. And with each step he took, the quiet fury inside me rose a little higher and burned a little stronger. Each step Josh took set off flashes of memory, snapshots of the kicking he'd given my brother. He had hidden out, waiting to ambush Adam. And for what? Because Adam had insulted him in the restaurant? With his head still down, Josh couldn't see me, which suited me just fine. I took a quick look around. There were three people further up the road but they were walking away from us. The late autumn night air was dark and cold and sharp, just the way I felt inside.

I smiled as Josh got closer and closer.

He was about two metres away from me and closing when he finally realized that something was wrong.

His head shot up. At the sight of me, his eyes widened, his mouth dropped open. And he bolted like he had the Devil himself after him – which, when you got right down to it, wasn't far from the truth.

Josh was fast.

But I was faster.

Rugby tackling him to the ground, I then dragged him up onto his feet, throwing him against the nearest wall just as hard as I could. The air left his lungs in a pained hiss for a second time in as many seconds.

'I'm sorry . . . I'm sorry . . .'

The words leaped from Josh before I could open my mouth. He put out his hands to fend me off but I knocked them out the way.

My hand was at his throat. I stared into his eyes without blinking. Slowly my fingers began to tighten around his neck.

'I'm sorry . . .' Josh squirmed frantically. 'I d-didn't m-mean to . . . He shouldn't have k-kissed me.'

I tightened my grip. Josh's face was turning puce now. He needed to taste some of what he'd dished out to my brother. Images of police, court, prison flitted in my head. My grip loosened, but only for a second. Josh had to pay.

My brother deserved nothing less.

And from the terror widening his eyes, Josh knew what was coming. He kept pulling away from me like he was trying to merge with the wall behind him. But he wasn't going anywhere. Josh's eyelids began to flutter shut.

Stop, Dante . . .

No. Damn it, he had to pay. Hell! There was a war going on inside me. Visions of Emma danced through my resolve.

Her smile kept biting chunks out of my hatred towards Josh. I needed to focus on Adam, not my daughter.

Emma . . .

Damn it. I was all mixed up.

Josh stopped pulling away. He unexpectedly leaned forward instead.

And kissed me.

I let go of him at once, scrubbing my lips with the back of my hand. Josh collapsed in a heap at my feet, coughing and spluttering as he fought to draw breath.

'You sick bastard!' I shouted. 'I'm gonna *kill* you.'

Josh put out his hands to try and push me away, but it did no good. Fists clenched, I aimed for his face and started battering him with all the fury that raged inside. He covered his head with his arms, curling up into a ball to try and protect himself. But it didn't make any difference, not to me.

'See,' he gasped out through bloodied lips. 'You hate us queers just as much as I do.'

His words jolted through me like a lightning bolt, stopping me in mid swing. Josh started to cry. Big awkward, embarrassed sobs racked his body. I stared down at him, his words clanging in my head.

Us queers . . . ?

'You . . . you're *gay*?'

Josh nodded, still sobbing at my feet.

'I . . . I don't hate . . . I'm not like you. This is about what you did to my brother,' I stuttered.

But who was I trying to convince, Josh or myself? Here I was standing over him, my fists clenched, my mind set on his destruction. I'd made up my mind to make him pay.

Pay?

Don't honey-coat it, Dante.

I'd made up my mind to make him suffer, to make him endure worse than he'd inflicted on Adam. I had it all figured out. It was cold and calculated and I'd thought of nothing else since the night it had happened. Dad and Adam between them could look after Emma if I got banged up, plus Emma would get my bedroom to herself that much sooner. The social services wouldn't take her away from the only family she knew, at least that's what I was counting on. Dad wouldn't let them take my daughter away from him. She'd be my one real regret, but if Josh got what was coming to him then maybe my brother could move forward and get on with his life.

An eye for an eye.

But then Josh had kissed me . . .

And any last lingering doubts I might have had about whether or not I could really hurt him flew out of my head and all I wanted to do then was not so much kill him as destroy him. I thought I hated him because of what he'd done to my brother. But that was nothing compared to what I'd felt when he'd kissed me.

So just what did that make me?

I leaned against the wall, my head tilted back as I tried to figure things out.

Next to me, Josh's sobs were beginning to subside. He inhaled deeply, fighting for control. I watched as he slowly got to his feet, spitting out the blood in his mouth. We regarded each other. Josh was shaking. I was still.

'Is . . . is Adam going to be OK?'

I glared at him. He could not be serious. My brother had escaped being six feet under by a hair's-breadth and Josh had the nerve to enquire about his health?

'Are you deliberately trying to wind me up?'

Josh shook his head. 'No, I . . . no . . .' The merest hint of a smile and it would've been me and him again, but Josh's expression remained sombre. 'Could you tell Adam . . . tell him I'm sorry?' asked Josh.

Fists clenched, I turned round and walked away.

It was way after midnight when I finally returned home. I'd walked for a couple of hours, just thinking. And my thoughts hadn't been pleasant ones, but they'd been honest. At first I'd seriously thought about going after Logan. When I eventually cooled down, I finally realized the extent to which we'd all been played, Josh included – not that I had any sympathy for that bastard whatsoever. But Logan was the one who'd wound us all up like mechanical toys and set us clashing and crashing towards each other. Some people like Collette and Adam had seen beneath Logan's mask. I hadn't. A lifetime ago, I'd dreamed of uncovering the truth and writing about it. Some joke when I couldn't even tell what was true and what was false when it was right under my nose.

So what should I do about Logan?

In the end I decided to just let it go. Logan needed sorting – but I wouldn't be the one to do it. To tell the truth, what I needed now was to be there for my daughter and my brother. They both needed me more than I needed revenge.

When I finally reached home, all I wanted to do was

collapse into bed and sleep without dreaming. Even though I tried to tiptoe into my bedroom, for some reason Emma stirred in her cot and woke up immediately. I groaned inwardly as she pulled herself upright. Tonight I could really do without Emma's teeth giving her grief.

'Go back to sleep, Emma.' I tried to get her to lie down again but she wasn't having it. I sighed. 'Emma, please go back to sleep.'

Emma held out her arms to be picked up. I gave in. Anything for a quiet life. I sat on my bed, holding Emma as she rested her head against my shoulder contentedly. I envied her so much. The world made far more sense to her than it did to me.

'Dada . . .' said Emma.

I froze momentarily. 'What did you say?' I whispered, holding her up so we were at eye-level.

'Dada,' she repeated.

'Who's your daddy?' I asked, then laughed as I realized what I'd said.

Emma pressed a finger against my cheek. 'Dada . . .'

I jumped up, taking Emma with me and ran for Dad's room. Switching on his light, I headed over to his bed.

'Dad! Dad!'

Dad sat bolt upright, blinking away, his eyes still glazed. 'What's the matter? Is something wrong with Emma?'

'Listen to this,' I told him. 'Say it again, Emma.'

Emma said nothing. His frown deepening, Dad looked at me like I'd lost my mind.

'Who am I, Emma? Tell Grandad who I am,' I coaxed.

'Dada!' Emma giggled and I laughed out loud. She'd

said it again. She really did mean it! I spun Emma around, lifting her high above my head and laughing up at her as she chortled down at me.

'Did you hear that, Dad? She said "Dada".'

'That's great. Well done, Emma. Now bugger off, Dante. It's one o'clock in the morning,' said Dad, falling back onto his pillows, his eyes closed, his whole expression pained.

'Dad, could you watch your mouth in front of Emma, please?'

Dad opened his eyes to glare at me. 'Dante. Go. Away.'

'But, Dad . . .'

The glare turned into a frost-ridden, laser scowl. He wasn't mucking around! I left his bedroom, still grinning.

'That's right, Emma,' I told my daughter as I put her back in her cot. 'I'm your daddy. And Daddy loves you very, very much.'

42

Dante

I wasn't the only one worried about Adam. They had unwired his jaw and the bandages were long gone but my brother was nowhere to be seen. He still wouldn't leave his bedroom and he barely spoke. When Adam did eat – at Dad's insistence or at my nagging – it was always alone in his room. He very rarely went downstairs, and once his outpatient appointments at the hospital were over, he never left the house. Adam's friends – male and female – came round our house to visit, but he refused to see any of them. After two or three times of the same thing happening, they stopped calling.

The left side of Adam's face was almost back to normal, but the right side looked like he'd suffered a stroke or something. His right eye still drooped noticeably and he only had about fifty per cent of the vision he used to have in it. There was a scar on his right temple and the skin over his right cheek was mottled and lined with scars where he'd needed a number of stitches to reassemble his cheek. The stitches had long since been removed but the scars were taking their time to fade.

And Adam insisted that he didn't want to see Emma and he wouldn't let her see him.

He'd emerged from his living stupor exactly twice in as many months and that was because Emma tried to enter his room. Both times he screamed for me to come and get her whilst yelling at her to get out. And all of this was done with his back to Emma. Both times he'd made her cry her eyes out, which I must admit pissed me off, but I managed to restrain myself. Just.

'There's no need to shout at her like that,' I told him. 'She only wanted to be with her uncle. She misses you.'

'You should thank me,' said Adam, his back still towards us. 'At least this way she won't have nightmares about my face. Could you take her and go, please?'

When Emma finally stopped crying, I tried to explain. 'Emma, your uncle isn't well at the moment.' I carefully picked my way through the words. 'Something happened to his face and now his face isn't the same and his heart is hurting and he doesn't want anyone to see him like that.'

Emma sighed, probably with more patience and understanding than I was feeling at that precise moment.

Poor Adam . . .

I racked my brains for some way to help my brother, for some way to get the real Adam back, but I just couldn't think of a way to do it.

We did get some good news. After my confrontation with Josh, a police officer came to our house two days later to tell us that Josh had turned himself in and that he was going to be charged with Grievous Bodily Harm under Section 18, which she was at pains to explain was a more serious charge than Grievous Bodily Harm under Section 20. I had to take their word for that. I passed the news on to Adam but he didn't bat an eyelid. I had to say it twice before I was even sure he'd heard me. There was no reaction at all.

My brother was broken and I had no idea how to fix him.

I still couldn't find a suitable job and Dad was working overtime as often as possible just to make ends meet. I'd finally given in and signed up for Jobseeker's Allowance. I really hated doing it, but Emma needed nappies and clothes and food and it wasn't fair for Dad to have to do everything by himself. Adam stayed in his room, Dad was tired all the time and I felt like the scrounger that woman in the shop a few months earlier had said I was. If it wasn't for Emma there would've been precious little laughter in our house.

Winter came and went with no change. Adam wouldn't even come downstairs to share Christmas dinner with us. Dad and I put on a show for Emma, putting up the Christmas tree and wrapping her presents to place under it and stuff like that, but to be honest Christmas was a big fail in our house. On the odd night when Emma woke me up with her crying because of her now emerging top teeth and I had to rock her back to sleep, I could hear Adam pacing back and forth in his room. And once or twice I'd swear I could hear him crying.

After the Christmas break, Dad insisted that Adam needed to go back to school.

'I can't. I'm not ready,' said Adam.

'Son, if you carry on like this, you'll never be ready,' said Dad.

'I'm not ready,' Adam repeated.

And that was that.

In the end, Dad was so worried, he called out our GP.

'D'you think I should tell him that Doctor Planter is on her way to see him?' Dad asked me.

I shook my head. 'He'd only tell you to cancel her or he'd phone the surgery and do it himself,' I replied. 'Wait till she arrives and then tell him.'

Dad nodded, deciding to take my advice.

It was almost an hour before Dr Planter finally arrived.

'Dante, run upstairs and tell your brother the doctor is here,' said Dad, giving me a meaningful look.

I thought Adam would hit the roof when I told him. Actually, I think I would've welcomed that. But to my surprise, he didn't. He considered for a few moments.

'I'll see her, but only if I can see her alone,' Adam said.

I went to the top of the stairs. 'Doctor Planter, would you mind coming up, please?'

As the doctor was entering Adam's room, I shook my head at Dad. 'Adam wants to see her alone.'

Dad frowned, but he didn't argue. When at last the doctor emerged from Adam's room, Dad and I were waiting on the landing, ready to pounce.

'How is he? Is he going to be OK?' Dad launched in. 'He can't go on like this.'

Dr Planter shook her head. 'In my opinion Adam isn't ready, physically or emotionally, to go back to school yet,' she informed us with a frown. 'He's not sleeping at all and

258

as a result is suffering from mental exhaustion, so I'm going to prescribe some sleeping pills.'

'Is that safe?' Dad looked worried. 'Isn't he a bit young for sleeping pills?'

'Well, it's certainly not a long-term solution. The tablets I'm prescribing are for short-term use only. Adam feels that if he could just sleep properly at night, he would greatly improve – and I'm inclined to agree. I'm only going to prescribe enough for two weeks, no more than that, but they should help him get back into a regular sleeping pattern. I'd like to see him again in a fortnight. OK? If he isn't making progress by then, I think some counselling might help.'

Dad nodded his agreement, though he wasn't entirely happy.

'Mr Bridgeman, I know Adam isn't keen on us doctors, but I really feel this is one of those occasions when you need to make him see sense,' she said.

'Don't worry, I hear you,' Dad replied. 'It's my fault. I should've called you out much earlier than this.'

Dr Planter wrote out a prescription for Adam's medication and headed off. And that was that. I don't know what I'd been expecting – a cure, some kind of instant miracle? Either way, I didn't get it. I stared at Adam's closed bedroom door and it felt like there was a whole ocean between us, rather than just a door.

My brother was slipping away from me and I had no idea how to stop it.

'I'll keep the pills and give Adam one to take each night,' said Dad once the doctor had left. 'That way we'll all know where we are and there'll be no chance of Adam taking two in one night by mistake. You know what your brother is like with tablets.'

I did indeed. And it was a measure of just how much my brother knew he needed help that he'd even agreed to take the pills in the first place.

Was that a good sign? Or was I merely clutching at straws?

I chose to believe it was the former.

43

Adam

There it is again, the knocking at my door. Dad or Dante? It doesn't really matter. I don't want to see either of them. Why can't they get that through their heads? I don't want to see anyone or speak to anyone. And I don't want anyone to see me. I'm so tired. Bone tired. Maybe the sleeping pills Dr Planter suggested will help. I hope so. I can't go on like this. I need to do something to get my life back. Everything I look at through my right eye is a blur and I have no peripheral vision in it any more. And even though all the mirrors in the house have been silenced, my fingers and my bedroom window still tell me the truth: my face is a mess.

Mr Marber, my surgeon at the hospital, tried to tell me that I was lucky. If I hadn't been at the hospital when my subdural haematoma decided to make its presence felt, I might've died. That's what he told me, I might've died. Was that his attempt to show me that getting beaten up had a silver lining? If so, he failed miserably. Here I am in my room and the future stretches out before me like some kind of relentless desert.

This is my life.

A life I'm too scarred and too scared to let anyone see. I tried to live my life out loud. What I have now isn't even a whisper.

It's silence.

44

Dante

After a fortnight, Adam insisted that the sleeping pills had done the trick and he didn't need anything else. He point-blank refused to go and see our GP about any further help and he still didn't leave his room.

So we carried on as before.

And as if that wasn't enough, Veronica made an appointment to 'discuss' Emma's future with Dad and me. And this time the visit was official. So that was another day Dad had to take off work.

On the day of her threatened visit, Dad warned me, 'Dante, don't get snotty and for God's sake don't lose your temper. OK?'

'What d'you mean?'

'I know you. You'll let her say what she likes about you but if she says something you resent about Emma, you'll flare up. Don't! Remember that you're doing this for Emma's sake, so just suck it up,' said Dad.

I nodded. Dad was right. I couldn't afford to be on anything but my best behaviour. Veronica arrived at our house at around two thirty and Dad escorted her into the sitting room.

'Can I get you a drink?' asked Dad. 'Tea? Coffee?'

'No, thanks. I'm fine,' said Veronica.

Outside the rain lashed at the windows. The view was wet and grey, a greyness which leeched by degrees into the sitting room.

'Where's Emma today?' Veronica asked the question with a saccharine smile.

'She's having her afternoon nap at the moment,' I replied.

'Well, we won't disturb her for the time being but I'd really like to see her before I leave.' The fake smile didn't wobble for a second.

'No problem.' I exchanged Veronica's smile with one of my own, equally as false. The last time I'd spoken to Collette, I hadn't been terribly kind. I didn't doubt for a second that Collette had passed on every word I'd said.

Dad indicated the sofa. Veronica headed for the armchair and sat down. After exchanging a glance, Dad and I sat down next to each other on the sofa. Veronica asked to see Emma's medical book which I was happy to hand over because all of my daughter's vaccinations were up-to-date. The polite conversation that followed was interlaced with questions. Amongst other things, she asked me whether I was collecting child benefit for Emma. I wasn't. I had assumed that wherever she was, Melanie was still getting that money. To my surprise, Veronica told me what steps I needed to take to make sure that I got Emma's child-benefit money instead of Melanie. And she gave me advice about getting Emma's birth certificate amended so that my name was also on it. That way I'd get full parental responsibilities and rights under the law. And I needed to pull my finger out for that one because it was best to do it before Emma was two. After that it got far more complicated. Getting my name on the birth certificate would also make it easier to claim child benefit for Emma, but to be honest I didn't want to draw too much official attention to myself. And I certainly didn't want to live my life from handout to handout. It was bad enough that I'd had to jump through hoops to collect Jobseeker's Allowance. I needed to find a decent job to support Emma and me. The last thing I wanted was to hop on the benefit merry-go-round. Too much pride, I guess, like Dad.

I kept expecting tripwires, but none appeared. The whole thing took close to an hour but I didn't even come close to losing my cool and a lot of what Veronica said was actually useful and informative. The only sticky moment came when Veronica asked, 'How's your brother, Adam, doing? I understand he was in hospital a while ago?'

'That's right,' said Dad evenly. 'But he's much better now and getting stronger every day.'

'I'm glad,' smiled Veronica. And this time, the smile was sincere. 'Is there anything you'd like to ask me or to add, Dante?'

'No, I don't think so.'

'OK then.' Veronica stood up. 'If I could just see Emma, then I'll be on my way.'

I led the way upstairs. Emma was still fast asleep in her cot. Dad, Veronica and I stood at the side of the cot watching her for a few moments.

'Is she talking yet?' asked Veronica.

'Yeah, quite a few words actually. And more every day,' I said, unable to keep the pride out of my voice. I bent over the cot to stroke my daughter's hair.

'She means a lot to you, doesn't she?' Veronica's genuine smile lit up her eyes.

'Yes, she does. She's my daughter . . .' Sod that. 'She's my world,' I admitted.

Veronica's grin broadened. 'Well, time for me to go. I hope I've been of some use to you both.'

'Yes, you have,' said Dad, holding out his hand. Veronica and Dad shook hands.

'Thank you, Veronica,' I smiled, holding out my hand also. She and I shook hands, a little firmer and a little longer than was absolutely necessary.

When she left, Dad and I exchanged a look of relief and smiled. That was the one bit of blue in a sky full of grey rain clouds.

Spring had finally arrived. It was the day before Adam's birthday and I wanted to do something extra-special for him. I couldn't buy him anything as I was stony broke. But I needed to do something to blast him out of his lethargy.

Leaving Emma in the sitting room, I headed upstairs to see my brother. Adam was sitting in his chair staring out of his window over our secluded back garden as per usual, his back towards the door. He was getting more and more sensitive about anyone seeing his face – even Dad and me.

'Hiya, Adam,' I said, forcing myself to sound upbeat and cheerful.

He didn't answer, but then I didn't really expect him to do otherwise.

'What d'you want for your birthday tomorrow?'

Silence.

'Come on. You must want something. And it'll be with love from Emma and me,' I told him, hoping he'd get the message.

'Can I have a mirror?'

I must've misheard. 'Pardon?'

'Can I have a mirror, please?' Adam repeated.

'What? Now?' I asked, confused.

'Yes, please.'

I wasn't sure about this, but Dad was still at work so I couldn't pass the idea by him. I thought of phoning him but it seemed silly to phone Dad just because Adam wanted a mirror. Wasn't that progress of a sort, the fact that Adam was ready to look at his face again?

I hurried off to get the bathroom mirror which Dad had stored in the cupboard under the stairs. Maybe . . . maybe I was finally going to get my brother back. Once back in Adam's room, I turned the mirror so that the back of it was towards Adam. He slowly turned to face me.

'Shall I hold it up for you?' I asked.

Adam nodded.

I turned the mirror round, before lifting it up till it was level with Adam's face. Time stood still as Adam studied himself. The scar on his temple was very faint, as were the scars left by the stitches on his cheek. His right cheek was no longer mottled but the skin wasn't smooth like before either. The most noticeable disfigurement was his right eye which was still noticeably drooping.

When at last Adam did speak, all he said was, 'You can take it away now.'

I put the mirror down and leaned it against the wall next to the door.

'I guess my acting career bites the dust,' said Adam.

'What're you talking about? You could still be an actor. Come on, my brother can do anything he sets his mind to,' I said. 'And if that doesn't work out, there are plenty of other things you could do.'

'I never made a back up plan, remember?'

'That doesn't mean you can't make one now.'

Adam didn't reply.

'D'you . . . d'you want to talk about that night?' I asked tentatively.

'Talking about it isn't going to change anything.' Adam shrugged.

'Didn't it help when you heard that Josh had gone to the police and given himself up?'

'Not really,' Adam said. We could've been talking about the colour of our roof tiles for all the emotion he displayed.

I needed to ask him the question that had been bugging me all these months. 'Adam, why did you do it? For God's sake, why did you kiss him?'

' 'Cause he . . . he kissed me first,' whispered Adam.

I stared at him. 'Huh?'

'D'you remember the night of your end-of-year do at the Bar Belle?'

I nodded.

'Well, after you left, Josh tried to kiss me. I wouldn't let him. So he punched me instead.'

Shocked didn't even begin to describe how I felt at that moment. 'Are you serious?' I asked.

'Why would I lie, Dante?'

'But when I asked you, you told me Josh had nothing to do with it,' I reminded him.

Adam shrugged. 'Well, I lied then because Josh was your friend and I didn't want to cause trouble between the two of you, but I'm not lying now. Josh really did try to kiss me.'

My eyes were beginning to ache from staring so hard at my brother. Josh had tried to *kiss* Adam? And then punched him instead?

'Your split lip,' I remembered.

'Yeah, that was Josh. The day after, he phoned to apologize and invited me out for a drink. And after that we started going out together . . .' said Adam.

I sat down, stunned, wondering if something had gone wrong with my hearing. I felt like something large and heavy had just fallen on my head.

I realized that what had landed on me was the truth.

'You and . . . *Josh*?' I said, dazed.

'We just hung around together, going to the cinema or for a meal,' said Adam, adding in a whisper, 'I was so happy . . . I thought I'd found someone. I thought we were together.'

Silence.

I couldn't have said a word then, even if I wanted to. That must've been the time when Adam had been out almost every night. He'd been very happy then . . .

Adam seemed to get lost inside himself for a while, as if he was remembering that time too. 'But Josh hated to be seen with me,' my brother said softly. 'And he wouldn't talk about things that really mattered. And he still put me down and made . . . homophobic comments when others were around. I really liked him, Dante. But I couldn't be with someone who was living a lie like that . . .'

'So what happened?'

'I dumped him.'

'You *what?*'

'Yeah.' The ghost of a smile flitted across Adam's face. 'Josh didn't take it too well though. He kept phoning me and he wouldn't leave me alone, so I put a block on his phone calls. I think that's what made him so angry with me.'

And now at last it all made some kind of sense; the antagonism between them, the strange looks, Josh's bitter comments. Adam was gay and didn't care who knew it, including me and Dad. Josh was gay and couldn't deal with it. All this time, all his derogatory comments about gays – and the person he despised most had been himself.

'Talk about messed up.' I shook my head, still trying to pull my thoughts together. 'All this . . . this chaos because Josh couldn't admit to himself that he's gay? For God's sake, it's not a disease you can be vaccinated against. You're born gay or you're born heterosexual. End of discussion.'

'And if you're bisexual?'

'Bisexuals are born . . . straddlers! A foot in either camp.'

Adam looked at me, a strange gleam in his eyes.

'What?' I asked.

'So being gay isn't just a phase?'

'Huh? Of course it isn't. What on earth are you . . . ?'
And then I remembered the conversation Adam and I had
had over a lifetime ago about the exact same thing. 'Damn
it, Adam.'

'What? I was just asking,' smiled my brother.

'Yeah, well, you've made your point.'

'No,' Adam replied. 'You made it for me.'

My brother thought he was so slick.

'So you and Josh . . .' I said, returning to the subject
uppermost in my mind.

'Yeah. Me and Josh.'

In spite of myself, I felt sorry for my ex-best mate – not
much, but a little – and that surprised me. He was the last
person who deserved any sympathy, not after what he'd
done and yet that's how I felt. But it was Adam's feelings
that mattered now; mine were irrelevant.

'Do . . . d'you ever think of Josh?'

Pause.

'All the time,' Adam replied.

Oh, Adam . . .

'Wouldn't it help to try and forget him and move on?'
I asked tentatively.

'How do I do that, Dante? Every time I touch my face,
I remember. Every time I take a breath, I remember.'

What could I say to that? When we were young, every
time Adam hurt himself, I'd fix him up with a plaster or a

drink or some sweets and then I'd give him a hug and we'd carry on.

But that was when we were both young.

'You know the letter I got yesterday?' asked Adam.

'Yeah?' I was the one who'd brought it upstairs for him.

'It was from Josh,' said Adam.

What the . . . ? 'Why did he write to you? What did he want?'

'Calm down, Dante.' Adam smiled faintly.

I took a deep breath, but lines of suspicion and creeping anger creased my forehead.

'He's not doing too well actually,' said Adam.

'My heart bleeds for him,' I said scathingly. 'Did he write to blame you for that? Where's his letter?'

'I threw it away,' Adam replied.

'Quite right too. Best thing for it. What else did he say?'

'Not much. Except he was sorry.'

Sorry, my arse.

My brother went back to his chair and sat down. I watched him for a few moments, my anger fading as I did so. Where was Adam? I longed for my brother to return.

'Adam, how much longer are you going to stay in this room?'

Adam didn't answer. He continued to stare out of his window, his shoulders slumped, his whole attitude one of defeat. I hated seeing him like that. It wasn't my brother sitting in the chair; it was just my brother's shell.

'Daddy?' Emma peeped round the door into Adam's bedroom.

Adam moved round in his chair so that we could no longer see his profile.

'Emma, I left you in the sitting room.' I frowned down at her. I hadn't realized she could make it up the stairs without me. And I only left the child gate closed if Emma was already upstairs.

'Heyo, Unckey . . .' Emma's version of 'Hello, Uncle' greeted Adam, the uncertainty in her voice very evident. She hadn't seen Adam properly in weeks and could still probably remember him shouting at her.

'Dante, could you leave, please?' said Adam, turning round further in his chair so we had a good view of the back of his head.

Emma toddled into the bedroom before I could stop her. 'Heyo, Unckey,' she said again. 'Heyo.'

Adam stiffened in his chair at the sound of her voice getting closer. He desperately wanted me to take Emma and leave, but something held me back. Emma waddled around the chair to face Adam. She looked up at him, then smiled, her arms outstretched.

Adam looked down at his niece.

Emma wriggled her arms at Adam, her meaning clear. Slowly Adam bent to pick her up. I released the air in my lungs with a hiss. I hadn't even realized that I was holding my breath. Adam placed Emma on his lap. I moved further into the room. My brother was holding Emma like she might break. I realized with a start that he was giving her a chance to bolt, to run and hide from his face. Emma reached out one small hand and stroked it down the scars on Adam's cheek.

'Hurts?' she asked.

'Yes,' Adam whispered.

'Lots?'

'Lots.'

'Kiss?'

Adam sighed, then smiled – the first real smile I'd seen from him in a long, long time. 'Yes, please.'

Emma clambered to stand up on Adam's thigh whilst he still held her. She leaned forward and kissed his scar-ridden cheek, then she wrapped both arms around his neck and held him as tightly as he held her.

And I could see from where I was standing that Adam was crying.

45

Adam

Emma wrapped her arms around my neck and pressed her good cheek against my bad one and hugged me like she was never going to let me go, like she could feel every single thing I was going through.

It was so strange to have her try and comfort me. I held onto her and once the tears started, they wouldn't stop. And still Emma held onto me. She didn't shy away from my face, not once. She didn't look at me like I was some kind of freak either. Instead, she just kissed my cheek and hugged me some more.

And what made it hurt so much was that it was exactly like when Mum used to hold me.

46

Dante

I woke up the next morning, feeling not just good but great. Adam had finally let Emma see his face. That had to be a good sign. I didn't expect miracles, at least not instant ones, but I refused to take the events of the previous night as anything but a good omen.

And I'd been called back for a second interview to work as a night-time cashier at the local petrol station. It wasn't exactly glamorous but at least I'd be making some money. As it was, I'd only been able to get Adam a card for his birthday. I couldn't afford anything else. But from now on things could only get better.

I got Emma out of her cot and after tidying her up, took her downstairs for her breakfast. Dad was already there. He'd beaten me to it.

'Morning, Dad.'

'Morning, Dante,' Dad replied with a smile. 'Morning, angel. I've made breakfast for everyone.'

'Bacon, scrambled eggs, sausages and beans on toast?' I asked hopefully.

'Croissants,' Dad replied.

I'd settle for that. I fancied something a bit tastier than

my usual cereal this morning. 'Shall I pop up and see if Adam might come down and join us?' I asked as I put Emma in her highchair.

'Is it likely?' asked Dad.

'He might. He let Emma see his face last night.' I grinned.

'Really?' said Dad, surprised. 'How did you manage that?'

'I didn't. Emma did.'

'Clever girl.' Dad smiled at her, before turning back to me. 'Well, no harm trying.'

I kissed Emma on the top of her head. 'Daddy will be right back.'

I legged it upstairs, taking them two and three at a time. I knocked on Adam's door.

'Adam, can I come in?'

No answer.

'Adam?'

Still no answer.

I opened the door and headed into Adam's bedroom. The curtains were open and daylight was pouring in but Adam was still fast asleep.

'Wake up, birthday boy,' I smiled. 'Are you going to come downstairs and join us for breakfast?' I walked over to him. 'Wake up, you lazy butt-head! We got you a birthday cake. D'you want to blow out the candles now, or tonight after dinner?'

I moved closer. Something crunched under my foot. I bent to pick it up. It was the fragments of a tablet. A sleeping tablet . . . But surely he'd finished those months ago?

How could there still be any left? Unless . . . unless Adam had saved them up?

'Adam?' I bent over him, shaking his shoulder. Adam's head flopped to one side. I shook him harder. 'Adam, *wake up!*' I shook him just as hard as I could now.

His whole body lay limp like cooked spaghetti and his eyes remained closed.

'ADAM? ADAM, WAKE UP. DAD . . . !' I yelled.

I was dimly aware of Dad running upstairs as I kept shaking Adam over and over, telling him, *begging* him to wake up. But his skin was cold and clammy and I was so afraid that I was too late . . .

The next ten minutes were a blur. Dad turned ashen when I showed him the crushed sleeping tablet on the floor. He immediately checked for a pulse. If anything, his skin turned even more grey when he took his hand away from Adam's wrist. Dad bent his head to Adam's face to check and see if my brother was breathing . . .

'Dante, phone for an ambulance,' he ordered.

I didn't need to be told twice. I phoned them whilst Dad pulled Adam upright, then hauled him off the bed. Wrapping one of Adam's arms round his shoulders, Dad started walking up and down.

'Adam, walk. D'you hear me? One foot in front of the other. *Walk.*'

Dad paced up and down, dragging Adam with him. I wanted to help but Emma started crying downstairs.

'Daddy?' she wailed plaintively.

'Go and stay with your daughter,' Dad ordered.

'I'll bring her upsta—'

278

'*Don't*,' said Dad fiercely.

'But—'

'Dante, she doesn't need to see this. Stay downstairs with her and let the paramedics in when they get here.'

Much as I wanted to argue, I knew Dad was right.

'Adam, walk. Come on. Walk,' Dad cajoled.

Adam groaned, his head lolling back, then slumping forwards like every bone in his neck had disappeared.

'Dante, go. Emma needs you,' said Dad.

Yes, and so did my brother. But I did as I was told and headed downstairs.

'Daddy.' Emma stopped bawling and held out her arms to me as I entered the kitchen.

'Sorry, love,' I said, lifting her out of her chair. 'I didn't mean to leave you alone.'

'Park,' said Emma.

'No, Emma. Not today.'

'Park,' Emma insisted, bursting into tears all over again.

'No.'

Emma howled like a banshee, her wail going straight through my head.

'Emma, we're not going to the park and that's final. We'll go some other day,' I tried to reason with her.

It wasn't working. I put her down. She was suddenly so heavy. But she didn't like that either. Her wail grew even louder.

'Park . . . park . . .' she demanded between screams. I couldn't take any more.

'EMMA, FOR GOD'S SAKE, SHUT UP.'

She stared at me for a stunned moment, then she really

let rip. If I'd thought she was loud before, it was nothing compared to what was coming out of her mouth now. She was really doing my head in. I glared down at her, my fists slowly clenching. I was less than a second away from losing it . . .

So I ran. Out of the kitchen and into the sitting room. I ran away just as fast as I could. Flinging myself down on the armchair, I buried my head in my hands, appalled at myself. I couldn't believe what I'd almost done. Emma's crying was getting closer. She peeped her head round the door, still sobbing, and looked at me with an uncertainty that twisted my guts.

I took a deep breath. 'I'm sorry, Emma.' I opened my arms.

Emma ran to me and I scooped her up. Her tears were subsiding now as I held her tight.

'Sorry, Daddy.'

'You've got nothing to be sorry about,' I told her, smoothing her hair over and over. 'I'm sorry I shouted at you. I'm worried about Uncle Adam but I shouldn't have taken it out on you.'

'Poor Unckey,' sighed Emma.

It took a while before I could trust myself to speak. 'Yeah, poor uncle.'

'Kiss, Daddy?'

I gulped, then gulped again. 'Yes, please,' I whispered.

Emma kissed my cheek. I kissed hers. And all the time, I couldn't stop swallowing.

It took a while, but I was finally able to say the only words that mattered to me at that moment. 'I love you, Emma. I love you very, very much.'

47

Dante

Dad made me stay home with Emma whilst he headed off in the ambulance with Adam. I tried to argue but Dad wasn't having it.

'I think Emma's seen more than enough of that hospital recently, don't you?' said Dad grimly.

'But what about Adam? I should be with him.'

'I'll be with him,' said Dad. 'You just stay here and take care of your daughter.'

But for the first time I was scared of what might happen, of what I might do if she started crying again and wouldn't stop. The thought of harming my daughter in any way sickened me, frightened me.

And yet I'd come so close . . .

I took my mobile out of my trouser pocket. I needed to make a call. Within two rings, the phone at the other end was picked up.

'Hello?' Aunt Jackie sounded annoyed.

'Aunt Jackie, I . . . I . . .'

'Dante?'

'Yeah . . .'

'D'you know what time it is? You know I'm allergic

to daylight before noon on Saturdays,' she said testily.

'Aunt Jackie, I . . . I need your help . . .' Why were the words so hard to say?

'What's happened?' she asked sharply.

I told her everything – all about Adam and the sleeping pills, all about me shouting at Emma and what I'd almost done.

'I'll be right there. D'you hear me? I'll be there as soon as I can.' Aunt Jackie hung up first.

Emma toddled up to me. 'Hungry, Daddy,' she told me.

I took a deep breath and switched on a smile. 'Well then, let's get you something yummy to eat.'

I took her hand and led her into the kitchen. Putting Emma in her highchair, I put some grapes, some orange segments and banana slices in a bowl and placed it in front of her. I stood and watched as Emma tucked in, wielding her spoon like a weapon as she attacked a banana slice. And I still couldn't get what I'd almost done out of my head.

I needed to get out of there.

'Daddy will be right back, Emma,' I said quietly.

I headed upstairs to Adam's room, needing to feel closer to him somehow. I pottered around his room, straightening up the stuff on his desk, moving his chair away from the window, smoothing his duvet, lifting his pillow to shake the filling. There was a folded sheet of paper beneath the pillow. I picked it up and, unfolding it, I began to read.

Adam,
I know I'm probably the last person you want to hear from and I wouldn't blame you if you put this letter straight in the bin but

I hope you will give me the chance I never gave you and read it through to the end.

As you probably already know, I'm in court soon. My solicitor tried to get the charge reduced to actual bodily harm instead of GBH but the police have photos and doctors' reports of what I did to you so that's looking unlikely. I've been warned that there's a serious possibility of me doing time. My mum has washed her hands of me and none of my friends want to know. I don't blame them. And believe me, I'm not trying to get your sympathy. After what I've done, I know that's impossible. If I do get sent to prison, it'll be what I deserve. I've accepted that. I thought of calling round to talk to you in person instead of writing this letter but you were right about me, I am a coward. But I need to say this to you. I'm sorry. I know it's just words and too little too late, but I'm really, really sorry about what happened. Even now I look back at that night and I still can't believe what I did.

I want to ask you for a favour. I know I have no right but I'm going to ask anyway. Will you write to me when I get sent down? I'll write to you and send you my new address once the trial is over. If you choose to ignore me, I'll understand. But I'm hoping you'll take pity on me and write back. I don't have anyone in my life now. Isn't it ironic? I was afraid of losing all my friends and family if I came out and stopped pretending to be something I wasn't, but I've lost them anyway.

I heard you haven't returned to school yet. Is it because, like me, you feel dead inside? Is it because life doesn't feel worth living any more? You once said that you and I were very alike, we felt and thought the same about all kinds of things. I didn't believe it at the time, but you were right about that as well. I guess that's why I think I know how you must be feeling right now. Betrayed.

I told you things I've never told another person, ever. We were close and I told you I cared about you, which was true (and still is), and yet I could do something like that to you. Now you think the world is full of hypocrites and liars like me, so what's the point? I can't answer that for you. Just know that not a second goes by when I don't deeply regret what I did.

I hope you will write back to me. I guess you're my last chance at feeling human again. But if you won't or don't or can't, I'll understand.

Take care of yourself.
Your friend,
Joshua

I sat down on Adam's bed and reread the letter from start to finish. So much for putting Josh's letter in the bin. I knew Josh had been remanded on bail but that was all I knew. The police had phoned Dad to tell him that even though the charges against Josh were serious, they'd remanded him on bail, allowing Josh to go home because he had turned himself in at the local police station. If he hadn't done that he would've been remanded in custody and would've awaited his trial in prison.

I read the letter one more time but it just made me even more confused. Was this why Adam had taken all those pills after all this time? Was Josh right about how Adam must be feeling? Had the letter reopened old wounds or had it just confirmed to Adam that they hadn't healed? I folded up the letter and reluctantly placed it back beneath Adam's pillow.

'Daddy? Daddy?' My daughter was calling me.

I headed downstairs, took her out of her highchair and held her tight until she started protesting and agitating to be put down on the ground. I led the way to the sitting room so that she could play with her toys whilst I stood in the doorway, just watching her.

Aunt Jackie was as good as her word. Less than twenty minutes later she was standing in the hall giving me a bear hug.

'How're you doing?' she asked.

'Better,' I said.

'Where's Emma?'

'In the sitting room, drawing.'

Aunt Jackie took my chin in her hand, scrutinizing my face. 'I am so proud of you.'

'For what? For losing my temper and almost hitting my daughter?' I said with self-contempt. 'For being no better than Melanie?' My aunt had to be joking.

Aunt Jackie smiled. 'But you didn't hit her. Thinking it and doing it are poles apart, honey. You remember that. You hang on to that. You walked away and gave yourself a chance to calm down.'

'But I nearly . . .'

'No one cares about "nearly". If "nearly" mattered, of the entire adult population there'd only be two nuns who weren't in prison,' Aunt Jackie dismissed with a wave of her hand. 'Stop being so hard on yourself. And I'll tell you why else I'm proud of you – you asked for help.'

At my puzzled look, Aunt Jackie smiled. 'It's a man thing, honey. You men can't stand to ask for help. You consider it a sign of weakness, as if people will judge you or get the idea – God forbid – that you're not coping.'

I opened my mouth to argue, but my mouth snapped shut without uttering a word. That wasn't true, well . . . not all of it.

'Adam is just the same, for all his chat about being in touch with his feelings,' sighed Aunt Jackie. 'Up in his room alone all these months, too much of a man to tell anyone just how scared he was and how alone he felt.'

'I'm not going to let him do that any more,' I said with determination.

If it wasn't already too late . . .

No. It wasn't too late. I'd feel it inside if Adam . . . Just as I'd feel it inside if I ever lost Emma. I didn't even want to consider that possibility.

'The days of Adam sitting up in his room alone are over,' I told my aunt.

'Oh yes?'

'Yes,' I said firmly. 'I love my brother too much to let him waste his life that way.'

'Have you told him that?' asked my aunt.

'Well, er . . . not in so many words. But he knows,' I argued.

'The way you know your dad loves you,' said Aunt Jackie. 'But I bet you don't mind hearing the words.'

She gave me a significant look, allowing what she'd said to sink in. That was the trouble with Aunt Jackie. She was as irritating as hell, especially when she was right. I guess, like Dad, I had trouble saying that kind of stuff. More we had in common.

'Have you heard anything from your dad?'

'Not yet.'

286

'Daddy?' Emma called out.

'Coming, Emma.'

'Where is my darling?' Aunt Jackie shoved me to one side and made a beeline for my poor daughter.

'Run away, Emma,' I tried to tell her telepathically. 'Or else brace yourself. Aunt Jackie is about to descend.'

I took a couple of steps, then stopped. What was it Aunt Jackie had said?

You men can't stand to ask for help . . .

It struck me that I wasn't the first guy to be a single dad at eighteen and I certainly wouldn't be the last. But there wasn't an awful lot of information out there written specifically for us. Maybe . . . just maybe I could do something about that? I shook my head, putting the idea on a back burner.

At this precise moment, I had more urgent things to worry about.

48

Dante

It was evening before Dad arrived back home, and thank God he wasn't alone. Adam was with him. I was surprised to see my brother back home so quickly, to be honest. I thought they'd keep him in overnight at the hospital at least. But I guess they needed the beds. I studied Adam but he didn't really look any different. Unlike Dad. Dad looked beyond tired, like he'd aged at least five years.

One of Dad's favourite sayings crashed into my head: *Another five years off my life . . .*

Only this time, it wasn't even close to being funny. I remembered when Emma had almost tumbled down the stairs, when she'd banged her fingers with the toilet lid, when she'd fallen off the end of the slide in the children's playground.

Five years off my life . . .

I wondered with a wry smile, would people be immortal if they didn't have kids?

'Hey, Adam,' I said.

'Hi, Dante,' Adam replied faintly.

'Adam, are you OK, love?' asked Aunt Jackie, emerging from the sitting room carrying Emma.

'I'm fine.' Adam didn't hang around to answer any more questions. He headed straight up to his room.

'What happened at the hospital?' I asked Dad.

'They pumped his stomach and gave him some kind of charcoal concoction to stop him absorbing any more into his bloodstream,' Dad replied. 'Luckily he took the tablets early this morning. If he'd taken them late last night and then choked . . .'

Dad didn't need to say anything else. He looked up the stairs after Adam, like he was at a loss as to what to do next.

'I'll go and speak to him, Dad.' I started up the stairs.

'No, I should . . .' Dad began.

'Please, Dad. Let me,' I said.

Dad sighed. 'OK. God knows I've tried but I just can't seem to reach him.'

I headed upstairs. Knocking once, I entered Adam's bedroom. He was back in his chair looking out over the back garden.

'Hey, Adam.'

'I don't remember inviting you to come in.' Adam didn't even turn around to look at me.

I sat down on my brother's bed. 'How're you feeling?'

'My throat hurts,' Adam replied. 'And I'm really not in the mood for another lecture.'

'I wasn't going to give you one,' I denied.

'Good, 'cause I just want to be left alone.'

No. Not any more. 'I read Josh's letter,' I said.

Adam stiffened for a moment. 'You had no right.'

'Neither did you.' And we both knew I wasn't talking about reading Josh's letter. 'Tell me something. Did that letter have anything to do with . . . with what you did?'

Adam finally turned round to face me. 'Dante, I can't live like this,' he said. 'Look at me. Look at my face.'

'You are more than just your damned face. There is more to you than that!' I shouted at him. 'Is that why you did it? Because of how you look?'

'No.'

'Then why?'

'Because Josh was right, Dante. What's the point? When you get right down to it, what's the point?'

I looked down at my lap trying to frame the right words.

'The point is, you have a family and friends who love you. You have a world out there just waiting for you to conquer it. You have a life that will be anything you make it. That's the point.'

'But the world is full of people like Josh who hate everyone – including themselves – because it's too much effort or they're too scared to do anything else,' sighed Adam.

'And how are the cowards who live like that your problem?' I asked.

'Dante, don't you get it? Look at my face. Take a good look. That's how they're my problem.'

And I did take a look. I clenched my fists and took a good look. My lips clamped together and I took a good look. My eyes narrowed, and still I looked. Anger, like a trapped bird, flitted inside my chest. Anger at Josh and Logan and Paul, anger at the whole world. Anger at myself.

'That's why you can't let them win, Adam,' I said at last.

'That's why you've got to keep getting up when they knock you down. But you don't just give in.'

'Dante, I'm tired.'

'So am I. D'you think this is where I saw myself at eighteen? D'you think this is what I wanted? But I'm not giving up.'

''Cause you have someone to fight for. You have Emma.'

'So do you,' I replied.

'It's not the same. And I'm scared, Dante.'

'Everyone's scared, Adam. If this last few months has taught me nothing else, it's taught me that.'

'But you're not,' said Adam. 'You're like Dad. You get on with life, no matter what it throws at you.'

I laughed harshly. 'Are you kidding me?'

'What're you scared of?' Adam asked, surprised.

'Damn, we'd be here until well into the next century if I went through the entire list,' I told him. 'I'm afraid of being a father. I'm afraid of being a bad father. I'm afraid of not being able to support my daughter properly. I'm afraid I might never meet a girl who wants a relationship with me 'cause I have a daughter to look after. I'm afraid that if I put my dreams on hold I might never get them back again. But most of all, I'm afraid of what will happen if Melanie returns and she wants Emma back. I dream about Melanie coming back and taking my daughter away and I wake up in a cold sweat.'

Adam got up and walked over to sit next to me. 'Don't let her. Take her to court if you have to.' He frowned.

I sighed. 'Melanie is Emma's mum.'

'Yeah, but Melanie abandoned her and you've been a great dad.'

'Have I? I came that close' – I put my thumb and index finger together and held them up for Adam to see – 'that close to losing it and hitting Emma earlier today.'

Adam stared at me, shocked. 'But you didn't?'

'I didn't. I walked away. But that's something else to be afraid of. I'm scared of turning into the kind of low-life scumbag who hits his kid,' I admitted.

We sat in silence for a while.

'You know what else I'm afraid of?' I asked.

'What?'

'Losing you.'

Adam looked away from me and down at his hands which were twisting in his lap.

'Please don't ever do that again,' I said quietly. 'What on earth came over you?'

'Jealousy.'

'Huh?'

'Emma came in my room, she kissed my cheek and hugged me and then you both left – and I was alone again. And I've never envied you before, Dante, but when you left with Emma, I was so jealous.'

Pause.

'Adam, I've been jealous of you my whole life,' I admitted.

'You have?' Adam said, surprised. 'Why?'

'You've always been a glass half-full kind of guy. My glass is always half-empty. And you've always been able to see the best in people. I'd hate to see you lose that.'

'Maybe I've lost it already,' Adam whispered.

'I don't believe that. I don't believe that for a second.' I shook my head, adding with a wry smile. 'According to Aunt Jackie, your trouble is you're being too much of a man. You think you can't ask for help and that you have to go through all this alone.'

'That's how I feel,' Adam admitted.

'Oh, Adam, you're not alone. Don't you know that?' I said, my eyes stinging. 'But that's what you wanted to do to me and Emma and Dad. We've already lost our mum. Not a day goes by when I don't think of her. But you obviously don't give Mum a second thought.'

'What the hell are you talking about?' Adam said furiously. 'I think about her every day. I miss her every second. You and Dad think that I was too young to remember when she died, but losing her was like having a hole shot through my heart.'

'Then how dare you?'

'Huh?'

'You remember what it was like to lose Mum and yet you wanted to inflict more of the same on Dad and me? You wanted to leave us behind to try and go on without you?'

Adam stared at me as my words sunk in.

'I'm sorry,' he said softly, looking down at his hands again.

'Adam, look at me.' I waited until he lifted his head and looked me in the eye. 'Adam, you're my brother and I love you. Very much. I don't want to lose you. I couldn't bear it.'

Adam's mouth fell open. He was staring at me like he'd never seen me before.

'It means that much to you?' Adam asked in wonder. 'I mean that much to you?'

'Of course you do, you super massive arse hole!'

'You'd better lower your voice before Dad charges up here thinking something is wrong,' said Adam, the merest trace of a smile on his lips. 'Potty-mouth!'

'It's not funny, Adam,' I said.

'I know. I'm sorry, Dante. I won't do it again.'

'Promise me.'

'I promise. You're not going to lose me.' Adam smiled. His hand moved up to my face. He wiped his hand across my cheeks. When he pulled his hand away, his fingertips were wet. Only then did I realize why.

'Don't you know that boys don't cry?' Adam grinned.

'Shall I tell you something I've only recently discovered,' I replied, not attempting to hide the tears rolling down my face and not the least bit ashamed of them. 'Boys don't cry, but real men do.'

My brother and I hugged each other. It was spontaneous and simultaneous and it felt really good.

'I guess I'd better go and help with dinner,' I sighed. 'Will you be OK?'

Adam nodded.

'Are you going to join us downstairs?'

'I . . . maybe tomorrow.'

'Definitely tomorrow. OK?'

'OK,' my brother agreed.

'I'll bring you up some food on a tray,' I said.

'Thanks,' said Adam.

I headed for the door but was reluctant to leave.

'Adam, I . . .'

'Dante, I'm not going to do it again. I promise,' said Adam. 'You're going to have to trust me.'

'I do.'

Glancing down, I noticed the bathroom mirror was still leaning against Adam's wall. 'I'll just take this away.'

'No, leave it,' said Adam.

After a moment, I left the room, quietly shutting the door behind me.

49

Adam

The moment the door shut, I leaned back to retrieve Josh's letter from beneath my pillow. I hadn't been lying to Dante about throwing it away. I did chuck it in the bin unread the moment I realized who it was from. But after a minute or two, I'd fished it out of the bin again. And I read it and reread it, waiting for the words to stop hurting.

But they hadn't.

Now my initial intention was to read it again, but once I had it in my hand, I was reluctant to even unfold it. I didn't want to read it any more but I wasn't capable of throwing it away either, at least not yet. In the end I buried it at the back of my bottom drawer, beneath a couple of jumpers I hadn't worn in years. The letter had brought back so many thoughts and feelings that I thought I'd dealt with.

Too many.

I'd taken the first couple of sleeping pills each night when Dad gave them to me, but after that I reckoned I didn't need them any more. And I never did like taking tablets, so I just collected them in some tissue paper and pushed them to the back of a drawer. But Josh's letter and Emma's visit had knocked me flat again. Not that I'm blaming either of them, and certainly not Emma.

She was so lovely. And I realized as she hugged me that it was the first time I'd been held in months. It was no one's fault but my own, but at that moment I'd felt so incredibly alone. Like I'd been buried alive and had a ton of loneliness smothering me, crushing me. I missed my friends, I missed school, I missed my life. The world was happening outside my door and I wasn't a part of it. And more than ever, I missed my mum. I missed being held and kissed and comforted by her. Whenever I was hurting she'd hug me until I felt better. But she'd died. And the hugging had stopped.

I'd lain awake all through the night just thinking how everyone, including me, would be so much better off if I wasn't around. And then all the pain and the loneliness would stop. And early this morning, I'd remembered the sleeping pills . . .

It was a stupid thing to do.

Stupid, stupid, stupid.

I'd realized that as I fell asleep. Tears of intense regret had escaped from my eyes as I'd lain in my bed, my head on my pillow, my eyes closed. I'd thought of all the things I had and all the things I would now never have because I'd taken those pills. I really had thought that was it.

But I'm still here.

I'm not sure if Dante believes my promise that I'll never try that again. But I do mean it. I'm not going anywhere.

I sat, surveying my room. The cream walls which had comforted me over the last few months now seemed claustrophobic and oppressive. I walked over to the mirror, still resting against the wall. My right eye drooped and my right cheek still had a couple of noticeable scars. But only a couple.

Hell! I was still standing. Ha!

Opening my door, I headed downstairs. I heard voices coming from the kitchen. Aunt Jackie's was the loudest as per usual. And I could hear Emma laughing. I love to hear her laugh. Something else I'd missed all these months. Taking a deep breath, I entered the room.

'Hi, all.' I smiled. 'D'you mind if I join you?'

50

Dante

Dammit! Adam's voice was so unexpected it actually made me jump. I stared at him like he was a ghost or something. And I wasn't the only one. Emma regained her composure before the rest of us.

'Unckey,' said Emma, toddling towards him, her arms outstretched.

Adam scooped her up, grinning at her. 'Hiya, Emma. How's my favourite niece? The rest of the family are doing really great impersonations of goldfish at the moment.'

My mouth snapped shut.

'Cheeky bug—!' Dad exclaimed.

'Dad!' I interrupted. 'Young ears are flapping.'

Dad looked apologetic but only for a moment. As Adam put Emma back down on her feet, Dad walked over to him.

'How're you feeling, son?'

'Sore,' Adam replied.

Adam and Dad regarded each other.

'Adam, I want you to know that if you need someone to talk to, someone who will listen without judging you, someone who'll always have your back, I'm right here. OK?'

'Yes, Dad.' Adam smiled.

And then, out of the blue, Dad hugged Adam. It only took a second or two for Adam to hug him back. A strange silence descended on the kitchen. As I watched, my eyes began to leak. Oh, hell! A quick cough and a turn of my head gave me an excuse to raise my hands to my face to mask my embarrassment. Dad let go of Adam and we all stood in awkward silence, unsure of what to do next.

'Me now,' said Emma, holding out her arms towards Adam and making us all laugh. I could've kissed her! My brother scooped her up again.

'Honey, you're just in time for dinner,' said Aunt Jackie.

'What is it?' asked Adam.

'Sausages, mashed potatoes and peas,' said Dad.

'I'm not sure my throat can cope with sausages, but I'll have some mash,' said Adam.

I got out some cutlery and Aunt Jackie retrieved some plates from the cupboard. Dad added more butter and milk to the potatoes and carried on mashing them like they were the enemy. Sixteen oven-baked sausages occupied a casserole dish resting on the cooker out of the way. Adam stayed in the kitchen, alternating between whirling Emma around and lifting her above his head.

'I wouldn't do that if I were you,' I warned him. 'She's only just had some juice.'

'She'll be fine,' Adam dismissed. 'Stop fuss—'

Emma puked all over Adam's T-shirt.

For the third time in under five minutes, there was a

stunned silence. I broke it first. I howled with laughter, followed by Aunt Jackie.

'Oh dear,' said Dad, before he creased up too.

Emma burst into tears. I took her from Adam's unresisting hands. He was still staring down at the mess on his T-shirt.

'You were warned,' I told him, before turning to my daughter. 'It's OK, Emma. No point in crying over spilt blackcurrant juice!'

Adam glared at me. 'You're not funny.' Then he did something I hadn't seen in a long, long time. He started laughing too. My clean-freak brother had sick down his T-shirt and he could actually laugh about it. He shook his head. 'Serves me right,' he said. 'I'll be right back.' He headed out of the kitchen.

'Don't drip on the carpets,' Dad called after him, putting the food in the oven to stay warm.

Ten minutes later, once Adam had had a shower and changed his clothes, we all sat down to eat.

'OK,' I said, picking up my knife and pointing it at Adam. 'Who are you and what have you done with my brother?'

'What?' Adam frowned.

'You spent less than ten minutes in the shower,' I told him. 'You're not Adam.'

Pause.

'Sod off and die, Dante,' Adam replied, displaying sparkling wit and repartee.

'Dammit, Adam, stop bloody swearing,' said Dad.

'Tyler! Tyler, really!' My aunt sighed.

And we all started laughing again. Emma started babbling away to Adam, and Aunt Jackie and Dad smiled at each other as they shared a memory about my mum and how she was always telling off Dad for his colourful use of language. I quietly and carefully put down my knife and fork and just watched them all.

At that precise moment, I was happy. And, at that moment, it was a feeling shared by everyone around the table. Before Emma arrived, we'd occupied the same house and that was about it. But not any more. There were no questions answered, no blinding revelations, nothing had really been resolved. But we were a family and we were together.

And for now that was all that mattered.

ABOUT THE AUTHOR

MALORIE BLACKMAN is acknowledged as one of today's most imaginative and convincing writers for young readers. *Noughts & Crosses* has won several prizes, including the Children's Book Award. Malorie is also the only author to have won the Young Telegraph/Gimme 5 Award twice with *Hacker and Thief!* Her work has appeared on screen, with Pig-Heart Boy, which was shortlisted for the Carnegie Medal, being adapted into a BAFTA-award-winning TV serial. Malorie has also written a number of titles for younger readers.

In 2005, Malorie was honoured with the Eleanor Farjeon Award in recognition of her distinguished contribution to the world of children's books.

In 2008, she received an OBE for her services to Children's Literature.

www.**malorieblackman**.co.uk

Boys Don't Cry: Questions For Readers

WARNING: THESE NOTES CONTAIN PLOT SPOILERS SO DO NOT READ BEFORE YOU READ THE BOOK ITSELF

1. *'She should've told me, given me a chance to wrap my head around the idea and step up. I should've been there. Not just for Emma's sake and Melanie's, but for my own as well. Why hadn't Melanie told me?'*
Why do you think Melanie didn't tell Dante about her pregnancy? Dante says that he doesn't know what his reaction would have been, but what do you think he would have said or done? Was Melanie right not to tell him? And if she had, do you think she may have made different choices?

2. *'Doing a runner is usually the man's province, not the woman's'* – Dad
'At least he's in his child's life. At least he hasn't done a runner like a lot of men do' – unknown woman (with child) in the shop
How fair are these statements? And why do you think both Dad and this woman might feel this way? If this is true, why do you think this might be so? And how does this attitude affect Dante's own struggle, for instance with social services?

3. *'You're threatening to take my daughter away from me for no other reason than my age and my gender.'*
Is Dante right to worry about social services being more likely to doubt his ability to be a single parent because he is a dad, not a mum? Can a single dad do just as good a job as a single mum? Is it easier or harder for Dante than for Melanie? Compare how each copes with the challenge of being a single parent.

4. Adam tells Dante that he and Dad are *'too alike'* (chapter 18). In what ways are they the same? Different? How does their understanding of each other change throughout the book?

5. *'I've known I was gay since I was thirteen. And what's more, I like it. Scratch that, I love it.'*
   Adam is very positive about his homosexuality at the beginning of the book, yet as events spiral out of control, it is clear that homophobia still exists in our society. How do both Dad and Dante react to Adam's homosexuality at the beginning of the book – and why do you think they might feel this way? Does Dante still feel the same way at the end of the book?

6. Dante realizes in chapter 38 how he has in the past tolerated a friend's verbal homophobia. Was he right to believe that *'It's just a word. It doesn't mean anything . . .'* Or are words a form of assault in themselves? Just one step away from what Dad describes as last-century *'gay-bashing bullshit.'*? How hurtful is 'just a word' aimed at a minority group? If you have read Malorie Blackman's *Noughts & Crosses* trilogy, are there similarities between the way noughts are described in that society and Josh's verbal insults of gays? What is the best way to deal with this kind of attack?

7. Why does Dante believe that Logan has acted like some kind of *'malevolent puppet-master'*?

8. At the end of the book, do you think Adam will keep in touch with Josh? What do you think he might say to him and do you think they could possibly be friends – or even more – in the future?

9. *Boys don't cry . . .* What influence on Dante and Adam's attitudes and actions do you think this belief has had? How do their views change throughout the book? And are there other beliefs they hold about 'men' that change? What attitudes do you have about what defines a 'real man'?

10. And finally . . . what do you think might happen if Melanie should come back and reclaim Emma? How do you think the story might develop?

Further Information

If you feel personally affected by any of the issues within this book, or would like further information, the following websites and helplines may be of interest. Helpline telephone numbers are given for the UK area; but there will almost certainly be similar support services within other countries. Your school or local library may also be able to provide information on help available.

And, of course, don't forget that you should seriously consider talking to your parent/guardian too, who may be more supportive than you think they will be. As Dante and Adam's father says: 'If you need someone to talk to, someone who will listen without judging you, someone who'll always have your back, I'm right here.' Many parents and guardians will agree with this statement.

A WORD OF WARNING

Please ensure that you are aware of the need for caution when using the internet. If you should receive bullying or inappropriate messages, images or other material over the internet, report it. The following sites give useful information on on-line safety and what to do if you run into problems.
www.thinkuknow.co.uk
www.kidscape.org.uk
www.childnet-int.org/report

Helplines and websites relating to issues within *Boys Don't Cry*:

Teen relationships and sexuality

www.nhs.uk/livewell/sexandyoungpeople for information about adolescence and relationships, including gay relationships, and an online sexual health advice service
www.fpa.org.uk for straightforward advice on contraception, sexual health and pregnancy. Information booklets are available and there are several helplines (all calls confidential):
FPA England 0845 122 8690 (Mon-Fri; 9 a.m. to 6 p.m.)
FPA Northern Ireland 0845 122 8687 (Mon-Fri; 9 a.m. to 5 p.m.)

Single parenting and teen parents

www.coram.org.uk provides specialist support to young parents across London. For further information call 020 7520 0311
www.parentlineplus.org.uk provides help and support for anyone caring for children. There is confidential email support, as well as a 24-hour Parentline helpline: Freephone 0808 800 2222
www.onespace.org.uk for lone parents
www.gingerbread.org.uk organization to help single parents. Helpline: Freephone 0808 802 0925
www.opfs.org.uk for one-parent families in Scotland. Lone Parent helpline: Freephone 0808 801 0323

Gay Issues

www.lgf.org.uk The Lesbian and Gay Foundation offers advice on coming out, sexual health and relationships, combating homophobia and provides advice by email (**helpline@lgf.org.uk**) or on the phone:
0845 330 3030 (local call rate; 6 p.m. to 10 p.m. staffed; 10 p.m. to 6 p.m. automated)

Emotional Health

www.samaritans.org for confidential support from trained volunteers for anyone **experiencing feelings of distress or despair.**
08457 909090 (UK); 1850 60 9090 (Republic or Ireland);
jo@samaritans.org (email)

International: Befrienders worldwide cover 40 countries. If you live outside the UK and Republic of Ireland or wish to use a language other than English, visit **www.befrienders.org** to find your nearest helpline.

www.getconnected.org.uk A young people's help resource for under 25s. Free confidential helpline on any issue, as well as email and webchat support (**4.30 p.m. to 10.30 p.m. everyday**) and Webhelp 24/7: an online directory of help.

Telephone helpline: 0808 808 4994 (1 p.m. – ll p.m. **all week**)